For my [...], Helen

DISPOSABLE

ASSETS

B. K. Lauren (Bobbie) 1/3/20 B

B. K. LAUREN

Original copyright entitled *The Winslow Affair*
February 2002

ISBN: 1470046466
ISBN 13: 9781470046460

For

Samantha

ACKNOWLEDGEMENTS

I wish to thank the following contributors to my book for their kind help and patience. To my dear friends, Joan Medlicott and Nancy Jo Feinberg both of whom encouraged me in this endeavor. Larry Smith, Sue Moss and Cindy Snow for editing, and without whose help I could not have finished. To Nikki Kolleda for introducing me to Gloria and Nigel Prescott who not only welcomed me into their home for an extended stay in Hamilton, Bermuda, but also introduced me to members of the Bermudan Banking community. I'd also like to thank my cat, Macavity, who persistently protected the technical equipment, both computer and printer (by constantly inserting his paw in the paper feed, etc.), adding a touch of comic relief when I wavered. And Bruce Lauren, to whom I am ever indebted for enhancing my love of nature and the sea, by teaching me how to sail and giving me the invaluable experience of both inland and off shore sailing.

PROLOGUE

The older man lay in a rumpled heap on the hardwood floor. The bump on his head had swollen into a large knot. Not unattractive under other circumstances; his graying pallor reeked of death. Prior to his fall, one would have guessed the man to be late middle aged. But death had a way of accentuating facial lines and crevices rendering its victims into waxen mannequins devoid of their human souls.

Before his death, the man had often pondered the question of his soul. Would it be snatched away as a final insult in his battle with death, winner takes all? Or would his free will whisk it away before Heaven or Hell could wrestle it into one of their ethereal cupboards?

A lone individual sat on the floor beside the body, his head smothered in his hands. He was much too distraught to ponder any questions about the soul, nor was he the type who ever would. Stunned by the events, he just sat there as tears trickled down his sun-tanned cheeks. Eventually the younger man regained enough composure to make the emergency call.

As for the dead man and his soul, he now knew the answer but he wasn't talking.

CHAPTER 1

Asia Winslow-Whitney discreetly maneuvered herself beside one of the ionic pillars near a side exit. As she glanced across the room at the dancers' reflections in the Ballroom's baroque mirrored walls, she was suddenly overcome with a sense of foreboding. Apprehensive that someone might notice her, she moved further into the shadows. Even the orchestra's soft, melodious sounds did not stave off her unease. Asia knew she had to leave. Leave as stealthily as possible.

The guests had been wined, dined and the Settlement House Gala was in full swing. She and her husband, Ian, had glided around the dance floor to the strains of Frank Sinatra's "Lovely with your smile so warm"…the perfect couple. It was shortly after, that Asia had slowly receded into the background behind the pillar, where she now stood.

During a final perusal of the ballroom, she noticed Ian with his arm around a stunning, dark haired young woman, one of the company's accountants. She noted how, as if by accident, his lips brushed her cheek as he leaned over and whispered intimately in her ear. In the past, he had been exceedingly cautious about his philandering at public events. Why this obvious change in his behavior she had no idea, but tonight Asia didn't much care.

This had been the worst year of her life. The death of her father had plunged Asia into a deep, penetrating depression. It had also forced her to take over the family's private international banknote company. Although apprehensive about being in charge, she had taken the reins and placed her most trusted employees in key positions creating the kind of efficiency that Asia knew would have made her father proud.

Now it was time to make her move. What she was now about to do was dangerous, and there was no one hundred percent guarantee of success. She knew if she stayed, she might never find out the truth about her father's death, a man under 60 brimming with health. Was it murder? Recent facts she had uncovered pointed in that direction. But then, she had met a blank wall.

'No matter how close I come to that conclusion, would anyone ever believe me?' Asia had pondered the question over and over again. She sensed a ruthlessness about the whole affair. Instinctively, she knew, that if she did not leave, she too might end up dead. Death was so permanent, and in this instance, with the kind of finality that would leave everything status quo. That, Asia could not accept.

'Stop procrastinating,' she admonished herself, 'it's now or never,' and she slipped quietly through the exit to an out-of-the-way elevator.

Upon entering her room, Asia caught a glimpse of her image in the full – length mirror. Her soft sensual cleavage accentuated the elegantly low cut of her tissue paper-sheer rose colored gown. This once-in-a-lifetime perfect dress clung to her slim athletic body. It was at that very moment that Asia was sure her only choice was to follow through with her plan. Her soft grey eyes filled with wonder earlier in the evening, were now filled with fear.

With a sigh of resignation, she placed her thumbs deep in the center between her breasts, and with a violent tug, tore the bodice well below the waist. She watched the dress fall in a rumpled mass on the emerald green carpet. The gown's variegated dull and shiny folds seemed almost a metaphor of the roller-coaster events she had recently experienced.

Twelve minutes after eleven. Time to get moving. It had taken five minutes and twenty-seven seconds to get from the lobby to her room. If her calculations were correct, it would be at least a half-hour to forty-five minutes before she would be missed.

Asia silently thanked the Plaza for having king-sized beds, as she reached between the box springs and mattress, pulling out fresh underwear, a pair of faded Levis, an undistinguished-looking blue oxford cloth shirt and an old navy sweater. She also removed a worn pair of cheap sneakers with no identifying tread and a dark-colored medium-sized backpack.

She moved quickly, tearing the rest of her clothes as she stripped. The clothes fell to the floor in a trail leading from her evening dress toward the bath. After redressing, Asia checked the backpack to make sure her passport, travelers' checks, extra copies of her money transfers, and registered mail receipts were all still safely intact. Next, she donned a pair of sixteen-millimeter orthopedic surgical gloves and wiped away all the finger marks throughout the room. The time was exactly eleven-twenty. Twelve minutes forty-four seconds, gone. One minute: sixteen seconds ahead of schedule.

Asia paused to catch her breath. 'How will my friends view this whole affair? Could they fully comprehend my desperation?' Her entire body tensed. Minute beads of perspiration accentuated the furrows on her forehead.

"Oh, hell! It really doesn't matter!" Asia shrugged. She had been subservient long enough. 'What other people thought was unimportant. It was the here and now that really counted.'

From the inside zipper compartment of her backpack, Asia took out a small plastic zip-loc bag. She removed one cotton ball, a small circular adhesive, two disposable syringes, and a rubber tourniquet. Now for the tricky part. Laying the syringes beside her on the bed, she rolled up her sleeve on her right arm. Then positioning the tourniquet on the bed, she lay down next to it. She placed her arm on the tourniquet, leaned over, grasping the far end in her teeth. With careful precision, she pulled. The pressure of her arm on the bed held the middle section of the tourniquet securely in place. Asia took the end nearer her body and forced it underneath. Silently, she congratulated herself for successfully tying the necessary knot. Asia pinched the vein directly below the tourniquet, creating a purple protuberance just under the skin. With meticulous determination she inserted the needle. She grimaced in pain, as she watched with morbid fascination as the blood flowed steadily into the syringe.

Filling the second syringe was easier than the first. It was as if an external force had taken control driving her forward, and the adrenaline rush Asia got from watching the flowing blood sent her mind racing with extraneous thoughts; the amazing number of things one could do in a short period of time. It took the average person less then seventeen minutes to eat a four-course meal. While the process of tying one's shoelaces took less then seven seconds. Approaching time from that perspective, she momentarily pondered how much of one's lifetime the average person actually wasted. At last, the second syringe was full. She pressed a cotton ball against her arm and stuck the adhesive firmly in place. Asia glanced at her watch. The whole process had only taken a little over four minutes. After tossing the syringe wrappings and paraphernalia into her small plastic bag, Asia stashed it back into the inside compartment of her pack. Then she pulled out two small scraps of industrial weight plastic and set them aside.

She wiped away most of her evening make-up giving her skin a natural, even color, with only a hint of lipstick. Her blond hair had been coiffed in an upswept style for the evening's gala, and the medium length, chestnut-brown wig she added was an easy fit. The change was startling.

The time, 11:29. Asia scanned the room. Then she swung the backpack over her shoulder and walked to where her dress lay crumpled on the floor. Holding the syringe in her gloved hand, she pushed. The freshly drawn blood spewed down on its taffeta folds. The mixture of shimmery soft rose and dark red blood was nauseating.

Continuing the bloody trail, Asia saturated the path of clothes and intermingled the crimson drops onto the hotel carpet. The dark red stains tinged the thick emerald pile in vividly distorted fan-like patterns. This magnified the amount of blood soaking into the thick green carpet. This Asia hoped would spread a falsified message of pain, brutality, and perhaps even death.

At the bath, she sprayed the door at chest level and paused, fascinated by the patterns and streaks that were created as the fresh blood ran down toward the floor. After splattering the bathroom mirror, she walked back toward the door allowing a few drops of blood to dribble down unevenly onto the carpet. Asia knew the blood had to be fresh.

As a final act, Asia wrapped her arm in a towel and karate chopped a nearby ceramic lamp. The splinters scattered onto the carpet among the blood-saturated clothes. 'Just the right touch,' she thought as she surveyed the room one last time.

The hall was quiet. She opened the door wide enough to slide one of the ragged-edged plastic scraps between the door and the jam. Then she slipped out, closing the door softly behind her. Asia hurried down the hall and made a right turn into the adjacent corridor toward a bank of service elevators. Pushing the button labeled "garage," she waited anxiously. The elevator ground it's way upward. Once she entered, Asia heaved a sigh of relief. So far, her plan had taken less than twenty-four minutes.

The ride down seemed interminable. Aware that someone else might need to use the elevator, she was prepared to crawl out the ceiling hatch onto the top of the car into its no-man's-land of eerie pitch-blackness. There, she would hang onto the steel cables and ride it out until the car was again free. A desperate and dangerous act, but ...

About half way down, she heard another elevator go into gear. The slight tremor as the two cars passed brought a smile to her lips. Asia looked at her watch; eleven thirty two.

"The laundry man making his rounds. Nothing like good planning," hoping he had parked in his usual spot. Her whispered sigh of relief floated off mingling with the stale elevator air.

As the elevator continued to ease down, Asia noticed a few hardly perceptible drops of blood fall from the syringe as she stepped out into the quiet semi-darkness of the underground garage.

"The final touch," she grimaced looking down at the syringe. Only an occasional bare bulb, protected by a wire encasement lighted the way, as she headed toward the ACME truck and the garage exit.

It was then she realized that it had taken fewer than thirty minutes to change her whole life.

CHAPTER 2

Riley Patterson steered the ACME LAUNDRY truck carefully out of the company compound and maneuvered it smoothly into the crowded city traffic. Riley knew his route by heart. It was routine. With Riley, routine was 'ace.'

The late fall air was crisp and fresh. Riley rode high above the cars with his elbow resting on the opened window. He was used to rush hour traffic now, and on days like today, at particularly long stoplights, he enjoyed watching his breath fog his rear view mirror.

As he waited for the light, he remembered how much he had always loved trucks. The rumbling sounds of dump trucks, the smooth hum of small delivery trucks and the roar of the semi's diesel engine. In Riley's eyes, they were magical. He watched how they would stop and go, and by age five he had realized that certain symbols controlled their movements. Once he had memorized the shapes of the signs, he demanded that his mother teach him the words and the meanings of each.

Riley's academic career had been woeful at best, and although ideas and books befuddled him, Riley could read every traffic sign by age six.

"It's because of those trucks," his mother had said. "My Riley just loves trucks, … singin' jingles and readin' them road signs, that's what my Riley does best."

It was always "my Riley this" and "my Riley that" from Mrs. Patterson, who doted on Riley no matter what his capabilities. Even though Riley's school placement had been in the 'Slow Learners' classes, when he advanced to high school he insisted on taking Drivers Education. When the school hesitated, Mrs. Patterson roared into the front office, red hair flying and nostrils flairing.

"What do you mean, my Riley can't take the drivin' class?"

"Mrs. Patterson…"

"Don't Mrs. Patterson me! If I was Mrs. High Falutin' Upper Eastside, my Riley would be in that drivin' class before you could shake a Jack-assed stick."

"Mrs. Patterson," the principal began again as he tried to maneuver her into his office. But Riley's mother stood her ground.

"Drivers Ed is an elective ain't it?"

"Yes." The principal betrayed a sigh of resignation in his voice.

"Then Riley elects it."

The next afternoon, Riley experienced his first driving class. To everyone's surprise, Riley was an outstanding student-driver. His abilities surpassed most of the other students and with the help of a "reader" Riley passed both the written and driving tests with excellent scores.

Yet, in hiring him, the laundry company was taking a chance. When he began, ACME assigned Riley to an old established route with customers the company had serviced for years. The other employees were supportive, and for the first two weeks a companion driver rode with him until he felt comfortable driving his route alone.

As usual, his rounds started with the mom and pop Delis whose hours were from 5 a.m. to 3:30. Their day slowed around 2:45, which was about the same time Riley began his daily route, and most were closed and shuttered by 4:00 or 5:00 p.m.

Riley took pride in the short cuts he'd learned. The occasional detours, although they made him a little nervous, became a challenge rather than a problem. Over time, Riley, who lived with his mother in a small one-bedroom apartment, developed a camaraderie with most of his customers, who offered him a bit of social fulfillment as well as a job.

However, tonight a minor accident at Fifth Avenue and 45th had slowed him down and made him anxious. He had been slightly tense all day, and it was beginning to show in his face. Meyer Leibovitz saw it too. Riley's round, youthful, unlined face with its elfin, bulbous nose and large angelic, brilliant blue eyes appeared to be unusually stressed.

"Seem a little edgy, Riley? Not an 'ace' day?"

"Aw! A fender bender two blocks back slowed me up."

"Hey, Fanny," Meyer called into the kitchen. "We got something to cheer up 'Mr. Do It Right Riley.'"

Leibovitz's was one of the few Delis that still made its own pastries and that extended their day. They stayed opened later, while Fanny prepared the dough for the morning baking of sweet buns, cakes, and cheesecakes, which were displayed in their revolving see through 'tempter domes'.

Mrs. Leibovitz came out with a box.

"Wouldn't you know, today I made too many cakes." She smiled at Meyer as she handed Riley a box. She also handed him a small brown bag that contained pastrami on rye and a Dr. Brown's.

Since the Plaza Hotel had begun its laundry renovations, Riley's boss had temporarily added the hotel to his route. Although this gave Riley extra overtime, the added stop had also proven to be stressful.

Riley needed time slots, and he needed his life to fit neatly into them. The Leibovitzes, who reminded Riley of the Jack Spratt family of nursery rhyme fame, showed a special warmth toward him and looked out for him in many small ways.

"We surely wouldn't want to lose you to another route," Meyer would tell Riley enthusiastically. "After all, you are one of the best laundry truck drivers we have ever had."

Every time Riley heard this, his chest would swell up like a peacock's and he'd grin from ear to ear. Thanks to Mrs. Leibovitz's generosity, Riley was able to munch a sandwich as he went about his route eliminating Riley's need for a dinner break. It also took away the worry those occasional glitches in the traffic flow caused. Riley knew he'd be on time.

"Like Broadway, you have my regards." Mr. Leibovitz waved him off.

Riley laughed and with a wave and a shout of thanks, he headed his truck out of the alley back to the main thoroughfare.

After the Leibovitzes, Riley moved onto his evening route of small homey, mostly Italian, restaurants in Little Italy. He liked the soft evening glow and cozy ambiance of these family run places. Riley often spotted kids sitting at a small table at the back of the kitchen imbued with the spicy scents of tomatoes, garlic, oregano and fresh homemade bread, doing their home-work in between stints at the sink washing dishes or carrying out the trash. At many, Riley exchanged the traditional fresh red checked table cloths for the soiled ones, getting an occasional masculine tussle and hug, accompanied with a 'Heya! Paesano!' greeting from his older customers. Afterward, Riley would ride in his truck laughing and repeating in his head an accented 'Heya! Paesano!' Yet he never seemed to get it quite right when he tried saying it aloud.

Tonight something was different. Was he going to have an accident? Hit some poor stray? That could mean an animal or a person the way people were being laid off work lately. Mr. Leibovitz had explained to Riley about big companies being taken over and about how the recession was causing a lot of homeless people to be around lately. Riley certainly didn't want to be one of them. What would he do without his truck, people like the Leibovitzes, and 'Heya! Paesano!' The thought had never occurred to him before. Suddenly, Riley's skin began to acquire a plasticine sheen and minute beads of perspiration dappled his forehead. Now he was scared.

As the evening wore on, he remembered his sandwich. The thick slices of rich homemade bread filled the pit in his stomach, and his body temperature soon returned to normal. Riley closed his windows to shut out the chilly evening air that was beginning to acquire a rancid staleness from the day's heavy city traffic. Dusk in the city no longer had the crisp clearness of streetlights and early evening stars, but rather the smoggy gray thickness of exhaust fumes that sucked at Riley's lungs and caused a burning sensation in his eyes and nasal passages. Tonight was especially bad and it exacerbated Riley's edginess. Something important was going to happen; it was in the air. Riley could feel it; he had

13

a sense for these things. Riley tried to concentrate on his driving, although he knew the unknown was inevitable.

"Get this evening over fast," he kept repeating to himself, "then it won't catch me."

Once Riley had heard 'timing was everything.' That expression came to him now as he moved through his next stops in a fog of anticipation and fear, hoping to keep ahead of it as if he were racing a tornado. Intuitively, Riley sensed there was no way to avoid the sense of impending doom.

By eleven o'clock, the traffic had let up enough that the sky was beginning to clear, and, although it was still coated with an infinitesimal haze, the crisp clearness began to return and a rich dark luminosity wrapped around the city glow.

As he drove across 58th Street past the Plaza's main entrance, he marveled at the array of brightly colored banners hung for the evening's gala. **1983, New York Settlement House Gala**, he read with some difficulty. It was clearly spectacular, but Riley knew this was not what he was anticipating. It was something different. Something more ominous.

He turned into the entrance to the hotel garage at exactly 11:19 p.m. He backed his truck carefully into its usual space just left of the bank of back-to-back service elevators. Even with his uneasiness, Riley had made good time. He was right on the mark.

"Ace," he thought, as he walked toward the back of his truck.

Riley opened the double back doors and lowered the ramp. He wheeled out two carts of crisp fresh white linens and entered the usual back elevator that had been left on hold, as it was every night for his arrival.

The hotel was his only customer that actually received whole carts of laundry, precisely eight daily. The manager of the night shift housekeeping staff had worked out an evening routine with Riley to get the sheets and towels to each floor station as expeditiously as possible. The morning crew would have everything in place just as they did when their own hotel laundry was operating. Riley's routine was to empty two carts at the sixth floor central linens station and then ride to the top floor. There he would fill the carts with soiled linens from the upper floors. It took him about twelve minutes to get his truck parked just right and the clean laundry up to the sixth floor. Tonight was no different. His apprehension did not interfere with his job. Yet, as he began his ride up the elevator, the tension was still there until something happened. He heard a long, low hum. At first, Riley was unsure; he had no idea what it was. But the sound, whatever it was, erased his anxiety and gave him a warm soothing, almost musical feeling. During the three months he had been delivering the hotel's laundry, he had never, until now, heard this or any other unusual or unique sound during his rounds. Riley listened rapturously to the low-pitched monotonal humming sound. He even stopped the elevator car and listened until the sound stopped. He was quizzical about the fact that it had begun so softy, then after a crescendo of humming had faded away. This was obviously what had been so foreboding to him all day, and he relaxed, laughing at himself for being so worried.

"Maybe I should tell Jose," he mused. Jose was his hotel friend. But instead, he decided to save it, and savor the lovely sound awhile longer for himself. Someday, just maybe, it might happen again and then Jose could hear it with him. Riley finished his rounds with the pleasant hum resounding in his brain, as he and Jose exchanged the last two carts of dirty laundry for clean. As he rode silently back to the garage level, he fixated on the single toned sonata he had experienced.

CHAPTER 3

Asia moved quickly through the bleak, muted light of the cavernous garage. She knew her sense of unease would not abate until she was well out of the confines of the hotel, but she had one last task before she slipped away. Walking swiftly around toward the elevators on the opposite side, she found the truck... ACME LAUNDRY. Taking the second scrap of industrial plastic, she slid it under one of the hinges of the truck's opened large double doors. Then she sprayed the last few drops of blood left in the second syringe on an inconspicuous lower corner of one of the carts. If discovered, Asia hoped the scant evidence would do little more than cause the driver a few sleepless nights and confuse the police just enough to muddy her trail.

An outsider might think she could have just walked away, disappeared, but there were other considerations. Suspected foul play was the only answer, and she needed time. After all, there was more at stake than just inconveniencing a laundry truck driver! There were World Wide Banknote and its assets, her father's reputation, and her life. Turning away from the truck, she removed her surgical gloves and threw them and the second syringe into another plastic bag and stuffed them both inside her backpack. Then she walked up the slight incline. As she reached the exit, a deafening clamor of bangs, crashes, shrieks and shrill shouts arose from outside the garage entry. Impulsively, Asia jumped back into the recesses of the garage doorway.

"Oh no!" Asia slumped when she realized her unforeseen predicament. Cautiously, she peeped out. In the hotel's narrow alleyway a ragtag, sallow, drunken man stumbled among a row of dented, green dumpsters. A scrawny, striped cat scavenged through the garbage at the end of the row.

Asia was sure he had not seen her, but she somehow had to get out of the garage without being detected.

"Get your fur ass outa here!" the man's flaying arm swung wildly in an inept attempt to discourage his feline competition. "Scat!" He shouted as his hand grazed the side of the cat's head.

"Yowl!" The cat's paw with claws extended struck out with perfect aim, scratching the back of its adversary's hand. The man stumbled, falling back. Seeing the blood, the victim was overcome with a seething rage. In one swift movement, he caught the cat by the tail and slung it high over his head. The cat slammed against the hotel wall. Its stunned, limp body slid down into the farthest bin. The vagrant sat for a moment seemingly dazed. Using his dirty shirtsleeve, he reached up and wiped away the sweat that trickled down his furrowed brow. Then, calmly as if nothing had happened, he turned back to his dumpster scavenging.

Asia watched, horrified. Suddenly, she snapped back to reality. There was no time to lose. Deciding the man was too preoccupied to notice, Asia cautiously exited the garage. The shadow of the hotel wall camouflaged her until she was able to turn at the end of the alley, out of the vagrant's view. Suddenly the startling brightness of the streetlights ignited an abrasive shock to her senses. She was out of the hotel, yes, but there was still an off chance that she might already be missed. Yet, she paused. 'One last look at the façade of her beloved Plaza,' she thought, 'no there wasn't time.'

It was a quarter to twelve. She walked quickly down Central Park South toward Columbus Circle, now an unnoticed medium aged woman, who blended perfectly with the infrequent late night passersby. Asia snuggled more closely into her old worn sweater, against the brisk, fall, late night air.

Going two blocks, she walked toward the Red Line Subway entrance at Broadway and the southwest corner of the Park. She was headed downtown on the number 2, 7th Avenue express.

The New York subway nightlife exuded an air of wanton decadence, poor blacks and Hispanics, tired cleaning ladies and the standard drunk sleeping it off. While many were seeking the safety of the bright lights, others were on their late night, long journeys home.

The train lunged out of the station with its side to side motion, causing a portentous flickering of the lights, created by a third rail. Unlike the tracks, this electrical rail, each section only 39 feet long, had large gaps. When the train switched from one set of tracks to another or moved too slowly, the lights either flickered inside the train or caused a momentary blackout to occur. This eerie third dimensional sensation would change when the subway renovations were finished. But now, it only added to the dismal surroundings and Asia's inescapable tension. Occasionally, a youngish couple got on or off, talking in hushed tones and laughing softly.

At the far end of the car a woman of indeterminate age, sat chewing, her jaws kneading in a constant circular motion. Periodically, spittle ran down her cheek. Each time, she wiped it away with the sleeve of the dirty faded green trench coat that hung on her emaciated body like an empty gunnysack on an undersized hook. Her gray hair, tightly matted from years of neglect, was piled atop her head. Random stringy wisps hung loosely about her face. A pair of rose tinted John Lennon glasses rested on the beakish, aquiline nose of her cronish, wrinkled face. She gazed out the opposite window with an unwavering intensity, seemingly knowing something in her heart she would probably never share. 'Sadly, one day soon, she will simply crumple,' Asia thought. 'A depleted mass, more fodder for Potters' Field.'

At the opposite end, stood a young twosome, each with the mixed racial features of the physically beautiful new mongrel breed. Their long lean bodies seemed coupled together, she standing on one foot with her other leg wrapped sensuously around him. Cooing, moaning sounds, they moved in a slightly undulating fashion.

"Were they really? Here...?"

The soft movement, and smell of a dirty, greasy haired young man, who sat down next to her distracted Asia's fascination with the subway's nocturnal travelers. Pressing his leg against hers, their eyes locked in a brief, momentary stare. The heat of his tepid breath smacked out at her as he began sliding his hand back and forth, slowly caressing the side of her leg.

Asia wanted desperately to scream and would have if her circumstances were different.

"No complications now, please?" She pleaded silently. Just then, the conductor walked in, and paused next to the old lady.

"Thank God for small favors," Asia sighed under her breath, relieved that the man had quickly removed his hand. Her stop, Wall Street was next. As she got off, she turned to make sure that she was not being followed. Even in the muted light, the rich rainbow palates of the occasional bold graffiti thrusting its messages bombarded Asia as she moved through the stale, silent shadows of the subway platform and up the stairs into the fresher air above. Here at the tip of Manhattan, she'd arrived just a few short blocks from the East River. Momentarily checking her watch, she turned, and walked purposefully down the street toward a small commercial marina.

It had taken her less than an hour from the hotel to the boatyard. As she walked the last familiar block toward the yard, Asia was sure that by now, she was definitely missed. Her gut feeling made her more certain than ever that by sailing out of the harbor, rather than taking commercial transportation, she'd be much harder to trace. Once they stopped looking for her body, someone might realize she was not really dead. Asia was truly sorry about having to trash her hotel room, and about the feelings of those she had inconvenienced by her actions, but she needed time, and she needed the authorities to believe her to be a victim of foul play; her body simply removed. Hopefully, for a while anyway, she would become just another Big Apple statistic.

To the right of the marina entrance stood the requisite dark green dumpster. Asia paused to toss in all the incriminating items from her pack. Then unlocking the marina gate, she silently picked her way through the circuitous path of hawsers, old cleats and ships' debris spread across the yard toward the dock. Onika, Asia's trim 30-foot fiberglass boat, was rafted next to a rust encrusted, old tugboat that floated lazily on its hawsers in the down river stream. Although she was not a modern spiffy racer, Onika was sleek and ready to cruise.

Carefully, Asia stepped onto the deck of the old tugboat. Softly, she walked across the deck, so as not to awaken the tug's skeleton crew. Upon reaching the other side, she grabbed on to Onika's portside halyard and swung herself stealthily aboard. She walked a few feet toward the stern, slipped into the cockpit, and unlocked the hatch board lock. Sliding out the companionway boards, Asia slipped below into the cabin darkness. Without turning on a light, she set her watch for 4 a.m., and lay down on the settee bunk to get some well-earned ZZZZ's.

Asia was awakened by her alarm. Right on time. She smiled as she heard the grinding gears of a garbage truck in the distance. Outside a thick mist shrouded the East River so thick the sound of the bell buoy was almost more visible than Onika's bow.

Asia put a pot of particularly strong coffee on the stove. While it perked, she opened the engine room door and checked the oil. She had done this the day before, but she still made a last check before casting off. Boats, being an entity unto themselves, had a contrariness that belied every precaution. Then grabbing her cup, she climbed into the cockpit. Casting the lines off the neighboring tug and giving a slight shove, she returned to the tiller. To the low, revenant hum of her small diesel engine, Onika glided gently into the mist.

CHAPTER 4

Detective Richard Crane picked up the phone with the enthusiasm of a bridegroom at a shotgun wedding. 4 a.m. My God. The one night he wasn't on duty. It wasn't often lately that he'd gotten a full night's sleep, and he relished it like an octogenarian potentate would a virgin 'screw'. Someone at the other end was mumbling something about the Plaza Hotel. What the H- did he have to do with the Plaza? Must be a dream, then without realizing it, he put the receiver back in its cradle. The incessant ringing finally forced him to grab the telephone again and growl into the mouthpiece.

"It's the Plaza, Sir," the voice on the other end began.

This dream was getting out of control.

"There's something funny there, Sir," the patient voice continued.

"Call Ringling Clown School. They deal with funny." The words hung suspended in his brain, and again he slid the receiver back into place. Only then did he begin to awaken from his deeply sound sleep.

Being notorious at the department for his acid behavior upon waking, the phone rang a third time and the patient voice on the other end began again.

"Are you awake yet, Sir?"

Crane grunted an apology and the voice continued. "As I was saying, there was a big social fundraiser last night at the Plaza Hotel, and one of the guests is missing."

Now Crane was really angry. "Haven't you made a mistake, Harry? It's my day off, remember?"

"I know it. You know it. But the mayor doesn't."

Crane knew it couldn't be helped. With a sense of resignation, he began to get his brain into gear. "Ok. I suppose Stan's coming over with the usual. Tell him I'll be out in fifteen minutes."

Reluctantly, Crane heaved his large sturdy body up and headed for an ice cold shower. Though it did little for his morning personality, it shocked his senses and sharpened his brain to its full mental acuity.

Shaved, with his tie slung loosely around his neck, Crane stood on the curb in the promised time. He watched as his partner pulled up in a 1979 Crown Victoria, standard department equipment. Stan knew better than to talk about anything until Crane had drunk at least half a cup of the strong black coffee, which was sitting in the cup holder between the two seats.

"It's moments like these, Stan, when I wonder if it's worth it." Crane paused to crumble his Styrofoam cup and throw it on the car floor.

Stan smiled. "Well, you're hell in the morning. But I can't see you lasting a week in your family's law office."

"What do you know about it?" Crane snarled. But they both knew Stan was right.

With an undergraduate philosophy degree from Harvard and a Michigan Law degree, he had naturally been expected to join the family firm. But compromise and negotiation were not his bag. It was problem solving he liked, methodically putting the puzzle together. And he loved the chase. Philosophy had honed his abilities, and he was relentless.

His family had been somewhat surprised when he chose to go to University of Michigan rather than Harvard Law. But that was nothing compared to their shock and consternation when he entered Michigan State Graduate School of Criminal Justice. They humored what they hoped was a passing fad. But Richard didn't have passing fads. He wanted to be a cop, not to spend the rest of his life rewriting wills, handling estates, or writing corporate contracts. Secretly, he believed his grandfather, Art Abernathy, whose father had begun the family law firm, and who had sat on the federal bench for many years, understood. Often the two of them would sit late into the night discussing the law and crime, and those who got away. His grandfather understood about the griminess out in the streets and why his grandson had made the choice. And like his grandfather, Crane was well aware that many people had gotten one of life's raw deals, that they often made bad choices hoping to square the dice; while others were just plain raw. One couldn't right those kinds of wrongs by writing legal briefs for the rich.

However, when he signed on to do the job, Richard didn't believe he owed society a fourth floor walkup, a semi-detached in Queens or Staten Island. Fortunately, Richard's grandfather had given him a substantial trust, so he was able to continue to live in the area of the city where he had been raised, the Upper East Side. The comfort his money afforded him became his respite from the dirt he encountered daily, and it isolated and 're-souled' him during the meanest days of his job.

Crane had risen quickly in the department. People wanted to work with him. He was smart and he was there when you needed him. He could be trusted. Eventually, knowledge of his background seeped out, but by then, he had proven his worth. Now, it was only the ice cold showers and the lack of sleep that made Crane occasionally question his choice of occupations.

"What do we know?" He asked as they neared the hotel.

"Not much. Some society dame. Funny name. Missing."

Crane chuckled at Stan's Runyonesque use of the word dame. Something, Crane knew, he could never pull off. "Damn! I'm not up to this. Some spoiled oversexed rich girl runs out on a fling, and we lose our day off. What's her name? Muffy? Bunny? Mitsy? I know exactly the type. My mother has introduced me to every one of them."

This time Stan knew Crane was definitely pissed.

"I'm telling you, Stan…" Before he finished his sentence, they had arrived.

Fortunately, there were no reporters. Either the word hadn't gotten out or this one was being kept under tight wraps. That, in itself was interesting. Hotel security was waiting and squired them into an out of the way elevator.

Asia Winslow, he mused during the elevator's slow assent. He'd heard that name before.

"Jeez-," Stan gazed around the room. Then he headed for the bath. But nothing. Just like they'd said. No body. Just blood. Blood everywhere.

Crane viewed the hotel room with his usual pensive, circumspect interest. His eyes followed the blood-spattered path of female evening attire that began at the bathroom door and went from there to the king sized bed. There was certainly enough blood. He knelt down studiously observing a sample. Crane had little doubt it was fresh, anyway fresh in the last twelve hours. He'd have to get forensics over to substantiate. The shattered lamp fragments scattered among the clothes, blood and carpet, finalized the grisly scene of evidence without a body. Obviously something had happened here, but Crane wasn't quite sure what. If one were to accept the evidence on face value, someone had raised havoc and put someone else through a final hell. But he wasn't quite sure. "This one's for Banner." He mused and Stan agreed. "Let's get moving."

CHAPTER 5

Annie Bloome stood before him, her clothes in a rumpled heap at her feet. Ian hungered for her. He ran his hands around her waist then down her long, ivory, sinewy legs. He watched as the slightest hint of a smile grazed her face then slipped away. Her rich black curls cascaded down her shoulders as she turned her large dark eyes away in a brief innocent blush. She was beautiful, and she was good. But it wasn't love. Ian had only loved one person his entire life, himself.

Annie began to unbutton his shirt. By the time she had loosened his belt and was unzipping his pants, Ian was hard and big. Even in the dimness, Annie Bloome's pupils dilated.

Bam! Like a Mack Truck. He slammed her hard against the hotel wall. His deep titanic thrusts, which began with a slow pulsating rhythm, caused her as much pain as pleasure. He knew it, but he didn't care. After all, for whom was she there? Somewhat dazed at first, Annie moaned. Catching his cadence, she responded with teasingly complementary movements. Suddenly, without warning, Ian swung her body around and slammed her down on the hotel bed.

"Oh! My God." Somewhat winded, it took Annie a moment to regain her tempo. Then she began to respond again with soft low cooing sounds. Annie was on the edge. Pain; pleasure? She wasn't sure.

She moaned aloud and wanted to scream, stop! She clawed the sheets and clutched the rungs of the brass headboard. Leverage. She needed leverage. She could feel his hot breath on her neck. Wham! Again bludgeoning, their perspiring bodies locked. Nirvana!

Ian lay quietly. After a moment, he lifted his upper body. She saw the curvature of the ripples of his backbone as he bent down. Bending his head she felt the touch of his tongue. Slowly, very slowly his tongue grazed her long crane like neck. He paused, and then he kissed her lips.

Now that he was finished, he lay silent. "I'm almost there," he murmured, his thoughts far away from what he considered just another pleasant, but otherwise mechanical performance. He had always needed these brutal little sexual forays. They were one of life's "perks," that he had to get elsewhere after he married.

"I'm almost there, too!" Annie thought, elatedly, for she had been preparing for this moment for years. Teasing, and titillating boys since she was thirteen, she had learned how to use both her brain and her body to get what she wanted. After she had lost her virginity on her old apartment building roof to Arnold Epstein, she had never looked back.

Annie wanted it all, surveying her assets, her choice was modeling; a quick buck, and lots of opportunity to be noticed fast, but she was too short. Fortunately, she was outstandingly beautiful and she was good at figures. Annie knew if she wanted to reach the top, she would have to work hard. After night school, she got a job in the accounting department at World Wide Banknote.

Once she had found her quarry, she was committed. She had played this man, pleased him and teased him for months for this. Gone to night school and elocution lessons for this. Helped him execute crimes for this and now she'd arrived.

The buzz of the telephone jarred the silence. Annie looked at her watch. It was almost five. Reluctantly, after an insistent fourth ring, she lifted the receiver.

"Yes?" she answered in a sleepy languid tone.

"Miss Bloome." The authoritativeness on the other end commanded her full attention as she heard her name repeated again. "Miss Bloome."

"Who is this?" Annie interrupted, no longer feigning sleep.

"This is the manager. I'm sorry to wake you, but there seems to be some trouble and we are unable to contact Mr. Whitney." The voice paused again.

Ian watched as Annie swore under her breath.

"As you are the only employee of World Wide Banknote staying in the hotel, we thought you might be acting in an administrative capacity, assisting, privy to the owner's schedule."

"I do have some notes here I can peruse but right at this moment?" she sighed. "At five o'clock in the morning, I really have no idea of the whereabouts of Mr. Whitney or Mrs. Winslow-Whitney." Ian's whole body jerked.

"I could look through my notes and call you back, or . . ."

"Miss Bloome, I know it's early, but would it be too much trouble for you to come down to the lobby so we could talk to you?"

"We?"

"Detectives Crane and Sorsky from the New York Police Department would like to speak to you." Annie could not conceal her deep sigh.

"It will take me a few minutes, but I'm happy to help in any way. May I ask what this is about?"

"When you get downstairs, come to the front desk and ask for the manager's office. We will explain to you here. Thank you, Miss Bloome."

"Ian, it was the manager," Annie said breathlessly, "they're looking for you! They assume I'm your personal secretary. Quick! I need some notes, an idea of Asia's evening schedule. I know yours," she said sarcastically.

"Well they assumed wrong, haven't they. And who are they?" There was a stoic toughness in his tone.

"The manager and the police."

"The police!" His eyes narrowed, his face became a twisted mask of brutality and his skin acquired a faded sallowness.

"For what? Did he say why?" Ian grabbed her arm.

"I don't know." She tried to release his grip. "Let go! You're hurting me." Annie was stunned by his brutish behavior and the chameleon way in which his features had instantly changed.

"The exact words, tell me the exact words." He twisted her skin even more viciously.

"Only about schedules; they only asked if I knew where you and Asia were."

Ian's grip tightened as she tried to pull away. Sobbing, she gritted her teeth in pain. Small patches of crimson showed through the ivory opaqueness of her upper arm where his nails had pierced her skin. His handsome face grimaced; mangled in an ugliness she had never before seen.

"They said they'd explain when I got there. I don't know! Let go, Ian, please!" She pleaded. Annie knew he was sexually abrasive, but she had never seen him like this.

Finally he dropped her arm as if it were part of a rag doll. The red blotches remained. Shakened, Annie massaged the redness and watched, shocked, as already the marks were turning into purplish, yellow bruises below the skin.

Ian's hands had become clammy. He didn't like the fact that the police had connected Annie and the room to World Wide Banknote. Under his breath, he cursed himself for agreeing to let her stay in the hotel. He didn't like surprises, and he didn't like situations or people he couldn't control. That was his problem with Asia. She was much brighter and more independent than he had realized before they had married. Yet, that had not changed his plan. But the police. Already?

"What could the police want?" He knew there was only one clue, but he was soon to get rid of that. With no other clues, it limited his ideas about what to do. One thing he knew for sure; this was not where he wanted to be found. Suddenly, he realized he had something he had to make sure of before he talked to any police.

"I've got to get out of here," he said as he jumped out of bed and began dressing. "This is one time you are going to have to wing it. Do the best you can. Tell them as little as possible. Use the pre-event schedule. I'm out of here," he said as he peeked into the corridor. Then he quietly slipped out and down the hall toward the bank of service elevators to the garage.

CHAPTER 6

Wind swept, watery ripples danced lightly across Sandy Hook Bay. Onika tucked snugly behind the long, flat, sandy spit of land, swung gently on her anchor. The movement of the boat caused an occasional sunbeam to stream through the starboard porthole and sprinkle its light across Asia's face. She repeatedly tried to push it aside with no success. Exasperated, she rolled over and with a kittenish snarl, covered her face with her arm.

'A speck in my eye,' she thought, half asleep, as she tried again to brush it away with her hand. A dog barked in the distance.

"Here Samson," the boys' voices carried across the water. Asia stretched her long, lean body. The barking of the dog and the boys' shouts caused Asia to finally open her eyes to the playful beam peeking its rays through the cabin port. She gazed at the chronometer on the bulkhead. 2:00 p.m.

Before sunrise, to mask her escape, Asia had sailed out of New York Harbor across the Hudson to Sandy Hook Bay on the New Jersey side of the river. She wanted to be well rested before embarking on a strenuous cruise, and her seven-hour sleep had been just right. The crisp, cool afternoon air filled the cabin with an energizing freshness. The dog barked again.

After putting on a fresh pot of coffee, checking the engine and making sure everything was shipshape below; Asia grabbed her mug and ascended to the cockpit above. Here she was greeted by an absolutely cloudless sky and bright afternoon sun. Typical of November's beginnings, it was excruciatingly cold on the water but Onika's cockpit had absorbed enough of the day's warmth to create a protective coating from the late fall chill. Asia put the engine in neutral and as she walked forward to the bow, she glanced over at the two boys on the shore with their hearty black Lab.

"Fetch! Samson, Fetch!" And the dog bounded after the stick, raced back to his masters and dropped his quarry at their feet, barking and jumping round and round, begging for the game to begin again. The boys laughed and waved.

"Where ya bound for?" One of the boys shouted as Asia waved back.

"Good Question. Just drifting south, I guess. That time of year," Asia replied knowing the truth might be dangerous, under the circumstances. Besides, she was not really sure of her final destination.

Once Asia had hauled in the anchor and secured it on deck and the chain in locker below, she headed Onika up into the wind. She released the roller-furling jib and set the main.

Turning off the engine, she tightened the sails and headed Onika out around the hook into the Lower Bay. 'One heck of a perfect day for a virgin sail,' she thought.

Asia's plan was to catch the outgoing tide and reach Ambrose Light by 4:00 p.m., while it was still light. 'I'm right on the money,' she mused. 'Just perfect.'

Rounding Sandy Hook into the bay was like leaving a country path and entering a boatman's super highway. Tugs and ferryboats plied their trades and freighters lay anchored, waiting until Monday to dock so they wouldn't have to pay an extra day's port fees. A shiny modern no nonsense cruise ship passed homeward bound in the distance and another could be seen coming out of the upper bay.

The tide was running about three knots. Aided by a following wind, Onika was whooshed down bay. It was about thirteen miles, eleven and a half knots out to the light. Asia was maneuvering the boat solely under sail, so Onika had the right of way. 'Out of my way,' Onika seemed to scream on her 'Space Mountain' kind of sail, fast and exciting with no stops.

'At this rate, Onika will reach Ambrose Light in time for tea.' Asia smiled to herself.

The day was so crisply clear that Asia could already see Ambrose in the distance. Its flashing light sat high atop the large four-legged structure visible for twenty-four miles in any direction. Besides the high flashing light, from dusk to dawn each leg was lighted on all four sides.

As Asia sailed past, its 15-second bell clanged a requiem that guided sailors in fair weather and foul. At Ambrose Light, Asia changed course to a windward sail. She was Bermuda bound, seven hundred seventy-four miles out in the Atlantic. Now that she was 'at sea,' Asia donned foul weather gear. Around her waist, she attached a long lifeline rigged to another line that ran from the mast, along the top of the cabin house, back to the end of the cabin trunk along the portside of the companionway hatch. Were she to be swept overboard by a foul wind or a crashing wave, she would have an umbilical chance of saving herself from the wind and angry sea. During foul weather, without a lifeline, she might get caught watching her small hearty ship sail away as she became victim to the open sea. Not a palatable thought. It was the tail end of hurricane season and like any sensible sailor, she wanted the odds to be on her side.

Onika yawed.

"Hot damn!" Asia exclaimed as the icy cold salt spray grazed her cheek. Wiping the spray on her sleeve, she rechecked her compass heading. Right on course. If the weather held, she figured she should enter St. George's Harbour in six or seven days.

Next, Asia searched aloft for any luff in the sails. She gained about a quarter of an inch of tautness by pulling in the main, which made all the difference in the set of the sail and the speed of the hull. The breeze gusted between 12 and 15 knots, spicy but not dangerous.

The sun descended into the sea and a crisp chill permeated the air.

"Stuyvestant Forever! Don't give up the ship,

Fair or stormy weather, we won't give up,

We won't give up the ship."

"This is probably nerves," Asia mused as she enthusiastically sang the second verse of the childhood Stuyvestant Sailing Club song at the top of her lungs.

"Friends and pals forever, Stuyvestant will live,

If you have to take a licking,

But don't give up the ship."

Asia had a healthy respect for the sea, and sailing off shore was no mean feat.

"Just remember, those initial tensions and anxieties during your first few days at sea are perfectly normal," Captain Sandy had told her.

"What the heck was I thinking?" Asia shivered, surveying the vast endless ocean surrounding her boat as the shoreline melted away in the distance.

"After a few days, once you get a routine, the fear will ease off. Myself," Captain Sanderson had sighed wistfully, "I rather like it out there. You're an excellent sailor. One of the best I've ever taught."

"But that was dingy racing around buoys, not the ocean."

"Nothing like dingy racing to teach helmsman-ship: that sense of wind direction, and the feel for trimmin' a sheet. That's what really counts offshore." He had given her a warm hug. "You'll do just fine."

After all, he had taught her to sail, and all about charts and navigation. He had taught her everything, and she knew he was right. She was a fine sailor!

As the night wore on, with only her masthead light and the small compass shell light, Asia was stung by the November cold. Although hurricane season was from June through November, she knew December would have been too late. The month of December was the beginning of the offshore winter storms no one even heard of, storms in which small boats were swallowed by gigantic waves with oceanic aplomb.

September, on the other hand, was too soon because of its peak season hurricane threats, while October and November both offered random brief windows in the winter oceans. Sailors like Asia were especially encouraged by the heartfelt kindness of the November winds, which normally created only an occasional squall and low-lying seas. Although it could be excruciatingly cold, the winds' calm and the abatement of the rougher seas were just enough that with any luck and good timing, one could make it to Bermuda unscathed.

As a first timer on an offshore sailing gig, Asia was scared, yet exhilarated, as Onika plowed through the relentlessly continuous waves, riding the small crests and furls, her sails cupped with wind, taut and secure on her strong masts. Onika's performance this cloudless night was a good augury for the future, as she became enveloped by the vast open sea.

CHAPTER 7

Annie Bloome was a showstopper. In retrospect, when the three men shared their first impressions, Crane's sidekick Stanley Sorsky said, "HOT!" Dan Healey the Plaza Hotel manager's first thoughts ranged from 'Beautiful' to 'Angelic.' Although loath to admit it, he remembered how he almost swooned as she stepped off the elevator and approached the hotel desk. Crane's first impression: 'TROUBLE!'

Annie walked into the room self-assured, well aware how her presence always affected people, particularly men. Even at five thirty in the morning she was a knockout in white wool slacks that accentuated her long slim legs, and a matching tunic top. She had full, shoulder length, black hair, ivory skin and red lips. Annie immediately saw the impression she had made on the manager and the shorter, stockier detective with thinning hair, but the third one, the one who took charge, was an enigma. He was not the common denominator she was used to.

'Better be careful with this one.' She surveyed him as the paunchier detective directed her to an overstuffed, paisley wing chair in front of the manager's desk.

'I've met tougher types than this.' Annie mused. Immured in her own self-confidence, Annie crossed her legs in a precisioned, provocative way which generally caused Adam's apples to quiver and most men to rethink their future plans.

However, the third man did not react the way she had expected. His stare seemed to penetrate through her to something on the opposite side of the room. Annie Bloom momentarily caught herself turning to see what was so interesting.

'Damn!' She had almost allowed herself to lose control.

"I'm Detective Crane and this is Detective Sorsky," the one in charge began in a droning monotone as the manager melted out of her peripheral vision. "We would not have asked you here at this hour if it were not important. I won't beat around the bush, Miss Bloome. Some events occurred during or after the Gala last night, which have caused the hotel enough concern to call the police. To begin, we'd like to get a picture of the evening events and also of the Whitneys. Your being the only World Wide Banknote employee staying at the hotel, we would like to impose on you for some help."

"Always ready to please."

'I'll bet you are,' Crane thought, brushing aside her coquettish tone. "Miss Bloome, can you tell us a little about the party last night? Any interesting, unusual or out of the ordinary events?"

"Nothing I can think of, but of course I don't make a career of going to these kinds of affairs, so maybe I'm not the best person to ask."

Crane noticed she had a kittenish way of swinging her head, rearranging her long waves of rich black curls as she talked. It was both provocative and distracting, yet he was sure it worked with most men, to keep their focus on where she wanted it.

'I really don't need this at five thirty in the morning,' he snarled to himself then continued.

"What exactly was your capacity at the event? Guest? Employee?"

"I would say both. World Wide Banknote gives out a number of tickets to employees every year. There is a drawing and everyone wishing to go submits his or her name. If you get lucky . . ." Annie paused.

"So you got lucky?"

"Well, yes." She wasn't going to tell him how lucky but she figured she could allow him that much.

"Then if you were a guest, for whom were you keeping schedules?"

"Schedules?"

"Yes, on the phone when we called, you implied your presence had some official capacity." Crane watched her carefully; certain she was a young woman with an agenda.

"Oh, yes! I'm a little tired."

"I can appreciate that," he waited.

"The employees with the invitations often come a little early and help with any last minute details. A program of events is distributed. I looked around for mine but I must have thrown it out this morning on my way back to the room. I'm sorry. I don't generally keep superfluous things around." Her smile radiated.

'I'm sure you don't,' Crane thought. "Seems reasonable to me. How about you, Stan?" They were a class act, and as Crane retreated into the background, Stan knew this was his cue to take over.

"What is your position at World Wide Banknote, Miss Bloome?"

"I work in Finance; I'm an accountant."

"An accountant," Stan repeated, "you must be a very valued employee. Did you talk with Mr. and Mrs. Whitney last night? Were you required to do any special jobs for either of them during the evening?" Stan allowed her little time to change gears from flattery to fact.

"Not really, I mean, yes, of course, I spoke with each of them, but I wasn't required to do any coordinating if that's what you mean."

'What is going on here,' she wondered.

"You say you spoke to each of them. Does that mean they didn't spend much of the evening together? As a couple?"

'Now I'm in for it,' she thought. "Actually, they were both moving around a lot, greeting guests; you know the whole society bit. I did see them dance together at least once during the evening. But I was having such a good time, I really didn't pay much attention."

Crane, who had grown up with cotillions and charity events found it odd that she had such a bang up good time. She had no escort. He knew mainly couples attended most of these events. Yet, he remembered once when his sister was dateless at one of these kinds of affairs. His friends and the husbands of family friends had asked her to dance; she was a known entity, one of their own social group. But this incredibly beautiful young woman was a threat to every wife in the room. No woman in her right mind would have loaned out her husband for a dance to a perfect stranger, unless it was to find out who she was.

"About what time was it when you last saw Mrs. Whitney?" Stan continued.

"I don't know," Annie thought hard. "It hadn't occurred to me. What? About eleven? Twelve-thirty? Until now, I hadn't thought about it. I hadn't realized Mrs. Whitney left so early. The ball must have lasted until well after three a.m."

"Must have?"

"Well, I left about ten till three and the party was still in full swing when I said my good nights."

"And about what time did Mr. Whitney leave?"

"Gee, I can't remember," pausing a moment. "But I think he was there much longer than Mrs. Whitney. In fact," she brightened, "he was there when I left. I thanked him for giving me the opportunity to have such a wonderful evening." She hoped she wasn't laying it on too thick.

"And that was the last time you saw him?"

"I...yes . . ." The word seemed to catch in her throat, "Why yes, of course it was!" She repeated herself, hoping the officer had missed her initial hesitation.

Stan and Crane exchanged glances.

"Miss Bloome, Mrs. Winslow-Whitney seems to be missing." "Missing?"

Richard Crane's words hung pungent in the stillness. "There may have been foul play."

"Oh! No!" Her face flushed and Annie caught her hand to her throat. How genuine her surprise was, Crane wasn't sure. If it wasn't, she put on one heck of an act.

Annie waited for more, but Crane wasn't giving.

"Miss Bloome, we would expect you to keep quiet about this, for now. After all, it may make a difference in Mrs. Whitney's safety."

Annie nodded in agreement.

"That's all for now. Thank you for coming down."

Annie realized she was being dismissed, and she still knew very little. Ian was going to be livid. She rose slowly, paused, and then headed for the door.

"By the way, Miss Bloome," it was Crane again, "why did you choose to stay at the hotel?"

Annie paused, this time she locked eyes with a man she instinctively knew could be her nemesis.

"I treated myself. This is quite a change for a girl from Queens, don't you think?" And she turned and walked out.

Crane waited until the door was securely shut before picking up the phone.

"Room 1610, thanks." Crane waited. "After the guest leaves room 309, check out that room too." Crane paused, "no, no dead bodies. Just make sure the current guest doesn't . . . You got it."

CHAPTER 8

The quiet hum of the Porsche 911 engine belied its power as Ian Whitney maneuvered the sleek low car though the incandescent grayness of the early Sunday morning, city traffic. The fine-tuned machine ran with precisioned race rally smoothness as Ian entered the empty freeway. Daylight lasted less than ten hours now, as the winter solstice neared, so his early morning, November ride on I95 North was shrouded in darkness.

Had the cops gotten onto him so soon? Had Asia found him out and called the police? Ian slammed his fist on the steering wheel. His hand smarted, but he didn't care. He thought he would have more time for those few small finishing touches. Tonight would have finished it off. Had someone mucked up his plan?

Infuriated, Ian's face darkened. The very thought of the police infuriated him but behind the wheel, he had no fear. The engine roared and Ian could feel his testosterone surge as he lead footed the gas pedal to the floor. He was filled with an erotic cockiness. Enraged, he cut the normal three-hour drive from New York to Providence by half.

This was excitement. Not those little whores who threw their bodies at him, trying to suck him into their hopes and dreams. The engine revved. This was real sex. A shameless masturbatic erection of unleashed power.

At the Wyoming exit, he left I95, traveling the back roads to circumvent Providence. The sun was peaking over the horizon as he crossed the Route 138 Bridge through Jamestown and the bridge through Newport. Going north, he reconnected with I95 then headed east on route 6 on the Cape.

His destination was a modest, weather beaten, gray cedar shingled house near South Wellfleet on the Outer Cape. The cottage that Asia had inherited from her grandfather was one of the few privately owned properties left, situated on the crusty Atlantic side. Nestled among a copse of pitch pine, red maple and beech, it was protected from the harsher winter storms by a massive sand dune that blocked the inhabitants' ocean view, but not the rhythmic pounding sound of the breaking waves.

Ian slowed his speed as the sun reached its full profusion. Full daylight meant more drivers. Route 6 was known for its high incidence of accidents, and a speeding ticket was the last thing he wanted now. Ian recalled his former life at home in London, the parties, the partners, a little 'coke' to juice it up. Unfortunately, his lifestyle was more expensive than the measly 50,000 quid his uncle paid. So Ian had gotten creative.

"What do you mean stealing from the till?" His uncle was livid. He had only taken from the family company's petty cash. After all, it wasn't much and wasn't he part of the family?

"A thousand pounds a month! You degenerate, sniffling little prig." Harsh words, Ian thought, and toward his only nephew.

'Why did everything have to be so hard?' Ian questioned, as he turned off the main road onto a sandy lane more like a path. All he ever wanted was his freedom.

Ian pulled into the semicircular drive and made an abrupt stop. Although his anger had lessened, his body was stiff from the long ride and upon getting out of the car, he walked with a fast staccato motion. His lean, Adonis body lunged toward the front door. He was safe here, out of sight of the world. Sure, there was a caretaker, old Weatherspoon, but he lived over Wellfleet way, and this was the only house on the road.

Once inside, Ian regained his composure. His facial muscles relaxed and a smile curled around his squarish jaw. Everything was in place. It had to be. He had taken care of it himself. It was nice to feel in charge, and Ian again believed his plan could not fail.

Shutting the door securely behind him, he surveyed the living room with its comfortable couches, claw footed over stuffed chairs and the hand made petit point rug. The highly polished wood floors mirrored the reflection of the long fireplace mantle. A number of years ago, Ian had noticed that in the reflection, there was the slightest slit in its wooden façade. Behind the rectangular, sliding wooden piece, he had found a hidden recess of perfectly defined proportions, ideal for his needs.

He moved eagerly toward the mantle. No matter what was happening in the city, over the years Ian had come here often to re-center his resolve and focus on his plan. Caressing his stash in his mind, he touched the right hand panel with just enough pressure to activate the spring. No response. Anxiously Ian pushed again, this time with slightly more force.

'What was wrong? Maybe it was jammed.' he told himself. He pushed the panel a third time. It remained stationary. Frantic now, he bent down, and tried to move the compartment panel by hand. Still it did not budge. Beads of perspiration covered his forehead and his facial muscles tensed. He gripped the small wood ax lying on the fireplace floor. Ferociously, he swung the blade, chopping at the panel, hoping that the spring would unlatch. But it didn't. He stopped momentarily to wipe his brow and survey the damage.

How would he explain this to Asia? Explain? Asia wasn't a factor anymore; as soon as he got what he came for, he would be on his way. Out of the staid, boring life he had been leading for the last eight years. Freedom!

He began again, feverishly chipping away at the mantle piece panel. As he hacked, sweat poured from his forehead and dropped onto the wood splinters that splattered the floor around his feet. His sweat soaked hair stuck, pasted to his forehead and his face reddened in anger. Finally a hole. He reached in and released the broken spring, jumping back just in time to avoid the mantle slat as it fell to the floor. Inside the open space there was nothing. NOTHING! How the hell could there be nothing? Six million dollars in United States Bearer Bonds gone! Kaput! NOTHING?

Unbelieving, he moved closer and thrust his hand behind the false front into the interior of the now hollow nook up to his shoulder. Emptiness. Aghast and chilled, he removed his arm and stood statue still for what seemed like hours, trying to absorb the situation.

Suddenly, swinging his arm, Ian smashed his fist into a gilded-framed mirror. Minute glass splinters embedded themselves in his hand and arm, creating pinpricks of blood in spider web patterns along his extremity. Stunned by the impact of his blow, he saw the face of a stranger in the splintered patches of mirror left hanging in the frame. As he watched, he realized it was his own smug, sardonic face that was changing into pure evil. Then without warning, his own high-pitched, piercing scream shattered the silence.

.

CHAPTER 9

It was late afternoon when the two detectives checked in at headquarters and found a lab report on Crane's desk. Attached to it was a note. "Drop by," was all it said. Stan, who hated the smell of formaldehyde and the sight of dead bodies, a real drawback in his line of work, begged off. Crane, on the other hand, rarely passed up an opportunity to talk to his old friend, Malcolm Banner.

"Maybe you can catch up with Ian Whitney while I'm gone."

"Yeah, maybe," Stan smiled.

Richard knew the first thing Stan would do was call his wife, Jeanie. Even with the hardships of his job, after twelve years of marriage and two kids, they still behaved like newlyweds.

. . . .

Malcolm Banner sat with his feet propped up on his massive, time-worn, mahogany desk watching smoke circles float upward and evaporate in the high ceiling wasteland he called his office. The fossilized desk had arrived with him and would go when he left. As Crane entered, he was fascinated by the hazy rays of light that filtered through the long, narrow, wood framed windows behind the desk. The permanently grime encrusted panes cast parallel lines of light and shadow across Banner, the desk, and the room. Heavy dark wooden floor to ceiling bookcases lined both walls on each side of the large cavernous space. One side was filled with books, pamphlets, and file folders overflowing in random piles onto the old oak floors. While on the other, placed in clutches, was an accumulation of jars full of unusual specimens, rocks and animal remains. Once Crane had circumvented an old gargoyle legged, refectory table placed between the door and Banner's desk, he paused to remove a stack of books littering the worn leather chair opposite the desk and sat down. The scent of the floating tobacco smoke softened the odor of formaldehyde and disinfectant that permeated the air from the morgue's lab next door.

"Other than the blood you saw in the hotel room and the bath, we found a bandage, one of those small circular types on which there was also fresh blood. Different blood type though. Too bad we're not equipped to do this new DNA testing. Deoxyribonucleic acid it's called. Discovered by some chaps at Cambridge. Scotland Yard's been using it for the last four years, since '79. British experts say the odds it can pinpoint an individual's blood are 189 million to one. The Brits claim it's already begun to make a difference in their criminal investigations."

"We've got to find a suspect first." Crane laughed, "and once we do, our courts and juries will still be leery of the science."

"That attitude won't last forever." Banner replied assuredly.

"So what do we have to work with now?"

"These bits of fiber string," Banner passed a small plastic bag to Crane, "were found among the shattered lamp fragments. I'd say sweater, probably old, wool. Generic. We'll do an analysis of course to determine the fabric and if we're lucky, we might even be able to determine the manufacturer. However, this is the kind of clue that will be almost impossible to trace to a specific individual."

Crane studied the lone navy strand. It had a fuzzy looking texture but not enough for the human eye to be able to distinguish any type of wool. But as Banner had said, they would process the small thread through every conceivable test.

"And these strands of hair," Banner continued pushing three more plastic bags across his desk. "We might get a little more from these, particularly if they match the missing person or some other known individual involved in the case.

"In this bag, is a piece of plastic we found caught in the door jam. We haven't much." Banner's slightly graying, tousled brown hair wreathed his head in ringlets and his piercing stare, through thick, horn- rimmed glasses gave the impression of a college professor not the pathology guru of New York City's forensic labs. Nor did he have that pasty pallid skin tone of so many of his colleagues who spent so much of their lives in windowless city morgues.

"Until we get some results back," Banner passed Crane the second plastic bag which held about a two by four inch piece of thick plastic, "this is probably our best lead. Industrial grade plastic used in the manufacture of heavy bags. The kind used by laundries or cleaning companies who have substantially heavier loads than found in your normal household trash or lawn debris."

"Maybe the hotel uses these, or a vendor. Someone whose presence wouldn't seem unusual," Crane felt a faint spark of excitement. "A list of plastics jobbers around the city... What about the elevators?" Crane rose and began to pace.

"One service elevator had a few bloodstains."

"That at least gives us a clue of how they or someone may have gotten her out of there."

"Until we get all the lab reports back we won't know for sure."

"Any fingerprints?"

"I think you know, fingerprints can't be lifted off material, so her torn dress is of no use to us."

Richard Crane nodded.

"As for the room, it looked as if it had been wiped down, so I've got someone checking for latent prints. In the elevator? Masses of them. Probably used by every employee in the place. I hate to admit it Richard," Banner continued, "but I'm somewhat baffled. Not by the blood or the little bits and pieces, but by the place itself. Although there was a lot of blood, the configuration was strange."

Richard Crane leaned against the bank of overloaded bookshelves patiently waiting for what Banner did so well.

"Blood is a liquid and like all liquids it responds according to the laws of physics. To the qualified eye, blood patterns tell stories. For example, if I punch you in the nose, which would be considered a low-velocity impact, the blood would drip straight down on the floor leaving big drops. Much larger than the drops caused by say, a bullet, which we both know creates pinpoint mist-like spots of a much smaller diameter. In that room, other than where the blood fanned out due to the textures of the carpet and the dress, there were streaks here and there on the mirror, but the rest of the blood was just a series of random spots, no smudges or splats from a body form."

"One would think if the victim were being stuffed into a plastic bag…" Crane caught his drift.

"But could it be that the victim knew her abductor or was taken totally by surprise?" Crane asked. "Or could the abductor have walked her out?"

Banner furrowed his brow. "This case ought to alleviate boredom."

"Stan and I flatfooted it all day and came up with zilch. Neither the guests, nor the hotel staff heard a thing. Other than a list of gala patrons, leads from the hotel ranged from zero to none." Banner detected a mixture of disgust and exhaustion in Crane's voice.

"Odd thing is, the woman's husband has come up missing as well."

"So you can't find the alleged victim and now the husband's gone too. Hell of a situation."

"We do know that at about three ten in the morning, he asked one of the waiter's for a bottle of Bouzy Champagne and two glasses."

"The guy's certainly got expensive tastes."

"Why not, he can afford it, or at least his wife can. Anyway, it seems that on his way to the elevators he asked which one was the fastest to the garage. Yet, when he got on, the bellhop noticed he went up instead of down."

"And I bet I can guess where you think he went."

Crane smiled. "You tell me."

"Voila!" Banner produced a fifth plastic bag containing a bottle with a missing label. "The trash, Room 309. We also got a lot of prints. Could be hubby's got something on the side?"

"The impression at the Plaza is the guy gets around."

"Did you meet Miss 309?"

Crane nodded.

"What's she like"?

"Cool. She's a real looker. Stan thinks she's hot. Another climber."

"Will she make it?"

"Who knows, a rung might break. Maybe it already has."

"Umm...Sounds like someone I'd like to meet." Malcolm paused. "You think you've got two victims here? A matching couple?"

"Maybe. My gut feeling? No." Malcolm Banner only reinforced Crane's feeling that something screwy was happening here. Something not quite real. Crane was tired and annoyed. He wanted to find this girl and be done with it. Coincidence or not, Crane had already decided Ian Whitney, the missing woman's husband, was no knight in shining armor.

CHAPTER 10

Ian awoke on the cottage floor, a rumpled mass. Dazed. At first, he was not quite sure where he was. He tried to rise, but an excruciating throbbing in his right arm limited his movement and he fell back. The hardwood floor felt cold against the slowly abating heat of pulsating pain. Finally he tried lifting just his arm and the acute pain again shot from his hand to his shoulder. A small pool of dried blood stained the wooden floor where his arm had lain, and the arm itself was riddled with a reddish brown glace of more dried blood over an infinitesimal pinprick pattern of glass splinters and dirt. Ian drifted. Was he dreaming? Awake? He wasn't quite sure.

Slowly, he regained consciousness. How long had he been out? Two, three hours? What time was it? Two p.m. It was the middle of the afternoon!

What the hell was happening? Then he remembered the horrifying events that had taken place before he passed out. First the police, questioning Annie. The very presence of the police gave Ian the hint of foul play, and if that weren't enough, the possible exposure of his affair with Annie Bloome.

But it went deeper than that. The missing bonds. He could deal with everything else. Save that. His whole body ached as he lay on the floor thinking. He had spent eight long years accumulating the cash. For eight years he had slowly converted the cash into United States Bearer Bonds. Whenever he had the opportunity, he would sneak up to the cottage and cache them behind the fireplace panel. Whenever there had been a glitch, skimming money from the company, he had taken care of it. Carefully covering his tracks with phony bills of laden, padded expense accounts, even fake petty cash chits when it was necessary. It hadn't always been easy, but he had succeeded. Jack Winslow's fondness for him had helped, as well as his fatherly concern for his daughter's happiness. Yes, he had survived.

Bearer bonds had been the perfect way to stash the cash. No account, or paper trails that the government or individuals could follow. Just bonds issued to THE BEARER. Anyone could cash them. No fuss, no muss, no names; invisible money. His kind of deal, and now they were missing. THAT was the problem! Anyone could cash them, no questions asked. Their beauty and their curse. They were so easily transferable. Possession was ownership. Just who the hell thought they owned his! This was going to take some concentrated methodical thought. He knew he couldn't steal six million dollars twice. Steal? Wrong! How could he consider it stealing? After all he had married her. Anyway, even if he could replace the six million, the FEC had just changed the law. Bearer- Bonds could no longer be bought by private individuals. He had to get them back. One thing for sure, he would not forget 1983.

'I'll call Annie…' he thought, 'find out about her interview with the police.' Slowly, supporting his arm, he got up and with halting steps maneuvered himself to the phone. No answer. He could feel his anger welling up again. He wanted to strike out at something, or someone. But this time he stopped himself. One bad arm was enough. He needed to control his temper and think. Finally he decided to call his house. See if he could find out what the police were up to, what they knew. After several rings their housekeeper Emma answered.

"What do you mean Mrs. Whitney is missing? She may be hurt?" He paused, listening. "Kidnapped! Oh! No!" Anyone listening would have heard his tone of genuine concern. "But she was supposed to meet me here at the cottage." A boldfaced lie, he knew and he hoped it wouldn't trip him up later. But what could he do? He had to find out what was happening? "Then I'd better call the police." He paused again. "Emma, if the police call again before I get to them, give them the cottage number." He could hear her soft sobs in the background. "If I leave here, I'll call. Don't worry, Emma, we'll find her."

Ian hung up the phone and considered the possibilities. Even if he had the bonds in hand, Asia's disappearance had put a damper on his original plans.

A quick trip to Mexico, sun, surf, babes on the beach - and no extradition. Six million could last a long time if one was prudent. A money transfer to the Caymans, there he'd even earn a little interest. But it had all gone bust. Even if he got back the bonds, if he left now, he might become the prime suspect. Tracking someone for missing money was one thing, but now that she was missing that was dicey business. Besides, if she never showed up, or was found dead, he might end up with not only the bonds, once he found them, but also control of World Wide Banknote. A real bonus. Leave now? No. It was obviously much better to stay and play the grieving husband.

But first, he had to find a doctor for his arm. Then try and figure out who had stolen his bonds. The police could wait.

CHAPTER 11

Crane opened a single eye and checked the time. After a 20-hour stint on duty with only three hours sleep and no day off, he had allowed himself to wake up naturally. No alarms, and positively no phone calls. Those were his orders. The president himself could have made a request and Crane would have declined.

Eight fifteen. His bedside clock seemed to yawn at him accusingly. Crane turned over in defiance and stretched. No matter what time he went to bed, he always awoke at six a.m., unless he was really bummed. Coffee. The thought stimulated by the need, gave him just enough energy to put his tired body into gear. Slowly, he maneuvered from the bedroom, through the living room and into the kitchen. Now, if only he could push the button on the automatic pot. Yes! Olympic gold! Then he wandered back to bed and slowly sipped his muddy black morning fix.

"ACME LAUNDRY," had been Stan's message, "they serviced the Plaza while their in-house laundry was under renovation. The plastic bags used by ACME matched Banner's scraps." Stan's message continued. He had dropped by the hotel and checked it out on his way home. Then he had called Crane. The paper work was already done; all Crane had to do was call in the request for a warrant. He and Stan were a class act, and together they functioned like clockwork. Crane went to sleep knowing there would be policemen impounding the laundry truck before ACME had a chance to finish opening its doors.

As Crane finished his coffee, he pressed for his messages. His mother had met another lovely young woman, this one worked in television, when could he come to dinner? Just what a cop needed in his life, another arm of the press. Never, Crane thought! Then he listened to his next message. Emily, his sister, bubbled over the new foal that had arrived, mother and baby doing fine. Richard smiled and gave a limp hurrah, although he was glad all went well. He'd respond to both later. Then he called the precinct. Having learned what he wanted to know, Crane grabbed a second cup of coffee and headed for his usual icy cold morning shower. He had no doubts about his biological structure being DNA, but he also knew the cups of black gunk he drank every morning seeped into the crevices of his brain and became his fuel. Bristling from the chilling shower, he had just finished dressing when his doorbell rang with a screeching sound only his partner could produce. Then he heard the latch as Stan let himself in. When Crane entered the kitchen, Stan was finishing a watered down version of the dregs in the pot.

"Truck driver's name is Riley Patterson." Crane smiled. "The desk sergeant says he made quite a scene, went absolutely ballistic about our impounding his truck."

"Yeah. I heard. Banner's just waiting for the report," Stan replied in his easy manner. "By the way, did you know that World Wide Banknote's offices are only a few blocks from here over on Park Avenue? I would' a thought they'd be located down in the financial district, where the action is."

Crane nodded with surprise. "Probably a better place to hide with their kind of clientele. After all, they don't trade money, they only print it."

"Your point being?" Stan questioned.

"They must have an occasional visit from financial heads of state or potentates wanting to bask at their picture on a sample bill. The Banknote staff could whisk them out of their limousines and into a quiet Park Avenue address pretty unobtrusively and none would be the wiser that the guy was even in town. I'd bet World Wide Banknote maintains their offices where they do to keep a low profile."

"Gotya! And the location's a natural, near the best hotels and restaurants, the theatre district and Fifth Avenue," Stan continued Crane's thought, seeing the merit of the expensive address.

Richard nodded.

"We're near enough, I figured we'd hoof it. Then we'd go back to the precinct and have our little chat with this truck huggin' Patterson afterward."

"The car?"

"I had Davis drop me off."

The thought of a brisk, Manhattan morning walk in the fresh winter air had its appeal and Crane threw on a coat. As they neared Park Avenue, Crane asked Stan the address. "Uhm," he murmured as they walked along the low, snug, four and five story granite buildings. Some had become private businesses while many still remained the original private residences and apartments that had always dotted Park Avenue.

"Some of society's grandest old ladies are still ensconced behind these unobtrusively neat little edifices." Crane mused.

"You mean most of this real estate is owned by a bunch of old biddies?" Stan responded.

"No, I mean that some of society's grandest 'Grand Dames' still quietly control 'real society', from behind the recesses of these almost opaque facades." Crane responded annoyed. "The younger family members, my father's generation, have moved to the more chic east side addresses with their views of Central Park, or to the Upper West Side, over with the newcomers, intellectuals and noveau riche. But these old girls are still here pulling the strings."

"That's what I said," Stan replied nonplused.

The façade of World Wide Banknote's respectable address abutted the sidewalk, creating an architectural right angle as the neat low, gray granite, stone building ended, and the sidewalk began. Indented into the building's flatness were darkly stained massive doors with highly polished bronze handles. Cat-eyed, sliced rectangular windows lined an upper floor on either side just above the entry. While metal framed, multi-square medieval Tudor windows balanced the edifice and enhanced its subdued, unapproachable presence of power and money.

Stan pointed out the almost indistinguishable highly polished bronze plaque with the company's name in small block script.

Seeing the building, Crane understood the merit of this expensive address, low key enough to be almost invisible. After all, this was a business that wanted invisibility, and almost everything these families did; births, weddings, and even deaths were cloaked in anonymity. A well-manicured English tweed who answered their ring abruptly interrupted Crane's thoughts.

CHAPTER 12

Inside the marble walled reception, the detectives were directed to a small Louis XIV desk where, and with quiet smiles and soft voices, their names and identifications were solicitously confirmed. Only then were they ushered into an inconspicuously situated elevator, with its interior walls lined with brushed brass, and brass and green leather covered handrails. A thick, red shaded handmade Turkoman Bokkara rug lay underfoot.

"Some operation," Stan said, as they were whisked at high speed to World Wide Banknote's third floor offices. "It's got class!"

The elevator stopped in front of wrought iron, glass paneled doors, which slid back to expose a modestly sized lobby, decorated with mahogany tables, small muted colored sofas and Audubon prints. The two detectives stepped out. It was only later on his way out that Crane noticed a small Rembrandt next to the elevator door and realized that all the furniture was antique Bermudan mahogany. Only at Winterthur in Wilmington, had Crane seen this fine a collection outside Bermuda.

A receptionist, seated at a small mahogany desk, nodded toward two comfortable sofas. A glass wall with mahogany honed, glass paneled double doors, to the left of the reception-ist's antique desk, separated the reception area from the more private offices.

Crane watched, waiting for the live action. A couple stepped into view, he in tweed, patched pockets, causally elegant.

"A regular Mr. Gentlemen's Quarterly," Stan mumbled under his breath.

But all Crane noticed was her legs. 'Start from the shoes up,' his boyhood pals had always joked, and for once he fol-lowed their instructions. Patent two-inch, slim line, heels with a buster brown strap, slender ankle, and just the right curve to the calf.

The pleats of her herringbone, hip stitched skirt swung softly just above her knees. Her matching top was cut like a rid-ing jacket; so perfect that Crane had the urge to register the size of her waist with his hands. The young woman was thin, about 5' 6", with soft curves in all the right places.

Her reddish auburn hair grazed her shoulders in a slight flip and as she turned, a casual smile lingered on her lips. She stunned him with her large, almond shaped, inquisitively pierc-ing, greenish-gray eyes.

Unlike Annie Bloome, whom Crane had to admit was beau-tiful, this woman's beauty, laced with a gracious natural elegance, exuded good breeding, good schools, private house parties and trips abroad.

"A rare specimen." Stan took a double take. Had he heard correctly? Crane was actually saying a 'WOW' under his breath just as one of the large mahogany doors swung open.

"Gentlemen," she said, extending her hand. Talk about poor timing. "Have you any word? I'm extremely worried about Mrs. Whitney. We all are. Please." With the movement of her arm she ushered them through the doors, into the inner-sanctum of World Wide Banknote's private world.

Her office was expensive and tasteful. She extended her hand, "I'm Cynthia Ryder, Mrs. Winslow-Whitney's personal assistant," she said as she directed them to two claw-footed wing chairs.

Her hand was neither as soft, nor her grip as delicate, as Crane had expected. Rather he was aware of roughened skin. Her movements suggested power and control and, as she seated herself behind the large half round mahogany desk, there was no doubt that in this room, in this office, she was in charge.

"Would you like some tea, coffee? No. News." Her tone was concerned and eager at the same time.

"I'm afraid we have very little," Crane paused. "Your employer seems to have vanished into thin air." Ryder's reaction was immediate.

"Yes! Asia was my employer. But you don't understand. She was my best friend. We met in college. We roomed together. We've been inseparable ever since. Why am I talking in the past tense? Do you think she's come to some harm?" She stopped, swallowed and she caught her breath; tears rimmed her large almond eyes. "You must find her. And find her safe."

"Maybe that's where you can help, Miss Ryder."

"I know nothing about this, officer. I couldn't even attend the Gala. It was the first time in the ten years I've worked for

71

World Wide Banknote that I've missed the fundraiser. And look what's happened."

Crane continued gently, "But if you could just answer a few questions. Give us some insight into this business. It might be helpful in getting Mrs. Winslow-Whitney home."

'Crane was being awfully nice to this dame that he knew nothing about. Not that he wasn't generally a nice guy but . . .' Stan couched his thoughts.

"Why don't you begin by telling us why you weren't there?"

"I'm an only child, Mr. Crane, is it? Mr. Crane. My parents died when I was ten and my grandmother raised me." Her voice resonated in a rich textured tone that reminded Crane of apple butter sliding off a knife. "She was in her nineties and had been in a nursing home in up state New York for some years. Because of her infirmity, oftentimes, I'd spend holidays with the Winslows who'd become a second family to me. My grandmother passed away last weekend. I have been in Albany since a week ago Saturday. I returned late last night, to this awful news."

"Yes, I can see you don't need any more . . . ." Crane paused. "But we do need your help."

Cynthia Ryder nodded. "Anything."

"Although there are clues of a mishap, we have yet to find Mrs. Whitney's body. Maybe we should start with World Wide Banknote. What is it you do? Whom would she have come in contact with? Grudges? Business problems? The kind that might make someone want her to disappear, that sort of thing."

Cynthia shook her head vehemently. "Banknote is a highly legitimate business, Mr. Crane, and probably one of the most financially solid privately owned companies in the country. Asia is highly respected in this business. The thought of anyone wanting to harm her is just too ridiculous!" A sob caught in her throat. "God! It's just too shocking."

The two officers sat quietly as she regained her composure.

"As for World Wide Banknote, we do just what the name implies. We produce paper money." She motioned toward the numerous framed bank notes behind her desk. "With a world population of nearly 5 billion, ours is a rather essential product. Last year alone, I'd estimate 50 billion new bills were produced by various bank note companies throughout the world."

"But I thought countries printed their own money?" Stan interjected.

"Some do," Cynthia continued. "The United States for instance, has the Bureau of Engraving and Printing and the Soviets have Gosnak. Interestingly, the operation in the USSR is still run by the same family that printed banknotes for the Czar."

"I guess it pays not to purge everyone," Crane smiled. "Some pigs ARE better than others?" She continued as if he had not spoken.

"Actually, until our competitors Rino Giori, an Italian Jew, and Otto Segfried, a former Nazi tank corps major, teamed up to manufacture and sell Intaglia Banknote Printers in the 1950s, seven families had a virtual international monopoly on the bank note business. Then a number of small, but very wealthy, countries bought Giori's and Segfried's machines and became their steady customers, needing servicing and occasional updating of the printers. As for the rest of us, we all lost major markets. China and Japan were two of the first in line to buy."

"Those are big markets to lose!" Stan blurted.

"You're absolutely right, but Giori and Segfried outsmarted even themselves. Both countries spent the requisite six million and each bought only one machine. The one that printed both bank notes and postage stamps. Then each country had their engineers set to work copying the parts of the original machines they purchased. The Japanese built sixteen copies of their machine and the Chinese made twenty-eight," she laughed.

Crane smiled, "Those inscrutable Orientals."

"Until the end of WW II, the production of banknotes was an exclusively closed shop," Cynthia continued. "If you weren't born into it, the only way in was through marriage. When Giori and Segfried broke the sacred tradition of secrecy, there were only eight major international bank noters: American Bank Note, Bradbury, De La Rue, Wilkinson, Giori, Giesecke & Devrient and Enschede, La Croix and World Wide Banknote.

Although Giori's actions cut into everyone's business, as always, the historically good friends of the bank note printers: colonialism, emerging nations, coups, and dictators remained. Every time there is a coup and a government changes hands, massive bank note orders with RUSH ORDER on them are received, keeping us from the depths of starvation. After all, no new dictator wants his predecessor's picture around, particularly on the currency."

"Oh yeah!" Stan thought as he surveyed the room.

"Of course," she continued, "over the years we have compensated and taken advantage of market changes. We contract to print postage stamps, food stamps, various stock & bond issues and recently, we have even been experimenting with hot stamp foils to produce holograms for credit cards."

"You don't do this all here?" Stan blurted.

"Our main factory is in Union Center, upstate. If you'd like to see the process, your're welcome anytime." Her warm, seductive eyes met Crane's.

"Sounds interesting. I just might take you up on that." Stan noticed Crane's manner changed after the invitation. "Then, you do not believe there could have been any business reason for her disappearance?"

Cynthia shook her head emphatically no.

"What about her family, personal relationships?"

"Her private life? Other then the loss of her mother when Asia was very young; up until recently, Asia's was a charmed life." Pausing, Cynthia sighed almost wishfully. "Her father doted on her, and she and her husband, Ian, were very much in love."

"Until recently." Stone faced, Crane solemnly mimicked her words.

"Yes. Earlier this year, her father Jack Winslow, died. They were very close and Asia took it hard."

"Had he been ill?" Crane questioned.

"No," her voice wavered. She paused and she moved her hands to her lap, barely maintaining her composure. "It was quite sudden actually. An accident." She gazed momentarily into the distance. A loss too much to bear? Crane and Stan exchanged glances. Then as quickly as the quiet had ensued, it had just as quickly dissipated. An almost infinitesimal hardness entered her tone as she began again. "Her husband Ian was there at the time. And although they have always had a solid marriage, her father's death seemed to put a wedge in their relationship."

"Then you're saying she believed her husband might have had something to do with her father's death?" Crane leaned forward and tapped his fingertips lightly on her desk.

"Oh! No! Her father adored Ian. After all, his mother is a De La Rue, of the English banknote family, a long time friend. This was a marriage made in Banknote Heaven." Cynthia laughed nervously. "Up until Jack's death, Ian and Asia were devoted to each other. The loss of her father has been a strain on both of them. I had hoped maybe the Gala might have helped to re-cement their relationship. I love them both. Unfortunately I was not able to be here."

As things got personal, Stan watched Crane's reaction. Was Crane's obvious attraction to this incredible woman going to get in the way? Stan had never seen Crane react to a woman this way, seemingly hanging on her every word. Of course, they had never run across a 'dish' like this before. Yet, something about this dame, for all her good looks and brains, didn't seem quite right. Stan could tell Cynthia Ryder was on the edge. It was obvious she cared a great deal about these people; their mess was her's, whatever it might be. 'Anyway, on the surface,' Stan mused to himself. But what about Crane? He was a good listener, a quality that made him such a successful detective. Usually, he'd let people talk until they hung themselves. But this time Stan was beginning to believe Crane was smitten.

"But what about you, Miss Ryder? Were you around when this accident happened?" The room went dead. Even Stan was stunned by the flatness in Crane's tone.

'Maybe I'm reading this all wrong.' Stan's confusion did not distract him from hearing her answer.

"No, Of course not! Jack died of natural causes." Momentarily stopping to catch her breath. "As I have already said, Ian was there at the time. But the inquest cleared him of all responsibility."

Inquest? If the man died of natural causes? Crane had the itchy feeling that there was more to these "really nice people" than their public persona implied.

"Speaking of Ian Whitney, Miss Ryder, we have not been able to find him anywhere. Would you, by any chance, know his whereabouts?"

Her reaction was swift and defensive, "Missing? I had no idea."

"You mean he hasn't called in?"

"No."

"I'm assuming he works in the business? Weren't you concerned?"

"Sometimes, Ian goes off for a few days, particularly if we've just finished a lot of deadlines. Typical of the way business goes; the bad timing, between the massive amounts of work and the gala, they have made this place a mad house." She paused as if collecting her thoughts. "Officer, Ian Whitney is a highly sensitive person. Wherever he is, whatever he's doing, I'm sure that if he knows Asia's missing, he's devastated. As for his harming her, it would never happen."

"We're not implying that he would. But we do need to talk to him. We need to make all the connections that might help us find Mrs. Whitney as soon as possible to assure her safety. If, by chance, she has been abducted, the longer it takes us, the less chance we have of finding her alive."

She nodded.

"Your offices are on the third floor of the building," Crane said casually. "What is on the other floors?"

Cynthia smiled. "The first floor is reception and a garden-drawing room, where clients may rest or freshen-up, the second floor is used for accounting and business and the top two floors were Jack Winslow's own private apartment. Asia has kept them closed since her father's death."

"Under the circumstances, we would like to see Jack Winslow's apartment, please." Crane was polite but firm.

"When?" Cynthia Ryder questioned.

"Now would be convenient,"

She hesitated…then reached into her drawer and laid the key on the desk. "I'll take you up."

"That won't be necessary, we can find our way. We'll drop by on our way out." Crane grabbed the key and he and Stan were out the door before Cynthia Ryder had a chance to object.

CHAPTER 13

Although Jack Winslow's home included two stories of the World Wide Banknote's building, the apartment was not enormously large. The first floor included an entry hall with a staircase to the upper floor as well as a continuance of the office elevator, which had a special key to allow one to ascend to the upper floors.

Off the hall, at the front of the building, was a neat eat-in kitchen with a small breakfast nook that overlooked the street below. In the center, a small formal dining area and at the end of the hall a large comfortable living room with floor to ceiling windows overlooking the small garden below. The second floor consisted of a master bedroom, large closets, two baths and a den.

"Wonder if this was our victim's room when she was small?" Stan pointed to the den.

"I doubt Winslow always lived here. Seems to me with a small child, he'd have needed room for a live-in staff. After all, a business like World Wide Banknote would not likely be a place for small children and their friends running about."

"Probably right. Couldn't have some sheik coming along tripping over roller skates in the hall." A bit nonplused, Stan knew his partner was right. Although Stan was well aware many Manhattanites had nannies, cooks and housekeepers, his background was with families who had to put their preschoolers and even babies in nursery schools or had the older kid next door baby sit until they got home from work. "So you think Winslow moved here after his daughter married?" Stan continued, as the two detectives perused the apartment, looking for links to the missing girl.

Winslow's clothes still hung neatly in the closet and personal brushes were laid out in a row on his waist high bureau top. It was as if a manservant had just tidied up and was waiting to serve. Other than a picture of his daughter on his bedside table and a clutch of family pictures on a small crotch mahogany refectory table in the den, the whole apartment seemed starkly devoid of personal items.

Crane picked up a picture and stared. She was younger here than in the shot the department had acquired. He wanted to respond to the face in the frame but he didn't know quite why.

Crane returned to the refectory table in the den. He picked up each picture individually. There were the typical graduation pictures, shots of children and adults making sand castles, a loving father and a small tot, and a clapboard New England seaside cottage. He was interested in them all but particularly the shots of the young Winslow girl. What was so perplexing about her, he wondered?

Suddenly he realized Stan was standing in the doorway, "Sorry, I just…" The sentence hung in midair. "Let's get out of here!" Crane turned abruptly, brushing past his partner as he headed back to the elevator.

....

Crane laid the apartment key on Cynthia Ryder's desk. "You've been very helpful, Miss Ryder."

"Anytime," Her smile would have melted an ice sculpture a foot thick.

Crane turned to leave. "Oh, and one last thing. May I have the name of Mrs. Winslow-Whitney's attorneys?" The glacial effect was unmistakable.

"Attorneys? Why in the world would you want them?"

'This woman sure can switch from bright to dumb faster than an idiot savant,' Stan thought.

"Abernathy, Huntington, Crane and Associates, 783 Madison Avenue, gentlemen," she said, looking from one to the other.

"I think I've heard of them." Crane smiled back.

"Actually there is a family cottage on the Cape. Sometimes Ian goes there when he needs some space. After a few days, Asia sometimes joins him. Maybe he's there. Maybe they're both there." Her tone was hopefully anxious.

"The cottage in the pictures upstairs."

"Yes, it's been in the family forever. Owned by Asia's grandfather, he left it to her when he died." The explanation was crisp and stiff.

'That Ryder dame's tough,' Stan thought as they rode back toward the station. 'If this is what Crane likes, he better watch out.' Stan was confused by Crane's behavior toward this woman. But he knew this was not the time to broach the subject.

"Well, well," Stan began, breaking the silence. "Abernathy, Crane, Huntington and the etc. Heard of them, eh? Getting damn close to home here, aren't we."

Crane grunted. It was the kind of response he gave when a fact didn't suit him, or he found it annoying. "Well, I guess I'll have to make time for my mother's latest dinner party." But he knew he wouldn't.

"But the question is . . . How many Muffy's can your mother get into the Crane dining room?" Stan smiled.

"More than in a 1978 Beetle." They both laughed knowingly. Although it was his mother's life goal, she hadn't married him off yet.

As they turned into the station lot, Stan said, "I can see why you like being rich, other than the money of course. So yeah! Everyone lives well . . . but the broads," Stan paused. "They're beautiful!"

Crane smiled. "On the outside." Crane repeated as if to himself. "On the outside."

CHAPTER 14

The two detectives were totally unprepared for the boy-man seated before them, his big brawny body and cherubic, childlike face streaming with tears.

"Nothing. I didn't do nothing. Just what Mr. Spankler said." At first, Riley spoke haltingly through his intermittent sobs. "Everyday I do as he says.... As perfect as I can. Otherwise he'd take my truck. I wouldn't get to drive... Mr. Spankler told me... Do your job and your truck's yours to drive as long as you want. Blood?" Riley's eyes widened in disbelief. "I don't know anything about blood. Why would I want to hurt someone?"

He paused as if thinking hard. "I know you just want my truck. I've been good to my truck. Why would you do this?" His sobs persisted.

"Look Mr. Patterson, please calm down. We don't want your truck."

"Then why did you take it? I didn't take anything of yours. I don't even know you." His body heaved back and forth as the words cascaded out in between his almost uncontrollable sobs.

Exchanging glances, the two men sighed. "Lets talk about something else. Lunch. Who makes your lunch everyday, Riley?" Crane asked kindly, speaking softly as if to a favorite small child.

"The Leibovitzes gave me a cake yesterday, a chocolate cake.... from the deli."

"The deli, huh?" The two detectives waited as Riley caught his breath and wiped his tear streaked cherubic cheeks.

"I bet they make great sandwiches."

"The best!"

"What's your favorite? Corned beef?"

"No, I like pastrami. Pastrami on rye." His reddened cheeks and eyes were tear stained and puffy as he blew his bulbous nose. Riley's slightly rocking motion was receding, although his tightly clinched fist full of soiled Kleenexes indicated his fear and tension.

"Would you like us to give the Leibovitzes a call? Ask them to come over?"

"Oh! No! They couldn't. They have their customers and Mrs. Leibovitz. She has her dough. They could never leave."

"Her dough?" The two detectives exchanged glances.

"Sounds important."

"Yeah! It's important all right. Mrs. Leibovitz makes cakes everyday. She takes pride in her fresh cakes."

"Sounds like serious business and you might be right," Crane said as Stan got up and left the room.

While Crane waited quietly for Riley to regain his composure and for Stan to return, he wondered what it must be like to view the world through Riley's innocence. Everything so black and white, good and bad, kind and unkind. To be such a gentle soul in such a harsh world. Crane doubted the brutalities of many of his own days and most of the people involved could comprehend Riley's kind of purity.

Moments later Stan ducked his head in. "The Leibovitzes should be here shortly. They're on their way."

"Mr. And Mrs. Leibovitz are coming here? For me?"

"Seems so," Crane smiled and nodded.

"I have a puppy, you know," Riley shared as he dropped the wads of Kleenex from his tightly clinched fists in the wastebasket Crane held out for him. "Its gray and white with white mitten paws." Slowly, his body relaxed. Gently he dried his eyes again, making a simple basket into the waste can with his last tissue. A slight smile crossed his face. "She has a big black ring around her left eye. Just like Spanky's dog," he continued, almost triumphantly. "If I'm not home to feed her, she'll starve...I'm a very responsible person. That's why Mr. Spankler hired me. That's why the Leibovitzes make my lunch. That's why I have Paws." Riley took a much-needed breath and straightened his collar. "That's her name, Paws. Do you like it?" Crane nodded again and smiled. "I wouldn't hurt anyone. Particularly a lady. My mom's a lady. I would never hurt my mom."

"Riley, you are probably right." Crane thought he'd try again. "But then tell me, how do you think that blood got on your nice truck?"

"I don't know. I wasn't gone any longer than normal." He paused a moment and thought. "Maybe it was because of the hum."

"The hum?" Crane watched as Riley's body stiffened.

At that moment, Stan entered with a warm rather roly-poly couple. They embraced Riley and he relaxed immediately.

Their trusting presence became the safety valve Crane needed to continue.

"Riley, tell us about the hum."

Mrs. Leibovitz reassuringly took his hand in hers.

"You know," he began, "I thought that low musical hum was something good. Something wonderful. I even stopped my work to listen. But maybe it was bad. Something bad." Riley slumped in his chair. A new awareness took shape in Riley's mind and his demeanor changed. Riley knew he was onto something, something important.

Crane perked up. He felt the same way. There was something here, and he had a good idea, but there was no way he was going to lead Riley.

Suddenly, like a lightening bolt, "It was a trick!" Riley shouted. "That's what it was, a trick, to get my truck – to hurt me. Why would anyone want to hurt me?" Riley was again becoming agitated, and wells of water formed in his eyes.

"What did you say?" Crane responded at almost the same staccato speed as Riley.

"Why would anyone want to hurt me?"

Mrs. Leibovitz patted Riley's hand.

"No, Riley before that. About the sound. What about the sound? Where was it?" Crane knew he was going too fast for the innocent young man, but he was in high gear.

"I don't know what you mean. It was just a good/bad sound. When I was on the elevator."

"Yes!" Crane responded.

Riley gazed at Crane amazed. "Did I say something wrong?"

"No, Riley. You said something exactly right, I think." Crane paused. "Riley, would you like to help the police with some detective work?"

"Detective work? What kind of detective work? I wouldn't have to arrest anyone would I?" Riley asked warily, with a hint of excitement in his voice.

"No arrests. Just go with us to the hotel and listen for the sound you described. Later. This afternoon." Crane explained in a serious tone. "Then we'd hear the sound too. It would be very helpful."

Riley grinned and nodded.

"Then we'll send a car. About three?" Crane looked toward the Leibovitzes for confirmation.

Mrs. Leibovitz smiled. "Why don't we go have a nice big lunch? Then you can go home and feed Paws and collect your thoughts. I think enough is enough. Detective Crane will see you later."

Crane nodded. They all knew Riley had had enough for now.

"Collect my thoughts?" Riley repeated, "I like that! It's ace. I'll just do that." Riley smiled. "I'll collect my thoughts as best I can. It's important to help the police."

"Christ! I could use my own pastrami on rye," Stan said as they watched Riley amble out between his friends, pointing at and reading aloud the EXIT sign as they went.

CHAPTER 15

"Hey Crane, you got a call." Davis' voice resonated across the precinct office. "Some guy by the name of Whitney. Line one."

"Bingo! Things are certainly looking up." Stan quipped.

"Mr. Whitney, Detective Crane here." Stan waited as Crane listened. "At this point we're not sure, but it's imperative we talk to you … as soon as possible." Crane paused again. "We are on our way." Hanging up the receiver, "He's at home. Sounds upset, but who knows." They both knew simulated upset was nothing new among their daily clientele.

"That's one pastrami sandwich out the window."

"Grab a doughnut." Crane replied tersely. "We need to get someone from forensics to check out which elevators ACME Laundry was authorized to use. We also want another thoroughly clean sweep of those service elevators that go from the basement to both the third and sixteenth floors." Before Crane, finished Stan was on the phone. "Tell them we're bringing the driver over this afternoon."

As long as he didn't have to spend time with Banner in the morgue, this was Stan's kind of job. Those forensics freaks were a good time away from their cadavers and slabs.

"Whitney's home is on the way. We'll check him out. Then go to Leibovitz's Deli around three." Crane paused, checking his watch and his partner's response as he rushed out.

"Forensics will be underway by the time we get there." Stan put down the receiver and followed.

"We'll play around. Have two elevators going opposite directions simultaneously," Crane suggested. "You know, have a good time."

Stan interrupted Crane with a long low whistle as they pulled up in front of the five-story brownstone, set slightly back from the street. "It's about half a block from Central Park. Private, yet convenient without the Fifth Avenue bustle and noise." Stan mimicked the typical local smooth, hard-boiled realtor spiel. "Not too shabby!"

Inside, they were ushered into a long living room that looked out onto a formal yet friendly miniature English garden. Curiously, Crane felt right at home. This was the kind of environment in which he had been raised. Small city gardens, classic taste, yet unlike so many people's homes of his background which reeked of 'decorator', this house had the same kind of hominess of pictures and personal touches that defined his own family's atmosphere. Just as he had done at Jack Winslow's apartment a few hours before, he picked up a photo of the missing young woman, and a pinch of memory nagged at him. Now he was sure of it; he had met this girl before. But where? He just couldn't quite dredge it up. It irritated him, made him angry because he felt it could be an important missing piece that would help him and maybe even save her life. Was he experiencing the sandbox effect; some event buried, he didn't want to remember? Maybe he'd made an ass of himself in front of her in college, or worse yet, she was one of his mother's 'Muffys.'

"No, I'd remember that." He remembered them all. So he could steer clear whenever the need arose. "Damn!"

"You'd remember what?"

So deep in thought, Crane was unaware he had spoken aloud, and turned on his heel toward the rich Etonian English accent. "I'd remember if I had met your wife at one of my mother's dinners."

Although Ian Whitney made every effort to saunter casually across the room to extend his hand, his movements were labored and heavy.

"I think not."

Crane ignored Whitney's sardonic tone, more interested in the nuance rather than the man's conceit.

"Asia is not much for dinner parties, and besides the only Cranes we know are our lawyers, Abernathy, Huntington, Crane & Associates. You know, Judge Abernathy and his family?" A snide smile crossed his face.

Stan quickly turned his back, pretending to be absorbed in a painting to keep from smirking in Whitney's face.

What an ass, Crane thought. Only this time he kept his thoughts to himself. "I see," was the only verbal response he could muster without laughing in the man's face. He could hardly wait for his grandfather, Judge Abernathy's commentary on this guy. But right now, Crane was more interested in how odd it was that the long sleeves of Whitney's crisp blue oxford cloth shirt were pulled all the way down his arms and tightly buttoned. It was certainly not the standard casual rolled up style one might expect in the privacy of this pleasantly temperature-controlled, private home.

"Detective Sorsky," Crane motioned toward Stan, who had finally gained enough composure to turn back around.

Whitney gave Stan a dismissive glance. His chalky pallor accentuated the excessively haggard lines that encrusted Whitney's otherwise handsome face. Crane's first impression was that Whitney was suffering from a serious illness. Then again, just perhaps the man was genuinely worried about his missing wife.

But Crane also found it strange, how Whitney kept his left hand stuffed resolutely in his cord's pocket, while his right, except when he had made the effort to shake hands, hung languidly, as if it were being pulled by an invisible weight.

"Are you ill, Mr. Whitney?" Crane asked.

"It's nothing. A fall at the cottage, an unfortunate little accident," Whitney countered with a sigh, brushing aside his obvious discomfort.

This guy was a real 'sod', but with his thick sandy blond hair, large grayish blue eyes, and accent... the accent got them every time. Crane knew this was just the kind of man women loved to mother. Whitney's hard, squarish-jawed features probably gave them the feeling of protection and strength. No matter what his current physical condition, Whitney was the illustrator's and Ad-man's dream. The kind of guy whose image every woman knew would fulfill her dreams. A real lover boy, who would emotionally do them in, then sweep them off their feet again and gain their forgiveness. Yet, Crane could see how women in general, and particularly an innocent young girl, could fall for him or even a needy, old gal. This guy oozed sensuality and sincerity. Bad news from anyone's standpoint. 'How,' Crane wondered, 'could Jack Winslow, such a shrewd businessman, have been so taken in by this walking, talking unmitigated self-centered bastard?'

"I'm so glad to finally be talking to you." The man's sarcasm had turned to charm. The resonance of Whitney's rich voice, imbued with his English accent, gave him a classy quality. Even in his obvious pain, he had the gestures and movements of an athlete.

"Have you found my wife?" He continued anxiously.

"No, Mr. Whitney we haven't which is why it's so important for us to understand the events of the evening she disappeared. Tell us about Saturday evening."

"You've had almost two days."

"Mr. Whitney, please. In cases like this, time is of the essence." Stan could tell Crane was losing his patience.

Ian Whitney gazed from one detective to the other then he began.

"The gala was its usual splendid event." He paused as if collecting his thoughts. "It went off without a hitch. I left about three in the morning to drive to the cottage. Asia was supposed to meet me there later. When she didn't show by afternoon, I called Emma. That's how I found out." Whitney told his tale in what sounded to Crane like short, flat, pre prepared sentences. Even his pauses had the ring of rehearsal.

"That's a long drive, particularly after a social function. Why didn't your wife ride with you?" Crane was genuinely interested in Whitney's response. After all, this was supposed to be one of those perfect couples, with a wonderful opportunity to exchange notes about a memorable evening.

"I find it exhilarating to drive up as the morning dawns, whereas Asia is more fastidious than I. She has to make sure all the grunt work is taken care of before she can relax enough to enjoy the ride. I guess I am selfish, but she allows me to be."

This, Crane conjectured, was probably the most honest statement they would ever get from this man. "Why didn't you come back to the city immediately upon hearing about Mrs. Whitney's disappearance?"

"I don't know. I guess, I just thought she was on her way. She'd been late before. Actually, I was really at a loss as to what to do. When a family event like this happens, I unfortunately tend to go into limbo, a sort of state of shock."

'Event?' Crane thought. 'Since when was a missing wife a 'family event.''

"… But you could have called the police…gotten more information; told them where you were. It's taken you over twenty-four hours to let anyone know your whereabouts."

"As I said, one doesn't always act rationally in situations like these." Whitney's snidely callused response grated at Crane's basic sensitivity for the welfare of his fellow man, let alone the individuals he loved.

"Have there been any calls? Here at the house?"

"Calls?"

"Asking for money, ransom." Crane paused, curious to see Whitney's reaction and hear his response. "In exchange for your wife?"

Whitney stiffened. "Not that I know of. Emma didn't mention anything."

"No notes in the mailbox?"

Whitney wavered again, "No! Anyway not since I've been home."

"And you've been home how long?"

"This morning. I arrived this morning. About an hour before I called you."

"You waited an hour before you called us?" The two detectives looked at each other. Whitney flinched, and Crane began again.

"The woman who answered the phone when we initially called, is that Emma?" Stan could tell Crane had had enough.

Whitney nodded.

"And her capacity in the household is?"

"She was Asia's nurse/governess when she was small. Been with her even before her mother died. Now she cooks and manages the house. Hires help, gets things repaired. Maintains the place."

"She lives in?" Stan continued.

"She and her husband, Evan Black, have a suite on the top floor."

"And the woman who answered the door…?"

"That's Beatrice, a daily. Been with us for about five years."

"We'll need to speak to those two women," Stan pressed on, "and we may need to put a tap on your phone. Although you realize a ransom call is questionable after the first two days when a victim has been snatched."

"Yes, whatever is necessary." Whitney responded as if pondering the situation and the request. Then he turned to leave.

"What car were you driving, Mr. Whitney?" Crane interrupted matter of factly.

"I have a Porsche 911." Whitney peacocked.

"And its location?"

"In the garage here at the house." More warily.

"We'd like to have our forensics people take a look at it."

"Am I a suspect?" Ian Whitney's response of shocked horror fell on the room with the thud of a cocktail party social faux pas.

"Currently, Mr. Whitney there is no suspect." Crane paused momentarily, and then continued, "it is for your own protection, as much as for ours."

"Be my guest." Whitney answered tersely as he nonchalantly reached into his pocket and tossed Crane the keys. Then he reached over behind the door and pulled a velveteen cord. "Emma should be here momentarily," he said.

But before he could turn and leave the room, Crane just as casually tossed the keys back. "We'll send someone over."

Whitney reached out but missed, and the keys fell to the wooden floor. Slowly, he shoved them to one side of the doorway with his foot.

"You do that." He said and walked out.

"Did you see that? He rang her." Stan observed. "He actually pulled a cord. Like in a Victorian novel."

Crane smiled.

CHAPTER 16

Within moments, as Whitney had promised, footsteps could be heard down the hall and a matronly, statuesque woman entered the room with an ancient golden retriever padding along side.

The dog's face had whitened around its nose and eyes, and grayish white hairs could be seen sprouting along the back of its head and down its neck. Its luminous brown eyes scrutinized the newcomers. Crane smiled as he realized, they were being 'sniffed' at a distance.

The woman surveyed the men quizzically.

"Mrs. Black," Crane began. He observed how neatly her big boned body and tall presence filled the navy dress with its starched white collar and cuffs, and her sensible, matching one-inch heels. The woman reminded him of the head mistress he had encountered over the years at his sister's school, and the dresses he had seen on the salesladies at Bonwits when as a child he had gone shopping with his mother.

"I am Emma Black." She said, taking her hand and smoothing her hair that was pulled back in a softly coiled chignon.

"We are Detectives Crane and Sorsky from …"

Although her outward composure remained, the slight quiver around her mouth and a quick spark in her eyes gave away her anxiety.

"You have good news of my Asia?"

"No, we are sorry, but no." The woman was obviously crestfallen. "But it might be helpful if you could answer some questions."

"Any way I can help." Crane heard the hope in her voice recede and watched her eyes dull. "Gentlemen, would you come with me, please?" summoning the two detectives to follow.

"Come along Spot," She patted the old dog gently on the head and turned out of the room and down the hall toward the back of the house.

'Spot?' The two detectives looked at each other, then back at the purebred, golden haired dog. Spot waited for Crane and Stan to leave the room, then followed closely behind. The two detectives grinned; not often were they the quarry rather than the guard.

Turning right, they entered a large country kitchen that looked out on a different view of the same garden Crane had eyed at the end of the living room. He also realized this brownstone was really two put together, much like his own. The long rectangular room was divided into two sections by a large antique refectory table. One side was dedicated entirely to cooking with built in industrial quality equipment and appliances. The two end walls were faced with used brick, with the upper wall of the cooking area imbedded with glass door cupboards, while a large used brick fireplace was the focal point of the opposite end of the room. On the back wall was a row of floor to ceiling white paned French door cupboards, which Crane observed stored everything from sets of china and glassware to numerous dry goods and spices; a well stocked kitchen.

The huge authentic European refectory table, which divided the room, had gargoyle carved legs and a wooden board across the bottom that met crossbars at each end to support the weight of the top. Crane surmised that the massive tabletop was a slice of a single tree, sacrificed for some long dead Germanic duke's pleasure. Facing the fireplace, a comfy leather couch much like the shabby piece in Cranes living room, abutted the opposite side of the table. A matching chair and ottoman were placed to give the user the warmth of the fireplace as well as a fine view of the garden beyond.

The London Financial Times and The Guardian newspapers were neatly stacked to one side, while The New Yorker magazine laid casually opened lying on top.

"Please sit." Emma Black waved her hand, directing them toward the couch. "Would you like a cup of coffee or tea and a snack?" She asked. It was obvious she was not expecting an answer.

Crane checked his watch. There was more than enough time. He and Stan, who almost salivated at the thought of food, settled on to the couch as a tray of coffee, tea, and scones immediately appeared.

Crane knew from Whitney's description, Emma Black had to be at least seventy, yet her carriage and demeanor were that of a much younger person.

When at last the woman sat down, the dog, freed from her post, lay down in front of the fire. Yet Spot never took her eyes off the two interlopers on her turf.

"Asia and I have spent many hours here together," the woman reminisced, "even when she was a child. This was her childhood home, you know. Her father moved out when she married, but I have been with the family since before she was born. Her mother had two miscarriages prior to Asia's birth. She was such a gift." The woman seemed desperate to maintain a connection.

"I am so sorry to prattle on like this. I'm just so nervous about Asia's safety. I am beside myself."

"We understand," Stan patted her on the shoulder. The woman obviously needed to talk, and both detectives knew they often learned more from witnesses and those closest to a victim by just listening.

"So you've been with the family a long time?" Stan continued.

"Over thirty-five years. I first met Mrs. Winslow through her distant cousin, Mrs. La Rue, and came out from England during Mrs. Winslow's first pregnancy. 'Three times a charm,' Mrs. Winslow had said when Asia arrived so pink and healthy. Too bad she died too young to see her precious child grow into such a lovely young woman."

"How did Mrs. Whitney's mother die?" Stan asked.

"Oh! It was awful." For all her self-control, it was easy to tell Emma Black wavered. "It was that Bloody horse! We could all see that Erasmus was in one of his snits, but Mrs. Winslow decided to ride him anyway. It was during one of the hunts up at Bernardsville. You know, New Jersey? That horse was always a mean, ornery creature." As she became more agitated, her English accent became more pronounced. "Mr. Winslow had often told her to get rid of that horse, but once a Winslow makes up their mind… All of them, including Asia, you can't stop them from doing what they are going ta do. Pigheaded, the whole lot of them. Anyway, if you've ever been up that way, you know. A landscape of hills, dales and little stonewalls. Lots of stones and rocks all over the place." Crane nodded. Both his mother and sister had gone to the hunt there more than once.

"Well I don't have to tell you the rest. Bloomin' horse nicked a wall with his hind leg, lost its balance, and fell right on top of Mrs. Whitney who suffered a broken neck. But it was a blow to her head on a rock that killed her." There was a snarl of anger in her voice. "Asia was five when it happened. So it was Mr. Winslow an' me, who brought her up." Emma Black's tone was more subdued now. "Mr. Winslow never rode another horse and although he did allow Asia riding lessons, she never really took to it. When Asia became old enough for boarding school, Mr. Winslow refused and kept her home sending her to Brearley here in the city instead." Crane and Stan could hear the exhaustion in Emma Black's voice. But she pressed on. "But you have no clues? Nothing to help find out what has happened?"

"Nothing." Crane responded. Although for other reasons, he was almost as exasperated as she. "Have you had any odd phone calls or ransom notes since her disappearance?"

"If I had, don't you think I would've called the police immediately!"

"Mrs. Black what people think they'll do and reality are not always the same. If someone has called and threatened Mrs. Whitney's life in exchange for money, we need to know." Crane was emphatic. "Now let's begin again. Have you had any calls asking for ransom for Mrs. Whitney's life?"

"No. There have been no communications about Asia at all. Why do you think I'm so worried? Ransom money would be no problem. If there were a note or a call, at least that might give a clue. But there has been nothing." The detectives knew she was being straight.

"Prior to the Gala, did you see any strangers milling around?"

"No. But if you think it would help to tap the telephone, as they do in detective novels, do so." Mrs. Black clearly wanted to help. It was obvious she was telling the truth, but Crane had had to be sure.

"Any odd happenings or events the last few months? Did Mrs. Whitney's behavior change or was she unduly stressed?"

"Her schedule was tighter than usual. But with the gala there is always extra work." Emma Black paused. "Of course with the death of poor Miss Cynthia's grandmother… Actually, since her father met his untimely death last year… Well, she just couldn't seem to get over it. It took some of her spark. She tried not to show it, but I knew."

Emma explained about Mr. Winslow's accident and how devastating it was for Asia. "After all, this was Asia's only living parent." It was obvious to the two detectives, that Jack Winslow's death was a great loss for this woman, as well as his child. Eventually the questions turned to the other help and Mr. Black.

"We met when Asia was a junior at Brearley. He was her English teacher. He's a Yorkshire man, so we had a lot in common. It was important to both of us for Asia to adjust to our relationship. So we didn't marry until she was a freshman in college. Being a bit younger than me, he still teaches. But he will retire soon. We live in a top floor suite here in the house."

Every time Spot heard Asia's name, he lifted his head, gazed at his mistress and wagged his tail. It was obvious to both detectives that Emma Black and Spot were the only ones they had met, who were really concerned – no, torn apart - by Asia Winslow-Whitney's disappearance.

Crane looked at his watch. As if it were a signal the somber dog rose and came over to Crane who felt the warm nuzzle of Spot's head in his lap. Spot seemed aware that these two strangers were here to find his mistress.

"One last question, if I may, Mrs. Black?"

"Anything?"

"How did Spot get her name?" Stan's question lightened the atmosphere.

Emma smiled and looked down patting Spot affectionately on the head. "When Asia was about three she found her father's Dick and Jane, Puff and Spot books and taught herself to read. One night at dinner she declared that all future dogs in this house would be named Spot." Spot lifted her head upon hearing her name. "This is our third golden retriever and our third Spot."

At the door the two men each smiled down at Spot and patted her on the head.

"We will keep you informed of any news." Stan promised.

"Thank you."

CHAPTER 17

It was one of those afternoons when everything worked. Crane had made the call to the Plaza Hotel explaining that their service elevators would continue to be out of commission for at least the rest of the afternoon, and Bob Stapleton from forensics was finishing his dusting job by the time Crane and Stan arrived with Riley and Mr. Leibovitz in tow.

"Hey! What is that guy doing over there?" Riley questioned as he stepped out of the police car, slamming his shoes down on the cement garage floor. The hollow sound of his metal tipped boots reverberated throughout the underground garage. Still dressed in his ACME Laundry uniform, Riley had added a Yankee's baseball cap with the beak turned backwards, a fashion statement everyone knew Riley would call 'ace' if he were asked.

"He's one of us, Riley." Stan replied. "His name's Bob Stapleton."

"One of us?" Riley was obviously pleased. "Hey, Mr. Stapleman, what's your job?" Riley shouted across the subterane basement garage.

"Clues," Bob smiled, "I look for invisible clues. Ones that can't be seen by the naked eye."

"The naked eye! OOOOH! That sounds like Halloween."

"I'm the one who found the spots on your truck."

Riley tensed.

"You really take good care of that truck." But before Riley had a chance to respond Bob continued, "How'd you ever land such a cushy job driving such a nice truck?"

"Took a test." Riley swelled with pride. "Said I'd be a good driver. I follow directions. And that I like people! But I'm not sure I like you," the words burst out.

"You help us today and we'll see if we can get your truck out of impound for you?" Stapleton gazed at the two detectives questioningly.

Stan smiled.

"Deal?" Bob questioned.

"Deal."

"Riley, we think we know what you heard, but we want you to listen and tell us for sure," Crane said.

Riley nodded. This he knew was serious business.

The rest of the afternoon was spent with the two back-to-back elevators going up and down in various configurations. It took only a short time for Riley to identify the sound. Then the three men concentrated on determining what patterns the elevators were in during the time Riley heard the sound and how much time the culprit had to dispose of the body before Riley was back down for his next delivery of linens to the sixth floor.

Without realizing the time, afternoon had become early evening.

"WOW!" Riley exclaimed as a profusion of light filled the garage. Riley whirled around. "It's like little stars in the sky." He looked up at the metal encaged light bulbs. "Hey! It's dark outside. That's why all the lights came on... I really would be a good detective."

Mr. Leibovitz and the detectives silently watched Riley gaze at the lights of the brightened garage.

Bang! Crash! Suddenly, a din down the alleyway outside the garage disrupted the quiet.

"It's a blinkin' rat, this time! Damn it!"

A lone man with his back to the doorway by the dumpsters was stumbling about swinging a large board.

"You're goina' be dead meat!" He shouted, as he wavered under the weight of his over-sized weapon. Moving noiselessly but fast, Crane grabbed the man's shoulder, breaking his fall, as a large brown rat scrambled away into the bowels of the nearest dumpster. "Careful man, their bites can be dangerous."

"What the.... I had a clear shot!" He replied. The reality that he hung like a rag doll in Crane's grip only increased his indignation. "...Copper ain't ya,"

"That's right." Crane responded, getting out his badge.

"Where'd you come from?" Startled, the vagrant stopped wriggling long enough to review his options. In the past, because of his small frame and agility, he had been able to wiggle in and out of most awkward situations. But as he turned, he realized Crane's hulking figure was blocking any opportunity of escape.

"The garage." Crane pointed to the others watching from the doorway.

"Well, I ain't doin' nothin'. Just lookin' around. That's all, just lookin' around." His words slurred. "Why are a bunch of men hangin' around the Plaza garage? Waiting for me?" The slightly inebriated man trembled. He'd met policemen before, but by the body language of this detective...he wasn't going anywhere fast.

"You come around here often?" Crane tilted his face away from the man's rancid breath.

"No. Nope, jus' passin' through. In fact, I was jus' on my way out." He answered as he tried to shake himself loose. But Crane held tight.

"You know it's going to be a damn cold night." Crane surveyed the man's crusty pallor. This stray wasn't someone new to the streets.

"Cold don't bother me none." The man pulled his dirty Mets cap more snugly onto his head and his neck sunk deeper into his tattered military camouflage jacket.

"Where you staying tonight?"

"Shelter up on a hundred seventy third." Crane winced, what a difference a few blocks made.

"Probably could use a good meal, too."

"No way I'm goin' over to Rikkers with all those crazy dumb asses. Six, eight rotters to a cell, havin' to keep one eye opened all night. Don't always get all your stuff back." The vagrant retorted sensing the direction of the conversation.

Riley stood next to Stan in the garage doorway, wide-eyed.

Stan walked over, "What's your name?" he asked as Crane continued to hold on to the slithery character.

"Name, rank and serial number, that's all you're getting from me!"

"Yea, Just state the handle your mother gave you at birth, soldier." This man sounded even more menacing.

"Al…. Alistair P. Sloane. Like in London, the square." A touch of his feisty spirit resurfaced.

"Stan, I think Alistair deserves a warm bed and a few good meals on the NYPD. Don't you?" Crane asked, ignoring the man's protestations. The vagrant slumped, defeated by the turn of events.

"Makes sense to me. Since we have guests, I'll call another car?"

Riley watched as Crane started to handcuff the tattered soul then changed his mind.

"Hey! You ain't goin' to leave my stuff, are you?" With the little fight he had left, the man protested, nodding toward a worn knapsack lying on the opposite side of the dumpsters.

"There's no way we're going to leave your stuff behind." Stan smiled as he walked over and picked up the bag.

"You're not going to make Mr. Sloan go to that Rikker person's house, are you?" Riley asked, shocked at what he had just witnessed.

"No, as a matter a fact, we are not." The vagrant surveyed Crane quizzically.

"What the hell's goin' on here, man?" Now, the vagrant was desperate to get away. "No handcuffs, no Rikkers. It don't make no sense."

"Try to do a man a good turn and he doesn't appreciate it. I got to cuff him, Stan," Crane lamented as Stan read him his rights.

"What am I charged with?" The man began shouting over and over as the police car arrived and Crane wrestled the man and his bag into the backseat.

"Vagrancy, in need of a few meals and a good night's sleep. See you in the morning!" Crane shouted back, and then gave the officers instructions.

By now, Riley was beside himself with fear for the homeless man's fate.

"Riley," Crane began, looking over at Mr. Leibovitz for some help, "that man is not going to Rikker's Island. Instead, he's going to a nice warm cell at our precinct, where he'll get three squares a day until Detective Sorsky and I can have him in our office for a little chat."

"After all," Stan continued, "if he's been here before."

"He may have heard something important…"

"Like I heard something," Riley finished Stan's sentence triumphantly.

"And he might even have seen something important like who put those blood spots on your truck. Now wouldn't that be 'ace'?" Mr. Leibovitz winked.

Riley nodded, and all the way home he tried to wink but could only create squints in both eyes instead.

"Well, Riley, it's been quite an afternoon," Crane said as the police car pulled up in front of Riley's apartment building. "You've certainly been helpful."

"Glad to help, Officer Crane," Riley replied as he exited the car.

"I hope you'll be available if we need to call on you again?"

Riley stood on the sidewalk and beamed from ear to ear. "I'm your man," he said. "Ace!" Then he abruptly turned toward the building, "I'm home, Paws," he shouted. "Oh boy, have I got a lot to tell you and mom." They watched Riley bound up the stairs toward the door as the car pulled away from the curb.

After dropping Riley home, Stan and Crane drove Mr. Leibovitz to the deli where his wife, who had closed up without him, was waiting patiently.

She sent Stan home with a leftover coconut cream cake.

"Jeanie and the kids'll be thrilled," Stan oozed as they drove back to the precinct.

"I can see the headlines now... 'Another policeman on the take.'" His enthusiasm made Crane smile.

CHAPTER 18

It was well after seven when the detectives got back to the precinct. Their 'ward,' Al, was dead asleep ensconced in his own private cell.

"Guy couldn't believe his good luck. Ate dinner and dozed off. Who is he, mayor's nephew?"

"We hope so," Crane replied.

"How long we keeping him?" The duty officer was baffled by this special treatment. "Why not just put this guy in the 'drunk tank' with the others?" he questioned, but Stan brushed the question aside with a shrug.

This was not the first time he considered Sorsky and Crane's requests mystifying. But 'what the hey,' these two got results, and it was a slow night. It wasn't like he didn't have an extra cell.

"We'll get to him tomorrow, but be nice. Don't want any dents in this beautiful package." Stan laughed. "Name's Alistair P. Sloane, see if his name comes up anywhere. Missing persons, military."

"Oh! And see if you can get him to clean himself up." Crane shouted over his shoulder as they headed out.

"What am I, a frekin' nurse maid?" But Stan and Richard were out the door.

Stan headed home with his precious cake, and Crane, after making a call, headed up town to the Carlyle Hotel on 76th.

Immersed in the events of the day, Crane hardly noticed the air filled twinkles of snowy dust that whirled around in the cold night air. As it hit the ground, it turned into a light slush that if it didn't melt, would turn into a brown mush by morning. He was looking forward to a quiet dinner, and the soothing sounds of Bobby Short wafted across the lobby from the Café as Crane entered the Carlyle's Bemelmans Bar. Waving to Tommy behind the bar, Richard settled into one of the chocolate brown leather banquettes along the wall.

The white-jacketed waiter smiled, "Glenfiddichs on the rocks with a side of water?"

Richard nodded. He appreciated this kind of service, especially after a day like this.

"Hungry tonight, Mr. Crane?" Like the rest of the members of the Abernathy, Huntington, Crane law firm who frequented the bar, Richard was a fixture. Knowing he was the Judge's grandson, the staff assumed he was just another partner in the firm. Although they were somewhat perplexed by his odd hours.

"Very."

"Your usual?"

Crane nodded.

Richard gazed across the room at the whimsical mural of picnicking rabbits in Central Park. Bemelmans, the artist and the bar's namesake, had represented all the seasons in his drawings, each with its own requisite activity. One of Richard's favorites was, Winter in the Park with its ice skating elephant. But he was content to watch as the rabbits had their family outing. Ludwig Bemelmans, famous for the Madeline books' illustrations, had painted the murals in exchange for a suite in the hotel for himself and his family for a year and a half.

"Smashing aren't they?" It was his grandfather, whose presence filled a major portion of the large booth as he slid in beside Richard.

"Black Angus burger, medium rare. Just the way you like it, Mr. Crane." The plate was placed before him with a flairful twist of the wrist. "Anything else?"

"Thanks Max, this is great."

"And for you, sir? Anything besides the usual?" He asked setting another Glenfiddichs on the table. Judge Abernathy smiled, shaking his head, and the waiter receded quietly into the background. Richard gazed at the tall statuesque gentleman seated beside him. Military bearing, that's how others described him. Yet Richard always contended that his grandfather's brush mustache made him appear a bit rakish, retired RAF or diplomat/ spy. The two men always had so much to share and never enough time.

The combination of Art Deco and Bemelmans whimsical murals with the dark richness of the fixtures gave the place a rather old world charm. Both men liked Bemelmans best in the evening after 8:00, when most of the 'cocktail' crowd was gone and before the evening entertainment began at 9:30. Then, there were only the soft whispers of the few early evening patrons and the unobtrusively pleasant sounds of a piano being played in the background, when one could relax, eat a perfect burger and sip a scotch in quiet harmony.

Richard recalled his excitement the very first time he and his little sister Emily had been brought here by their mother to see the murals. He was not quite six and the fantasy of it all remained with him over the years. The Madeline books had just been introduced to Emily, so mother thought it only fitting that she sneak children into the bar to see Bemelmans' 'Central Park Four Seasons.' Although the staff was quite amiable about the children's presence, Richard's mother approached this visit the way she did most events, as a secret adventure. Now that her children were grown, Mrs. Crane applied her same sense of enterprise and enthusiasm to her current project of finding a suitable spouse for each. This both Richard and Emily knew, was not entirely altruistic, but rather to fill their mother's need for grandchildren, so she could carry on with her life full of the mysterious through fresh eyes.

"Now, what's so important you had to drag an old man away from a warm fire?" Arthur Abernathy's eyes twinkled as he chided his grandson.

"Bad joke tonight, gramps," Richard was tired. "What can you tell me about a young woman? Name's, Asia Winslow." Crane continued. "Family owns World Wide Banknote."

"Not much. Why?"

"Seems she's gone missing. Saturday night, during or after the family's annual Settlement House fundraiser at the Plaza."

"Don't say."

"Cut the crap, gramps. I know the Winslow family are clients of the firm. Probably have been forever. I also know Ben Huntington and his sister were at the Settlement House Gala that the banknote company supported Saturday night. I suspect representing the firm." Richard took a big chomp out of his burger.

"You're right, Winslow family's been with the firm almost from the beginning. Jack Winslow was a nice man, straight shooter, but I don't know the daughter," he paused taking a sip of his scotch. "Just because my name's on the plaque doesn't mean I'm involved with the day to day workings of the firm anymore."

Crane nodded.

"Although I understand," his grandfather began again. "She started working in the firm the last few years after graduating from college. Missing, eh? Doesn't sound like the kind of thing a member of that family would up and do, just take off."

"I didn't say she ran off like some unruly drug addicted adolescent. I mean missing as in suspected foul play."

"Really! Clive didn't mention anything about it to me. You interview him?"

"Stan did."

"We weren't about to advertise the actual facts."

"Which are?"

"Her Plaza Hotel room, a lot of blood, no body. We've kept it under wraps."

"Terrible! Father's been in the grave less than a year and now the daughter's missing. Have you notified the family? The firm?"

"Actually, the husband who had also been missing finally called in today, forty-eight hours after the fact, and I just found out about Abernathy's being the family's lawyers today."

"Why are you speaking to me about this, here? Now?"

"Stan and I have been running our balls off," his grandfather winced at the term, "for two days, and we've got no leads." He certainly wasn't going to discuss their elevator theory, nor the vagrant they had drying out at the precinct. "This is the first chance I've had. Damn! I thought you might have some off the record insights into these people. Who they deal with? What makes them tick? Friends? Enemies?" Richard was talking in a frenetic almost shouting whisper. Why was his grandfather making this so hard?

"Richard, years ago, the firm made up a series of standard legal contract business forms for World Wide Banknote that suited their specific needs. Whenever they make a deal, all they have to do is fill in the blanks. Since then, except for the rare contract that needs special immediate changes, we do no legal work with regard to the business. Occasionally, we deal with the family's personal legal needs; a deed, trust, will, but otherwise nothing. These people are very secretive. I understand it's the nature of the business, discretion necessitated by the kind of clients they have. They even have all in-house accounting. Nothing leaves that Park Avenue address unless federal law mandates it," Art Abernathy spoke in measured tones.

"Then I guess it's another dead end." Richard sighed.

"I'm sorry I can't help you. But at least I can buy you another scotch." The two men settled in quietly sipping their drinks. The judge seemed saddened that he was of so little help.

However, Richard had already moved on. His thoughts were on the trip to Wellfleet he and Stan would have to make, if they didn't get the right answers by phone. The visit that needed to be made to Albany, and also the visit he was sure to make to the banknote factory in upstate New York. But most of all, Crane's mind wandered to the homeless drunk who was sleeping it off at the precinct.

CHAPTER 19

Stan was already at the precinct when Crane arrived a little before eight.

"How's our guest?"

"Hey, the guy's a real space cadet. Down in his cell banging on the bars shouting brutality." The duty officer responded.

"Two Alistair P. Sloanes. What's the odds on that?" Stan passed Crane a series of printouts.

"Pretty unusual. Both vagrants. Both born in the city. Only one way to find out. Had his breakfast?"

The duty officer nodded.

"Bring him up. If he can answer our questions, who cares." Stan was pumped.

"Morning, Mr. Sloane, take a seat." Crane extended his arm toward a wooden chair across the table from where Stan was already seated.

The wary-eyed man heard the door shut behind him. There was definiteness about it. He stood perfectly still at attention. Although he did not move his head, his gaze shifted from one man to the other. He had been here before. He tried to recall, 'If he let them interrogate him slowly, there would be less pain, or was it better to ram hard and have the pain more intense yet quickly numbing?'

"Mr. Sloane," Richard tried again. "We have a missing person and we had hoped you could help us out. After we're done talking, you are quite free to leave."

The man had heard that before too, and he knew from experience once they had you, they never let you go. He had made up his mind. Like a caged animal, he suddenly lunged. Crane was down before he knew what hit him. Sloane was on Crane's back pinning him to the floor. His hands reached toward Crane's chin. A snap of Crane's neck and it would be all over. Stan spun around out of his chair. Grabbing Sloane's two arms, Stan wrested them behind his back and handcuffed them before Sloane had a chance to make the fatal move. Lifting him off the floor, Stan threw Sloane onto the chair. "NOW SIT!" he shouted.

Sloane sighed; his actions had made it official. He was an offender. Sitting statue still, Al Sloane knew what came next. But he also knew it would be fast. Angry captors exacted quick revenge.

"We want some answers and we're tired of being nice. GOT IT BUDDY?"

Crane scrambled up.

"You ok?"

"A little winded," Crane rubbed the back of his neck, "just caught me unawares."

Relieved, Stan continued inches from the man's face. "Now let's try this again."

"Wait. I think we need some coffee."

"You need coffee, Al and I can wait. Can't we Al?" Stan was pissed as for Sloane; he just waited. The pattern never changed.

"NO, I mean all of us need some coffee." Crane went out the door and came back with the pot and three Styrofoam cups. "Coffee Al? I'll even taste it for you if you want." Crane took a sip out of each one. "For God sakes, un-cuff the guy, Stan."

Sloane felt the manacles loosen on his wrists. Wait! This wasn't the way it happened. They were supposed to hit next, with a big fist in his face, knocking him off his chair. This picture was all wrong. 'What the hell was going on?' Al began to sob.

'Here we go again, Crane games,' Stan mused to himself as he un-cuffed the man then reached for a cup. "Am I going to get your germs?" He asked Crane as he took his first sip.

"How about it, Al? You can even have this one I'm drinking. By the way, which Alistair P. Sloane are you, Peter or Pierpont?" Stan became a player.

"He's Pierpont, aren't you?" Crane interjected. "Which one was it? Hanoi Hilton? Alcatraz? The Zoo?"

"Farnsworth."

Crane gasped. He had read POWS' accounts, and for a US military officer, Farnsworth was the worst.

Alistair Sloane had answered softly, as he rubbed his wrists where the handcuffs had been. Then cautiously, he reached for one of the two coffees left on the table. "'68 to the end." Whispering his words.

"West Point weren't you? Class of '63. Went to Nam fall of '67."

"Four years." Sloane nodded.

"You've had a rough time," Crane paused as he put down the file. He couldn't imagine being a ground soldier in Vietnam. The Vietcong made Francis Marion look like a boy scout when it came to guerrilla warfare.

"Look at me Al." Crane sat across from Sloane trying to make eye contact. "This is not one of those hellholes in Vietnam." Hoping more reality would set in. "You are at the NYPD." He paused. "We've got a missing girl. We need your help."

Slowly, Al Sloane realized the man before him was pleading. Pin sticking tremors began all over his body, as if he were afraid the scene might change again. Was it in his brain or reality? He wasn't quite sure. There were times when violence overtook him; whether man or beast, it was all the same. He had no control. His had developed a primal sense of survival. Yet, this moment was so real. "I can't help you. I've never been in that alley before." Yet, he was beginning to remember.

"But we clearly heard you say, 'it's a rat this time.' This time Al, this time. Think about it. What was it the other time?" Crane accentuated the words. Al's focus was on something across the room. Stan followed Al's gaze to the blank wall opposite.

"A cat! Poor damn dead thing." Al turned his face away.

"Do you know which night it was?"

"Ah, hell, I'm there every night," he laughed, as if he had just pulled off a childish ruse. He began again slowly. "Ya' see we have it all divided up. The whole city. Tough on newcomers. But the Plaza's my turf. Some guys like the garbage, trash. Gives 'em an income. Others food." He explained to the amazed detectives. "I'm a food man myself. Pickins' are good at the Plaza. Generally, I'm there later. But last night I had things to do man, things to do. You F- it up." The words tumbled out.

"But we gave you a warm dry place to sleep and meals."

"Hell, I got a place to sleep. And money, I don't the need trash. As for meals, don't you guys get it? I eat like a king, man. A king. I got the Plaza!"

"What about last Saturday night? Anything out of the ordinary happen then?" Stan asked.

"Saturday, Monday, they're all the same to me."

"What about the night with the cat? That night seems to stick in your mind."

"Yea, now that you mention it, one hell of a night. One thing after another. The place was ablaze."

"There was a fire?"

"No, Man. It was the lights. Like a damn marquee out front. I got there late. There was this truck. But that happens every night, always arrives just before I leave. Then the cat."

Stan and Crane realized Sloane was trying to put it all in order.

"Then, then…the phantom."

"You mean a person?"

"No, the Phantom, man, the phantom. Like a wraith moving along the wall."

"A person?" Crane tried again.

"NO! It was something…dark and black and wide…disappeared at the end of the alley." Sloane's grizzly, unshaven face convulsed in horror. Now Sloane couldn't be stopped. "I was flipped. Couldn't leave that alley for hours. NO WAY! Slept there most of the night. The roar woke me; fast black car sped out of the garage. Didn't even stop at the street."

"What time was that?" Stan interrupted.

"Like I'm wearin' a Rolex? How the hell should I know? Early morning, still dark. Daylight, I left. Thought twice about going back."

"But you did."

"Yea, same night. A man's gotta eat. After all it's my turf."

"Anything strange happen after that?'

"No, been a sweet dream ever since."

"Mr. Sloane, you've been very helpful. Is there anywhere we can contact you if we have some additional questions?" Crane asked.

Al Sloane looked cautiously from one detective to the other, "You mean that's it? You're really going to let me go?"

"Why wouldn't we? But we would like to have a contact address, phone number, where you sleep?"

Sloane pondered. Crane could tell he wasn't going to give away too much. "Every afternoon in Central Park, Simon Levin takes a walk; on the Plaza side of the park. If he doesn't know where I am, hell he'll sniff me out." Al Sloane gave the two detectives a devilish smile. "Course there's always the Plaza, I spend a lot of time there." He laughed again nervously.

"Before you go, is there anyone you'd like us to contact?"

Sloane paused, then he shook his head.

"Your personal items are at the duty desk," Stan said as he opened the door.

"Here's my card. If you think of anything we missed, or if you ever need..." Crane's words hung in thin air as he extended his hand.

Alistair Sloane hesitated. It had been a long time.

Crane opened the door and escorted Sloane to the duty desk where he picked up his belongings and walked hurriedly out of the precinct and down the station steps.

"Fruitcake," the duty officer commented.

"Oh, he saw something, alright." Crane turned to Stan, ignoring the statement "But right now, he has to sort it all out. Give him some time."

"Right. I suppose with what he's been through..." the thought lingered in Stan's unfinished sentence.

But the day had just begun for them both. Stan was off to Albany and Crane to the Banknote printing plant in upstate New York.

CHAPTER 20

Three days she sailed. Three days of listening to the constant hollow drumming of the never-ending waves pounding against the fiberglass hull. When the wind picked up further offshore in the deeper seas, the more resounding it became. Often, in a particularly deep swell, Onika would yaw and then re-center herself. The first time, Asia thought a whale had hit her. Once she gained a better understanding of these random swells, Asia was able to compensate, and maneuver Onika more comfortably. Although she had rigged the boat for self-steering, during the day in between deck work and her other chores she liked to steer Onika herself. At night, she turned on the masthead and running lights, tied down the wheel and dozed at first somewhat fitfully, for who knew what was out in that vast ocean. Yet each night as Asia became more confident and adjusted to the rhythms of the sea, she caught enough hours of sleep necessary to maintain her strength and spirit.

People have written whole books about single-handed sailing. For some, it was 'the challenge', for others 'money', a sailing contest they had entered with the promise of fame and financial compensation. There were also sailors, like Chichester, who needed to prove they could succeed, and some who really just enjoyed the whole aspect of that 'man against nature relationship', risking one's life for the thrill…the adrenaline rush. Asia laughed as she recalled how Moitessier, who, after crossing the finish line of the Single-handed Golden Globe race, didn't head up to London to get his prize, but rather just kept sailing. Asia remembered the message he sent to his publisher: "I am continuing non-stop towards the Pacific Islands because I am happy at sea, and perhaps also to save my soul."

Asia was certainly impressed by Moritessier and the other sailors whose feats she had read about, but to sail around the world, although awe inspiring; she could not even fathom such a feat. How different her goals were from theirs. Albeit, she loved sailing, but she had no convulsive drive to prove anything to anyone. Her act of leaving by sea was only because she wanted to stay alive. She wanted to save the family company and have time to try and discover if her father's death was really accidental.

Asia's mind wandered back to the inquest into her father's death. She recalled her thoughts that day as a damp winter wind blew across the bleak, flat Cape Cod landscape. She remembered every image every word. Grief stricken, even with Ian and Cynthia by her side, it was an effort to climb the steps of the old Greek revival granite Barnstable courthouse, Cape Cod's county seat. Upon entering the courtroom, Asia reflected on what a strange atmosphere for an inquest with its frieze designs of flowering palms and Ionic columns behind the judge's bench. Rather, one expected a great orator the likes of Daniel Webster, or stringed chamber music to be taking place here in this beautiful antiquated atmosphere. And why an inquest? Shouldn't the cause of her father's death have been cut and dried.

Ian was the first witness called, and in his usual manner he dazzled everyone in the courtroom, acting the quintessential son in law.

"At first I didn't understand. We were talking, and then all of a sudden my father in law seemed to lose his balance; just keeled over, hitting his head on the fireplace mantle as he fell. It happened so fast. Well to be honest, I lost my bearings. I couldn't think…."

"Do you know if Mr. Winslow might have been ill at the time?"

The prosecutor asked.

"He did have a cold." Ian stopped as if in thought, "It was quite severe, as I recall… What were Mr. Winslow and I doing there?"

Ian had paused as if regaining his composure before answering the prosecutor's next question.

"Discussing a surprise party for Asia, my dear wife's up and coming birthday."

"And you couldn't discuss that in the city?" The prosecutor continued.

"We could have, but Asia's very clever and it never fails that even though she may pretend, she always finds out. This time, we had hoped we'd beat her at her own game." Asia recalled how Ian had turned giving the grand jury one of his most alluringly innocent, handsomely boyish smiles.

"If we had been nearer the family doctor, a hospital," Ian had paused again, this time as if overwhelmed, confused. "I don't know, maybe with help, we could have saved him. I just don't know. I'm not medically trained, you know." His voice cracked as if in forlorn defeat. A soft sigh was heard among the female jurors.

Asia remembered, too, how Ian's pandering to the crowd had made her cringe. It was then, for the first time, she actually questioned Ian's involvement in her father's death. No longer did Asia question the need for an inquest.

"But no, he had not had previous heart problems and the autopsy had ruled out a stroke." Both the coroner and family doctor had stated. She sat very still listening, as Dr. Ballard had continued with his testimony. "Mr. Winslow did have a cold."

That was certainly true, Asia recalled. But she also knew that her's was much more severe at the time. She was laid up in bed for over a week, while he was out gallivanting around the countryside. After all, he had obviously felt well enough to drive from the city to the house in Wellfleet.

The Doctor droned on, "Yes, as Mr. Ian Whitney testified, Mr. Winslow did have a serious head cold which may have caused him to have a dizzy spell causing him to pass out, thus causing the fall in which his head accidentally hit the fireplace mantle and his untimely death."

"The way the body was positioned when we arrived implied that is what took place, and there were no marks on the floor that made me suspect otherwise."

When the Grand Jury returned with a determination of accidental death, Asia knew there was something terribly wrong. She wanted to stand up and shout, "My dad wasn't that sick! Something else happened."

But because she didn't know what, her grief and self-control had kept her silent.

Suddenly the boat yawed, snapping Asia back to reality.

"Ocean sailing certainly gives me lots of time to think." Her boat, Onika, was a good listener who never criticized. "Did I tell you," she went on, "that bastard Ian has been stealing from World Wide Banknote." Although Onika was new to her life, they had created an interdependence that had developed into a fast friendship. "And something else, I don't think dad's death was an accident. Was there a link between the missing funds and his death? I was so stricken with grief at the time, I didn't see the signs." She paused to take in the thoughts she had kindled so long, yet only now was daring to express aloud. "Do repeatedly spoken messages sent into the universe often enough become truths?" She pondered the idea then scoffed it off. "I can't prove it yet, but certain things just don't add up. That's why I trashed the hotel room and disappeared, in hopes the sensationalism would bring enough attention to dad's death to reopen the case." Onika yawed against an extra large wave as if in shocked response. "This single handed sailing isn't half bad… and at least I have you to talk to. Ok for you, girl?" Onika hummed along among the waves at a steady clip. "Good! I must be pulling a Josh Slocum, talking aloud to myself like this. Next, I'll be hallucinating and I haven't even been out here four days." Asia Laughed." Aw heck! It fills my time. And maybe I'll figure out some answers."

Asia paused to do a 360. The sky was an immaculate, rich robin's egg blue that blended with the crisp coolness and gave the horizon an enigmatic sparkle, enveloping the sea and cloudless sky together into a symbiotic sharing of nature. Yet, a slightly darker periwinkle hue hung in the far off port horizon. Being so caught up in her musings and random ramblings to the little boat she had come to adore, Asia gave it no thought.

She recalled how some months after her father's death she had found a tap on her phone. "Was I next?" She questioned. "I sure wasn't going to wait around to find out. Get out while you can, that's my theory. I like a challenge, but the one I just left was more than I bargained for… there is no nobility in the physical and financial survival trip in which we have embarked, old girl," initiating a deep gruff Major Hoople tone. "This trip is for expediency." She paused, frowning in dismay. "What was Ian thinking…that World Wide Banknote existed for his personal asset accumulation? Obviously! And what were we, dad and I? Disposable assets?"

A cool brisk wind filled the air brushing Asia's cheek. It blew wisps of her pony-tailed hair away from her face. Asia remembered when she was making her plans, how she had made all of the calls that really mattered from pay phones. Some from the banks of telephones at Grand Central Station, where one became another member of the teeming throng. Her first call was to Bermuda, to her godfather and her father's closest friend, Aubrey Tinkerton. Together, they decided upon a mutually beneficial calling time, when Asia could talk unhampered by lurking listeners. Then, she arranged a visit to her former sailing master at the Stuyvestant Yacht Club on City Island. He was another of her father's close friends, and her mentor since childhood. He had retired long ago, after his wife died, yet he still lived in their stucco cottage on the bay side of the island. Asia was not sure if she was ever followed, but a visit to Captain Sanderson had always been a common event in her life. She believed Ian, who considered Ted Sanderson somewhat of a dolt and an elderly hanger on, would find her visits, even if he knew about them, of little consequence and no threat. So Captain Sandy became her co-conspirator, and his City Island home a safe haven for her plans.

Asia gazed across the vast sea. A spray of salt water smacked her hard and a particularly large swell slammed into Onika's starboard side, causing some unconventional rattling below decks. Once back on a steady course, Asia left the helm and leaned down the companionway to be sure everything was ship-shape. Returning to the wheel, Asia anticipated her future landfall. So far everything had gone well and she knew that although the temperature had begun to change, because of the tempering effect of the Gulf Stream, Bermuda would still be much warmer than New York. There would be fewer sailboats, and berths would be easier to find. June was the big race month, the Marion to Bermuda and Single-handed races on the odd years, and the Newport/Bermuda Race on the even. She loved Bermuda during October and November. It would be quieter now; slowing down from the wilder paced season, which began in April, and would come to a standstill with the January chill. Tourists and sun seekers were already moving down the pleasure chain to the Bahamas, Jamaica, Mexico and the Caribbean.

Only serious sailors would be arriving now. Those like Asia, who would be using Bermuda as a stopping off port on their way to warmer climes. It was the standard first leg for northeastern mainland cruising sailors on their way to the Leeward and Windward Caribbean Island chains.

As Sandy had said, she was beginning to get a healthy pleasure from ocean sailing as Onika plowed into the incredible force of the sea, its comrade at arms. With all these self-satisfying musings, Asia had not noticed a line of crepuscular rays of rain that filled the distant horizon. The sky darkened. Suddenly everything was happening at once. The winds had picked up with gusts of 45 knots and more. Onika yawed. The jib and main began flailing in the air. These first winds, like a classic white squall, had a gray hardness that came from nowhere, knocking Onika broadside so hard that Asia lost her balance, falling onto the cockpit deck. With the support of the self-steering rig, she lifted and re-steadied herself. She could feel the gale force wind beating at the sails and knew there was no time to waste. Heading up into the wind, she reefed the main sheet and secured it down. The jib, she remembered, "I have to secure the jib."

Asia crammed sail ties into her pocket and crawled onto the deck moving forward to the bow. Taking a deep breath, she loosened the jib sheet and dropped the sail. "Oh God! Please don't fall into the water." She grabbed as much of the falling sail on the deck as the incessantly howling wind would allow. "Don't get wet." She pleaded as if to a living relic. "I'll never be able to lift you out." As Asia pulled, the wind's strength whipped the sail back and forth with a cracking sound. It reshaped the sail into bellowing puffs. The harder the wind beat, the harder she fought to pull the sail down flat on Onika's deck. Where the heck did this come from, she thought, as she tied the jib down along the side of the deck, securing it tightly to the stanchions as she crawled aft, working as she went? "And where was I?"

Constant winds continued battering the little boat. At first Asia thought that after the jib was secure, she would be able to get back on course with a reefed mainsail. But these winds were out for vengeance. As if a giant sea monster had regurgitated the whole ocean in one wave on to this one small boat alone in the middle of an angry black sea. There were only two choices: let the main rip or take it down entirely. Quickly, she checked her safety line, to see that it was still securely attached around her waist. Being careful not to slip, she hoisted herself onto the cabin trunk. With sail ties clenched tightly between her teeth, Asia crawled slowly toward the mast. As she dropped the main, it began beating itself against the mast, furiously whipping around the tall spire then swinging again aft toward the stern and forward again. It slapped against her face and shoulders with a stinging cadence. Fighting the wind's great force, she braced herself on her knees against the steadfast boom as she hauled in the sail and tied it down with a superhuman strength she had not known she had.

Just as Asia slid down the cabin topside to crawl onto the deck back to the cockpit, she slipped. The powerful waves that slammed against Onika's hull threw Asia against the lifeline netting. Her head hit a stanchion. Momentarily stunned, she sat up trying to remember where she was. The boat rocked again, the rail riding the crest of the sea. Then the rains came. A deluge from Mother Nature began to pound the deck. The rhythmic cadence resounded in her ears, soaking her body and springing her mind back to reality. "Oh God!" Tears rolled down her cheeks and she wondered why she ever believed she was capable enough to survive an offshore single-handed sail. Then she slowly began crawling down the deck toward the cockpit. She wasn't concerned anymore if Onika could stay on course. Rather, it was a matter of her little boat staying upright enough not to take on too much water. Like an attendant dame at sea, Asia helped guide her stalwart friend and carapace against the resoundingly enormous black waves that surged onward toward their weathered destination. But the wind and rain pitched and battered the small boat till Asia's only answer was to tie down the wheel and hove to. Onika might lose ground but at least the hull and sails would stay intact.

Oblivious to its final blow out as the winds, rains, and seas tempestuously attacked, Asia, overcome with exhaustion, slipped into the cabin below. Neither the screeching hiss of the wind in the halyards nor the continual resounding drumming of the waves against Onika's fiberglass hull stopped her from falling into a deep dreamless sleep, letting Onika drift in a relentless sea.

—

CHAPTER 21

"A Florentine jeweler is said to have gotten the idea, …back in the 15ᵗʰ century. Quite simple really." Cynthia paused a moment as she and Crane watched the large presses through the office bay windows as they moved in their steadily patterned, back and forth motion below. "Ink an engraved plate and apply it to a sheet of paper and you get a printed impression."

Crane watched as she moved toward the door. Her slimly cut black wool slacks and snug fitting turtleneck sweater accentuated her athletic body. This woman was a rich, stylish package of sexuality.

"Actually, what the engraver does is hollow out an image and spreads ink on the whole plate." Motioning him to follow, she continued. "Then the surface of the plate is wiped off and only the ink imbedded in the indentations remains. The final print leaves a slightly raised impression. It's called intaglio," she shouted over the din that roared through the opened door as she and Crane stepped out onto a long metal catwalk to get a better view of the massive Maehel-Gross-Dexter and Koebau-De-La-Rue-Giori single and multicolor intaglio presses twenty feet below.

"Over there," Cynthia shouted again as she pointed toward a far wall.

"We're printing banknotes for Nigeria's new government under General Bahuri. Thank God for coups. They have a three-colored banknote. The more colors, the harder it is to counterfeit. Of course who'd want them?"

Her face made the shape of laughter, but because of the roar of the presses it exploded into silent sound. "It's the United States that should take 'note'!" she shouted again. "Mark my words. Once manufacturers figure out how to make these new copiers produce color, there is going to be all kinds of trouble."

The strong steel catwalk with its chest-high railing ran the length of the north wall of the old brick building. The doorway separated the second floor office wing from the press area, and management had created this overlook to be able to survey the press works from a pinnacle vantage point.

"Really?" Her black leather flats momentarily distracted Crane. "Because of their green and black two color format, I suppose?"

"You're right on the money. Some Arab terrorists have already started counterfeiting 'hundreds.' Who's next?" She yelled at the top of her lungs, as they moved slowly down the catwalk toward one end.

No dumb bunny, Richard mused to himself as he eyed Cynthia out of the corner of his eye, recalling a recent directive from the FBI on the very topic.

As he followed, he remembered laughing upon hearing his mother tell his sister Emily that 'people of our class never wear heels with jeans, or with any other pants or slacks for that matter.' Maybe Cynthia Ryder was his mother's class. He hadn't decided.

"The press below us is printing federal government food stamps, and the press next to it is printing holographs for credit cards. We also print private company and corporate stock certificates and bonds for bond issues, national and commemorative stamps for various countries and government treasury bills as well."

"This is quite an operation!" Crane shouted back over the noise as he followed Cynthia Ryder through the door to her office. "What happens to the business if Mrs. Whitney is not found?" He had already asked the same question at his father's law offices, but he wanted to hear her answer. "After all, this is a private company."

"It depends on who's responsible doesn't it?" Cynthia's clipped response hung in dead air.

"Meaning?"

"Well," Cynthia could feel her throat catch, "if she has come to harm and an outsider is responsible, then Ian and I would continue to run the company, with the approval of the family board, of course. However, if Ian had anything to do with her disappearance, then I suppose it would be quite a different scenario."

"During your previous statements, Miss Ryder, you stated that except for a brief period after her father's death there was no question about the strength of Ian Whitney and Asia Winslow's relationship." Crane and Cynthia were back in her office. His notebook was out and there was no question that this was an official interview. "What about their relationship, Miss Ryder?"

Cynthia knew she had dropped a bombshell. Although he was just a small wrinkle in the plan, she realized she did not quite have this man in her pocket as she had previously thought. "Look, I didn't mean to wash dirty laundry in public." She paused. "I'm Asia's closest friend, for God's sake. But Ian's been very distraught lately. After all, he was there when Jack Winslow died. It drove a wedge between them. They were silent at first, but it has affected their relationship very badly. And now this!"

Crane could certainly attest to Whitney's stress after the previous day's interview. Ian Whitney was distraught, all right. So with the thrust of a direct hit by a high-speed bullet Crane demanded. "Tell me about Jack Winslow's death."

Turning her back to him, there was a momentary hush. "Haven't you read the accounts?" There was a slow, sexual, smoldering edge to her voice as she turned toward him.

"Yes …"

She was so close; he could feel her hot breath on his skin. Right then he could have pulled her to him and kissed her hard. The room had heated up like a Florida summer day at the beach with ninety-percent humidity. Crane could feel tiny beads of perspiration form on his forehead. It was too Mickey Spilane. And this was reality. Crane looked at her. He realized he'd almost been had. And, as for the answer to the shoe question, he knew that too. Modulating his voice, he moved away toward the black leather, brass studded chair opposite her desk and sat down. He spoke in a slow soft definite tone. "Yes, but I want to hear it from you."

Her desk was now the battleground between them. The lines were drawn.

"Keep in mind that I wasn't there. So what I'm telling you can only be considered hearsay."

Crane nodded. No question, she knew her basic law.

"As I understand it, Jack and Ian were at the Wellfleet cottage, talking in the living room. Jack was leaning against the fireplace mantle, and all of a sudden he became weak, lost his balance and passed out. Before Ian realized what was happening and could respond, Jack keeled over, hitting his temple on the mantle edge and crumpling onto the floor. There was nothing Ian could do. Ian who is 'Mr. Suave' in both business and social situations, fell completely apart as he usually does when it's a personal or emotional situation."

"How do you know that? That wasn't in the report."

"Because he told me. Do you think any man wants to look like a wimp? Especially publicly. Anyway, he pulled himself together and called 911, and they sent the police. That's the inside story as I know it. But other than the personal comments from Ian afterward, I have the same source of information as you, the news."

"And now explain to me what will happen to the business if Ian Whitney is found even somewhat culpable for his wife's disappearance?"

"I suppose I would run the company, with the family's approval of course, until one of the grand nieces or nephews comes of age and chooses to enter the business. Banknote families generally don't sell. This is a closed shop business and its secrets are well kept commodities, even today."

"So, Whitney's relatives would not inherit?"

"No, the terms of the marriage contract are that relatives on his side may not become direct working partners, only the children from Asia's marriages can inherit the business and work in it."

"Then essentially, this company would always stay in the Winslow family?"

"Look at her name. Asia Winslow-Whitney, and all her children were to have it too."

"So other than as an employee, neither Ian nor you could ever become working partners in the business?"

"Right," she answered in an icily irritated tone.

Crane had already surmised this from talking to his grandfather, but he wanted to hear it from her. "What if something happened to both Ian Whitney and Asia Winslow, until an interested heir came of age, you get it all?"

"I can assure you, I would be considered by the family as keeper of the flame."

"And is there anything missing?"

"I beg your pardon?" Her face became almost ashen in relation to her lacquer black clothes. "Missing. Why would anything be missing?"

"Just thought I'd ask. Sometimes situations are more complicated than they seem on the surface and one likes to cover all the bases."

An interesting reaction, he thought, as the color returned to her cheeks.

"No. Not that I know of," she said as she rose from her seat. This interview was obviously over for her.

Crane agreed, so he decided not to bait her anymore and graciously stood up to leave.

As he walked out of the building, a blast of cold air heightened his senses. Putting the key into the ignition, he laughed recalling Stan's comment as he headed to his car for his drive to Albany to check out Cynthia Ryder's weekend movements.

"Give me a grievin' mafia widow any day," Stan had said. "The dames in this case are somethin' else."

As he pulled out of the parking lot, bypassing Binghamton down through the snow-shrouded countryside of Route 17 to the City, he knew Stan was right.

CHAPTER 22

Stan Sorsky's Albany run was no more productive than his partner's to the other side of the state. By traveling the freeway on the west side of the Hudson River, Stan avoided the small towns and hamlets on the old road that dotted its banks. As he neared the Catskills, a new snowfall covered the landscape; its small drifts eddied by the wind. The trees stood rigid, their bare limbs cloaked in shimmering icicles like tinsel ladened holiday trees. By mid morning the sun's rays melted patches of snow, leaving white spidery expanses on the barren earth.

It was refreshing to get away from cement and glass, traffic and noise. Although the heavy winter snows had not yet arrived in New York, Stan did not look forward to the inconvenience of snowplows and piles of dirty-pigmented slush that always lined the city streets.

He had grown up near the city in a family of three generations of NYPD police, yet Stan loved the country. Unlike Crane's grandfather, Stan's had a different point of view about filial responsibility.

"We come from a long line of police officers," his grandfather pontificated. "It's every male's obligation to the community and the family to join the force. It's our tradition," was his mantra. Of course, both his sons had joined the force and he brooked no dissent from any grandchild.

Stan did what his family expected, but he was the first family member to get an AA degree, before he joined up. He finished his criminology degree during night school at NYU, and married Jeannie right after graduation. Keeping his nose clean, his path to detective was easier than most. Although he had all the skills necessary to be successful, secretly he hated blood and morgues and found the endless hours an imposition on his family life. Jeannie, also from a police family, understood the long hours and dangers that came with the job.

What he valued most was Jeannie and the kids. They had agreed at the onset, that their sons would not be pressured into any occupation. Ben, the elder of the two, well read and academic, was the scholar and Stan suspected they had a future professor in their midst. As for Tommy, he was the wild card, athletic and devilish. Like his brother, he did well in school, but was definitely on a different path. He was already tall and lanky for his age and although 'white men can't jump,' Stan suspected Tommy might prove the naysayers quite wrong. Whatever their choices, Stan felt sure neither would become a cop.

As Stan watched the changing terrain, he reflected on his relationship with his partner Richard Crane. Everyone on the force who had worked with him realized there was something different about Crane. It was only after he had covered a few backs and saved some lives that his background and connections surfaced. By then, he was one of them. He and Crane had certainly saved each other's skin more than once. Right from the beginning, they had meshed. Crane often took the lead and Stan liked that. They had skills that complemented each other and although they had grown up in uniquely different physical and financial environments, their value systems were exactly the same. Often, no matter what the situation, it was as if each knew exactly what the other was thinking.

They had become a highly successful team on the force. More importantly, they had developed an endearing friendship, with each family welcoming the other with open arms. Richard Crane was the main reason Stan would probably stay on after his pension came due. He and Crane made space for each other's fears and foibles creating a camaraderie that made the daily grind of the NYPD not only palatable but also almost fun.

Albany was looming in the distance and Stan put his mind back on track to the business at hand. The Spring Hill Retirement Home was nestled in a high valley on the outskirts of the city. A neatly manicured hedge of boxwood bordered the long gently winding drive to the building's entrance. Behind the home was the city, but the building was surrounded on three sides by raw land, horse farms and dairies whose white and wire fences sliced the countryside into neat patchwork partitions. The H shaped building sat on a large knoll indented into the landscape, overlooking the farms and valleys below. As the car moved closer, Stan could see that the large covered veranda wrapped around the entire building giving the residents several protected vantage points from which to enjoy the views.

The grueling cold suckled by a whipping wind blasted Stan as he exited his car. Rushing into the building, he was sure his breath would form icicles dripping from his mouth if he remained outside too long.

'Gees it's cold.' Stan noted that the double door entrance opened onto an enclosed vestibule, with a reception area beyond. Removing his gloves, he headed for the receptionist's desk. Stan was immediately ushered into the director's office. It was a room that exuded the kind of confidence families of current and future residents expected in such a facility. Stan appreciated the hot coffee and buns Mrs. Marlow, the director, had standing by.

"I understand you had some interest in Mrs. Honeycutt and her granddaughter Ms. Ryder. Detective Sorsky is it?" The tall matronly woman paused. "As you probably know, Mrs. Honeycutt died last weekend and was cremated on Sunday. I would hope this has nothing to do with Mrs. Honeycutt's death," she'd continued with a slight hint of anxiety.

"Not at all. We're mainly interested in confirming Ms. Ryder's where- abouts last weekend and a general overview of her relationship with her grandmother."

Mrs. Marlow gave an almost imperceptible sigh of relief.

"When did Mrs. Honeycutt die exactly?"

"It was early Friday, approximately five in the morning. We called Ms. Ryder about 6:30, and she came directly. She arrived about eleven Friday morning and did not leave until after the cremation."

"And you know she was in the Albany area the whole weekend?"

"I am quite sure. Because we are somewhat out of town and many of our residents' relatives travel quite a distance to visit, the north wing has small suites set-aside for families. After all, most want to spend an optimum amount of time with their loved ones during their stay in the area. Ms. Ryder made use of our facilities last weekend. But I do find it strange that she had her grandmother cremated so quickly."

"Mrs. Honeycutt was an unusual sort, other than a rather wry sense of humor, she was quite matter of fact. All business. They both were for that matter."

"In what ways?"

"Well I...." Mrs. Marlow stopped mid sentence, seeming to think better of what she was about to say.

"Look, we are not investigating a fraud. We have a missing person. Besides, these people are no longer your company's clients, and if World Wide Banknote wasn't interested before, it is their last concern now." Stan paused to let the situation sink in. "So if you would please continue... anything that could help us?" God! Stan thought, all that TV crap about taking a person in a room and making them crack was so much bull. In reality, cops spent much of their time being psychologists. Stan had given it his best shot and now searched the woman's face for some kind of compliance.

"The billing for instance." Finally, to Stan's relief she slowly began again. "Although her company, World Wide Banknote paid the bills, Ms. Ryder demanded that the checks for any refunds and the end of year statements to be held and handed to her personally, rather than mailed to the Banknote company. She was quite precise about this. I remember once when a random refund was sent to her company by mistake and she was livid. She even threatened to move her grandmother to another facility if it ever happened again. Needless to say we were vigilant about handling the accounts the way she requested."

"And World Wide Banknote never questioned the lack of invoice charges or monthly statements?"

"No, never. I found it an unusual way of doing business. But as we were never questioned by any of her company's people, I just assumed, she was a valued employee who had negotiated a wonderful company perk."

"Did World Wide Banknote ever overpay the bill?"

"Every month always $500 more than was necessary, which was very convenient for us when we needed to bill Mrs. Honeycutt's account for extra services or changes in medications. We gave Ms. Ryder a quarterly statement and settled up any overages at that time."

"Fascinating. Did Ms. Ryder come to visit her grandmother often?"

"Every two months, like clock work. Arrived on a Saturday late morning, sat with her grandmother for two hours, took care of business at the office, then left. In three years the pattern never changed."

"And did her grandmother look forward to her visits?"

"I think the idea of someone coming to visit is anticipated by all of our residents, but like so many events in life reality isn't always what it's cut out to be." Mrs. Marlow gave Stan a weak smile. "More coffee?" She asked as she automatically filled his cup.

"About the cremation, wasn't that a little fast? I didn't know anyone could get a death certificate that fast and over a weekend too. Sounds impossible to me."

"I would agree with you Detective, but when you have the right contacts, I don't think there's much you can't do. She just made a phone call and her grandmother's Certificate of Death was here Saturday noon, like clockwork. As for the cremation, it seems Mrs. Honeycutt's will stated she wanted immediate cremation, no embalming and no services. There's Kurt's Funeral Home over the hill and it was done Sunday afternoon, just like that."

"What about Mrs. Honeycutt's belongings?"

"Oh, that was easy. She told us to dispose of them anyway we saw fit."

Stan had experienced the deaths of numerous aunts, uncles and four grandparents. He had watched family members slowly sift through the deceased's belongings, or because of grief, leave their things stuffed in drawers and closets for a younger generation to sort out. Stan was amazed. "And she just walked away taking nothing?"

"No. She took three things; a book, a music box her grandmother often played and a picture. I noticed it once on her grandmother's bedside stand. Such an unusual picture. I ask Mrs. Honeycutt who they were but all she would say was... 'They are the past.'"

Stan waited.

"It was of a small frail girl, I would say about eight or nine, in a thin dress standing next to an emaciated woman of medium height who was as poorly clothed as the child. The woman's hand was on the child's shoulder, and they were standing on the rickety porch of a small, one story row house." Mrs. Marlow sighed and then reflected. "If you must know, I have always felt there was some darkness about those two women I never understood." Her mood instantly changed. "Well, I know it's not much, but I hope I've been of some help."

"Thank you for you time." Mrs. Marlow watched as Stan stepped out into the vestibule.

He could feel the vibration as the incessant wind rattled the outer doors. "Does it always blow like this?" he called back.

"The verandas are often somewhat uncomfortable, even in summer. I didn't pick the site, I only work here." She sighed.

"Sometimes you do what you gotta' do." He understood. Then he braced himself for the biting blast of air that would smack him in the face as he stepped out into the bitter cold. 'The location was like a beautiful mistress with an evil intent,' he mused as he drove away.

Stan's next stop was Kurt's Funeral home.

"Just a rubber stamped signature, like they all are." The owner explained.

But other than getting the name of the individual whose name was stamped on Mrs. Honeycutt's Death certificate, he found the funeral director's comments even less revelatory than the ones he had obtained during his visit to Spring Hill.

As he drove back to the city, he rehashed the conversations he had earlier in the afternoon. It was obvious. There was no way Cynthia could have spent the weekend in both Albany and New York. Nevertheless he found some of the information he had acquired not only perplexing but also disconcerting. It was if he had been given a new version of a Cat's Cradle with no directions. Wasn't that what a Cat's cradle was all about? No direction. Stan laughed at his stupidity.

CHAPTER 23

L ike many of the cramped two-story houses on the street, the original brick façade had been covered with white vinyl siding. Decorative cement blocks lined both sides of the walkway and continued across the front, delineating the minuscule front yard from the public sidewalk that ran parallel between the property and the street. A light snow powdered the yard, and two matching red and green ceramic gnomes stood playfully as if on guard on each side of the steps leading up to the front door. Although this was the Queens address listed in Annie Bloome's personnel file, the name on the letterbox by the side of the front door read Benetonelli.

Stan rang the bell and waited.

"Comin' comin'." The rich, mellow voice with a slight Italian accent called from inside. "It takes me longer, ya know." A short squat, barrel chested, elderly woman dressed in black, steadied herself with her cane as she peered out, making sure to keep the locked screen door between herself and the two strangers. "If you're sellin'? I don't buy nothin'." The emphatic words spilled out of the puckered slit of a mouth that moved among the furrowed creases of the old face. Her eyes twinkled with deceitful mirth, as a hint of a smile changed the patterns of her corrugated expression.

"Detectives Sorsky and Crane, ma'am, New York Police Department, and we're not selling a thing." The two detectives smiled back as they showed her their badges. "But we would like a word with a Miss Ann Bloome, if this is the correct address."

At first, a little confused, the woman repeated the name, "Ann – You mean my granddaughter, Angelina Benetonelli, maybe? She change her name for that high-falutin' job she take in the city. Thinks it sound better. All my life, I am Benetonelli and I do just fine." As she motioned the two detectives toward the living room, aided by her cane, she hobbled, bow-legged to the stairwell. Leaning on the banister edge, she used her cane to point the detectives toward a plastic covered cherry red-flocked couch with baroquish carved wooden legs. "Sit! Sit!" She commanded. "I'll call her. Angelina. Angelina. You come now please." Her voice resounded throughout the house. Movement could be heard on the floor above as Mrs. Benetonelli slowly made her way to a tan Barko Lounger opposite the couch.

"You have a beautiful granddaughter, Mrs. Benetonelli. She must get lots of calls from young men," Stan started conversationally.

"Oh yes!" She beamed. "Not so much the local boys anymore. She refuse them so much. But from the City …"

"Yes?"

"Grandma!" Even wearing no makeup, in jeans and a tee, she could have stopped traffic. "Just what is so important that you could not have asked me at the office?"

"No, no, Angelina! You mustn't." Her grandmother interjected. "It's the police, Angelina."

"I know who they are, Grandma, and they have no business being here." Her venomous tone stung the air.

"Miss Bloome, we are sorry if we have invaded your privacy, but because the disappearance of Mrs. Whitney is such a sensitive matter, we thought you might be more comfortable talking at home." Stan continued.

"See! They care about you, Angelina." Mrs. Benetonelli spoke softly.

"Let's get this over with, gentlemen," her granddaughter demanded, as she glared at him with an acid stare.

The questions were basically the same ones she was asked the morning after the gala, with one exception. And her answers, although sounding more rehearsed this time, were as innocent as before. Unlike the last interview, Stan asked all the questions. Occasionally, Annie looked out of the corner of her eye quizzically at Richard Crane who sat silently, seemingly disinterested.

"The books, Miss Bloome, have you noticed anything unusual about the books?" Stan asked.

"The books?" She paused as if not understanding the question. "Oh, you mean the accounts. No ... why would anyone fiddle with the books? After all it's a family owned company. They'd be stealing from themselves." Crane observed her pupils dilate as she protested her employers' innocence.

"We were thinking more in terms of large cash flows because of an unusual debt or a major business slow down. Some unique financial event that compromised the owner's income, Miss

Benetonelli?" Crane paused. "Something that may have precipitated Mrs. Whitney's disappearance." Annie Bloome swung around and locked eyes with Crane whom she knew had purposely used her original name when he interjected the question.

"World Wide Banknote is a very solvent company, Detective Crane." She answered venomously.

Stan's gaze went from one to the other. Except for a few hardened criminals, who were obviously going down, he had never seen anyone with such an intense dislike for his partner as this beautiful young woman. It was apparent that the animosity she exhibited toward him during the hotel interview still lingered, and it was also obvious that Crane didn't care.

"Well," Crane said casually, "I guess that's about it, Miss Benetonelli. Detective Sorsky and I can see our way out." And they did.

. . . .

The ride back to the precinct over the Queensboro Bridge was slow but steady. "So we're back to the husband with his solitary trip to Wellfleet and no other admitted alibi," Crane said in a disgusted tone.

"But any guy who can screw a gorgeous dame between 3 and 5 a.m., kill his wife, stash her body God knows where, drive to Cape Cod and leave no tell-tale clues, either didn't do it or is a master criminal."

Richard knew Stan was right.

"But what if he's been fiddling with the books. He might have cause," Crane countered.

"No judge would give us a warrant to look at the company accounts with what we've got now." Stan was right again.

"It's obvious that woman's lying." Richard retorted. "After all 'she's not the straightest arrow in the sheath.'"

"So what do you suggest we do?' Stan smiled.

"Have you considered that maybe someone else drove his wife to the cottage?" Stan pondered Crane's new idea but before he had a chance to reply, Crane continued. "I think we'll take a little trip to Wellfleet."

"You got to be kidding. The Cape. ..."

But Crane was not. "We've got a few days off ..."

"Look, it's my anniversary. Jeanie would never go for it."

"I'm well aware what weekend it is. Even if the Pope were shot in Shea Stadium, everyone knows that you have this weekend off every year no matter what." Crane paused. "We'll take her with us. Drive up to Providencetown in my car, and Jeanie can hang out while we check the guy out. We'll talk to the people we need to and see what we have to see. Then you can take Jeanie out for a romantic dinner and spend the night at the Providencetown Inn, while I 'veg' somewhere else appealingly quiet. I've already made the reservations and reserved an extra car, if you want to stay more then one night. My anniversary present to you two." Richard grinned sheepishly. "Jeanie thinks it's a great idea. Anyway, I'd like to see where and how Whitney, while alone, did so much damage to himself."

Stan wasn't surprised. Crane and Jeanie were often in cahoots behind his back. Although Richard had a loving family with whom he spent a great deal of time, neither he nor his sister, Emily had married and had kids which was why Crane's mother was always introducing the two of them to all her friends' bimbo children and single relatives. Over the years, the two detectives became more than partners. They were friends. Sorsky and Crane, the precinct's odd couple, one from Brooklyn, the other from Manhattan's Upper East Side. Interestingly, it worked, and Crane had become a loving uncle to Stan and Jeanie's two boys.

"Well, I can't fight city hall." Stan clichéd. "Wait one damn minute!" Stan drew out the words on a long breath. "What car? You don't have a car!" Crane didn't answer. "Unless you mean that old piece of junk you had from college, forget it. I'm not taking the mother of my children anywhere in that."

"I just bought one."

"You bought one?" Stan repeated Richard's words. He knew Crane spent very little. Other than his comfortable apartment in the brownstone he inherited from an elderly maiden aunt and his yearly vacation, Crane's budget, in relation to his income, was financially staid.

"When?" Stan demanded, circumspectly. "What kind?"

Richard bit the bullet "A Jaguar," he said.

"You've got to be kidding! You always said your parents had a matching pair, one for the house and one for the garage."

Crane ignored Stan's statement. "They've vastly improved the electrical system, so I bought one of the new '84 models as soon as they came out. An S3 XJ6 saloon. Beautiful car. Handles like a dream. It sort of glides." Richard Crane was rarely euphoric about anything. "After all, I do own one of those rarities, a garage in the City."

"A garage? What? When and how did you get a garage?" Stan was astounded by the turn of the conversation; it was certainly a change from the Winslow-Whitneys. "What did you do? Dig a hole under your house?"

"Remember when my sister Emily was dying to buy her horse farm up near Skidmore in Saratoga where she teaches?"

Stan nodded, still in shock.

"And she asked me to buy the house Aunt Grace left her next door to mine so she could afford the farm?" Crane continued, "and I did?"

Stan nodded again.

"On Emily's side, I left the entry and stairs and converted the living room into a garage. You saw the contractors working. They finished at the end of September. Guess you didn't notice the new door to my kitchen, when you were there the other day. Really nice job, I might add."

Stan didn't need to ask how Crane had gotten the proper permits through the city. Crane knew the right law firm, and Stan laughed until his sides ached. "And of course, we would not like to put it to waste."

"I'll pick you and Jeanie up at 7:30 a. m. Ought to be a grand day for a drive." Crane replied ignoring Stan's sigh as he parked the department's five-year-old car in the precinct lot.

CHAPTER 24

As Asia came up the companionway onto the cockpit deck, she noted with pleasure the thin line reflection of the mast in the chrome of the compass binnacle hood. It was going to be a glorious day.

The storm had taken two days and nights to blow itself out. The third morning, Asia found that other than a purplish-yellow bruise on the left side of her head and a rousing headache, which was finally abating, the primary pieces of her body were still assembled in the proper order. As for Onika, Asia happily found surprisingly little damage to her sturdy boat. She immediately put her stalwart friend back on course and found that the winds and currents had pushed Onika much less off course than Asia had expected. There was no help for the loss of a five-gallon canister of extra fuel, but the tangle of sheets and lines here and there had to be put right, and Asia had Onika shipshape by noonday's end. After her tasks were done, there were no more pratfalls of gusting winds or bad weather. Onika sailed again at a steady clip on her windward course for the next five days.

By her calculations, she was only half a day from Bermuda. When she finally sighted the distant dots on the horizon, she knew she was within twenty knots of the Islands. Asia also knew that coral reefs, which had been created by the caresses of the warm Gulf Stream waters, extended 12 miles offshore encircling the Islands. Juan de Bermudez was the first to thwart Mother Nature's protective shield, invading the islands' pristine protected harbors and cays in 1503. Asia too, having succeeded in using celestial navigation to fix her position with the sun and stars, and weathering the Gulf Stream, would soon arrive in Bermuda, a small speck on an ocean chart. She was secretly thrilled with her single-handed success and glad for a daylight approach for her landfall.

Captain Sandy had warned Asia that the northern approach into St. George's Harbour, which she was about to undertake, was dicey at best, day or night, with ten miles of offshore shoals of doughnuts and coral heads. There was also a tide that ran as much as two knots in an easterly wind, which could create a choppy ocean surge as the sea and land converged. But she was in luck. The winds were light and visibility great in the exquisite morning sun. Keeping well east with a 226 heading toward St. David's head, as Captain Andy had instructed, she entered the Narrows Channel. Soon she was at buoy number 1 and on her way into St. Georges Harbour through the Town Cut Channel toward the town dock.

After clearing customs and immigration, Asia headed over to Mullet Bay at the western end of the harbor. The town dock was free for visiting seafarers, however it was also conspicuous. Mullet Bay on the other hand, was a dockage and anchorage for locally owned boats. It was a great hurricane harbor, and directly on the main road to St. George. Not terribly pleasant but obvious.

"Always hide things in plain sight. Then they are more likely to be overlooked," Aubrey had said. Mullet Bay was a perfect camouflage for Onika.

How Aubrey had secured the berth for her boat in this crowded marina was unfathomable to Asia. But this was one time when one of her most hated expressions 'the rich can get away with anything' was a most appreciated truth in her life.

"I'm here!" she exclaimed when she telephoned Aubrey at his office.

"And you have mail," Aubrey countered.

"A package?" She asked anxiously.

"A package."

A deep winsome sigh could be heard from Asia's end of the line. "I'll take the bus. We'll open it together at dinner." She laughed. She envisioned his smile as she grabbed her duffle and was off.

Having been to Bermuda many times, Asia knew she couldn't rent a car even if she had wanted to. Rental cars were against the law. She didn't want a record of one in her name anyway. Visitors got about the islands by moped, bus, taxi, or by the frequently run ferries in Hamilton Harbour. Putting around on a moped had its appeal, but today Asia rode the bus. The ride through the gently rolling green landscape dotted with an occasional elegant hotel, private homes and ocean views had always taken her breath away. These little islands, dropped down in the middle of the Atlantic Ocean, were one of nature's jewels. It was little wonder the Bermudans had so many protective rules. No rental cars, a one car per family law, and stringent building codes; property ownership rules for foreigners and laws of immigration were strictly enforced.

The package had made it here and so had she. One was no good without the other. Asia was enjoying her bus ride across the island and her sense of relief became a sense of success and euphoria.

Two down, she thought. Now to finish the job. Then to clean up the mess I've left behind. The hardest part was over – getting away undetected. She believed her acts must have put some wheels in motion that now could not be stopped. She could hardly wait to see the New York papers Aubrey had promised to save. Hopefully the right questions were being asked and … and …

"Give it a break," she whispered to no one. "You're in Bermuda – life can't get much better than this," she mused while leaning her head out of the bus window and feeling the fresh Bermuda breeze.

At Waterville roundabout, Asia left the bus and grabbed a taxi down Harbour Road just beyond Lower Ferry. Tinkerhouse, Sir Aubrey's ancestral home was in Paget Parish across from Hamilton on Hamilton Harbour. The house sat long and low above the shoreline, a rambling edifice built of Bermuda's traditional cream-colored, quarried limestone. The thin slabs of limestone were also sliced for roof tiles that became hard and strong when exposed to the weather. The thickness of the block walls not only gave protection from storms, but also protected their inhabitants from heavy winds and summer heat. Left alone, the stones turned gray with age, but Tinkerhouse was painted a soft, muted yellow with white push-out wooden louvered blinds and a whitewashed roof giving it a distinctly Winslow Homer façade. When Asia arrived, the house beckoned her with its messages of solidarity, warmth and love, a feeling of home.

CHAPTER 25

"I'm home!" Asia shouted, as she entered the warmly familiar, old yellow house. Greeted with Aubrey's bear hugs followed by his expressions of relief that she had finally arrived helped her feel safer than she knew she really was. After all, it was only a matter of time. Then came the barrage of questions.

"The most exciting part was the big storm!" And the stories began.

Aubrey's eyes widened; he was still the same burley, over-sized man with piercing blue eyes and commanding presence she had always known. Asia's father had often said Sir Aubrey was both respected and feared in the world of international finance, but with her, he was just a big pussycat.

Jack Winslow and Sir Aubrey Tinkerton had been friends since boyhood. They had gone to different colleges but were together again at the Harvard Business School. Each had been the other's best man at their weddings and when Asia arrived, Aubrey had become her godfather.

Growing up, Asia had spent a great many vacations at Tinkerton House and Aubrey, whose wife died young and who had no children of his own, became almost a second father. Tinkerton House and its staff had watched Asia grow over the years, and the house and its occupants had become a cocoon that enveloped her with warmth and love.

Their first evening together was a celebration. Cook made a splendid welcoming dinner of Asia's favorites, curried conch chowder, wahoo, a local fish sautéed with bananas and onions, and syllabub, a mixture of Guava jelly, crème and wine, which Asia knew was concocted to leave the diner with a hypnotic, mellow aftertaste.

After dinner drinks were served in the library, a large rectangular room paneled with cedar planks from an ancient shipwreck that had been salvaged by one of Aubrey's long dead relatives. The books were meticulously categorized much like a real lending library. Often Aubrey explained his precise nature with 'To have an organized mind one must live in an organized environment.' Or 'Clutter is the road to mistakes,' Asia had heard both of these so many times she would laugh and say them with him when he began.

"There certainly is no clutter here," she would tease in every room they happened to be together in throughout the day.

The library, with long paned windows and a fireplace built from antique nine-inch bricks brought from the old Royal Navy Dockyard, was the oldest part of the house. Aubrey had grown up at Tinkerton House and had inherited the property from his mother when she died.

When they were finally alone, Aubrey opened his safe.

"There you are, my dear," he said as he handed her the modest sized, rectangular package wrapped in brown paper and twine.

"And there they are," Asia laughed, as she removed the final tape and opened the lid, "six million dollars in bearer bonds. Money my dear husband siphoned off World Wide Banknote and our personal accounts over the last nine years."

"That's almost a million dollars a year. Damn good return, I'd say. But he did have to put up with you dear heart," Sir Aubrey teased.

"Oh! Pooh!" Asia replied, as she packed the spilling notes back in the box and handed it to Aubrey to return to the safe.

"Tomorrow, after lunch when you are rested, I shall fetch you and your package and we shall go to the bank so that these can be properly converted into hard currency and secured in an appropriate privately numbered account. I shall be much happier when, like you, they are safely placed out of harm's way."

After a well-earned rest, Asia awoke the next morning and thought about Ian. She was aghast that it had taken so long for the money to be missed. Yet, she did not believe that was the true situation. Over the years, after Ian had joined the company, she had heard comments about misplaced money transfers. They were mainly from countries where coups had recently taken place. During the change in the power structure multitudinous assets often mysteriously disappeared. The new leaders, unable to immediately trace all of these assets, always covered the supposedly missing transfers to World Wide Banknote rather than lose face with the company that produced their image for posterity. She recalled hearing her father's rumblings the last few years and discussions with Ian about missing assets. As she lay in her bed, it dawned on her that it was not her father's lack of knowledge about the missing funds but rather his inability to trace their path. Bearer Bonds, being a totally anonymous financial instrument, had obviously never entered her father's mind ... and, as for Ian, she knew her father was blinded by his charm. Asia remembered her own infatuation with the handsome young Englishman. She also recalled her reservations about the marriage. She had ignored her discomfort about the union because it gave her father so much pleasure. She made it work because that was what was expected, and in the beginning, she believed Ian had made an effort as well.

The aroma of the Bermuda island breakfast wafted through the room and jarred Asia back to the present. Jeanette entered with a tray   overflowing with boiled potatoes and codfish, fresh bananas, eggs and stewed tomatoes mixed with onions and spices.

The car arrived at exactly 1 p.m., and that afternoon Asia was quietly squired into the bank's inner sanctum and Aubrey's offices.

"The papers have been prepared to invest the money in a tax exempt company. There is no income tax, capital gains tax, business tax, or any tax on the accumulation of profits. The only cost to you is a five percent fee," Aubrey explained.

Five percent of six million dollars was a fat chunk, Asia calculated. Nevertheless, this was minimal next to the loss of the entire six million if Ian had gotten away with his heist. No matter, these were the Bermudan banking rules and they too had to make a buck. Service, after all. "I understand," she said.

"As you have more than the minimum one hundred twenty thousand dollars necessary, I have written the terms so you may enter the reinsurance end of the financial markets, if you are so inclined. It is an excellent way to invest as the Bermudan government has minimal regulation."

Asia did not interrupt but listened carefully with an occasional nod of understanding.

"Gori's and Segried's sale of banknote producing machines has allowed more and more outsiders and countries to enter into the banknote business, encroaching on the eight families' worldwide monopoly. It might be time to consider other financial ventures," Aubrey suggested.

"That has been a worry of mine for some time now. Ian's little private savings account just might be put toward the reinvention of our family fortunes." Asia said with a sad smile.

"Exactly my point. Warren Buffet, Ross Perot and many other United States and European insurers already have companies well entrenched here and they are improving their bottom lines daily. When you are rested, come with me, and we'll begin your new financial education. I don't want you wasting your time while you're waiting around for the turn of events," Aubrey continued. "It is the least I can do for your father and you, my love."

Asia's simple "Thank you," expressed it all.

CHAPTER 26

Richard Crane nestled down on his well-worn, cracked leather couch. Propping his feet comfortably on the coffee table, he gazed contentedly out at the winter starkness of the small walled garden. It was Sunday, the day before Christmas, and a heavy snow covered the ground leaving white-flecked touches on the lone fir tree, now festooned with colored bulbs, that dominated his view. The fireplace in the cozy, masculine room, with its wall of books and French doors that folded back in summer opening onto a small covered terrace, had a warm glowing fire that suckled every nook and cranny with the rich lights and shadows of its flames. This was his sanctuary away from the dirt and pain that he dealt with daily in his job.

Richard appreciated his home, an inheritance from his Great Aunt Grace. She was his sister Emily Grace's namesake, who had left them each contiguous Upper East Side Manhattan townhouses. Emily, who taught at Skidmore in Saratoga in upstate New York, spent little time in the city, unlike Richard, who had made the first floor and garden his permanent home. A smile crossed his face as he recalled the weekend Emily had come to him with her proposition.

"Richard, I got tenure," she exclaimed breathlessly, "and now I can buy it."

"Congratulations! Calls for a champagne dinner. And whatever IT is, it's your gift from me."

"It's a horse farm! Just outside Saratoga! Just perfect Richard! And with the Skidmore girls bringing their horses to school with them, it's got a built in clientele. Isn't it super? And I just knew you'd help." Emily blurted out words in quick staccato. Richard was amazed that this graduate of MIT and full professor in chemistry could act just like she looked. A pixie.

"Whoa! I can certainly get you a nice gift, but a horse farm is a little out of my financial league."

"I don't mean buy the horse farm for me, you dunce, I meant you could buy my house next door, make yourself into the slum landlord of the upper Eastside and I could buy my farm. After all, neither of us could ever sell the property to an outsider. Aunt Grace would turn in her grave."

Richard knew she was right.

"But this way," she continued, "it stays in the family, and you become more of a real estate mogul than you already are. I get a permanent home where I work and elevate my guilt."

Richard had already converted the rest of his house into nicely proportioned flats that more than paid the taxes and insurance on the property. So he snapped up Emily's, creating a second floor pied-a-terre for his friends and Emily's use, and converted the upper floors into rentals, adding them to his small but lucrative real estate empire.

Richard's mind wandered back to the present. As he poured his coffee, he was reminded of how much Stan chided him about his daily consumption. Hey, maybe Stan was right. However, this was Sunday, Richard's favorite day of the week, when he didn't have to work. He was not cutting back today. Screw Stan and his health bulletins; he was the one with the paunch not Crane.

By a quirk of fate and massive amounts of overtime, Stan and Crane had struck pay dirt and gotten two consecutive days off during the holidays. Although Richard always attended his parents' Christmas Eve fete as often as his work allowed, Crane considered his Christmas visits with Stan and Jeannie one of the most enjoyable parts of the holiday. Their two boys, Tommy and Ben, considered Richard their surrogate uncle, and Richard fawned on the boys as the children he had not yet had.

Seeing the Sunday papers lying patiently on his doorstep, Richard stepped out and retrieved them from the damp, chilling cold. Heading back to his warm coffee and hot buttered muffin, he settled in for a quiet morning. 'Can't get any better than this,' he thought, enjoying his quiet sanctuary. Then the phone rang. Damn! No one called on Sunday. They knew better, unless it was a family emergency. Resigned, he picked up the receiver.

"Have you seen the Times?" It was his Grandfather who continued before he had a chance to reply. "You might look on page 2A."

"Hold on, Gramps." Richard put down the phone. There it was under METRO SECTION.

Police Baffled Over Disappearance
Of Missing Heiress
'Asia Winslow-Whitney, heiress to the World Wide Bank
note fortune, disappeared from her family supported
Settlement House benefit held at the Plaza Hotel.' B1

"I'm surprised it's been kept out of the press as long as it
has." Richard was already scanning page B1. "It looks pretty
generic."

"True," his grandfather paused. "The story is in the tabloids,
too with a slightly different slant. You might want to take a look
at those as well."

"Thanks, I'll call you back," he said as he hung up the phone,
sighed and picked up the Times. The story under the Missing
Heiress headline, although slanted toward the suspected foul play
angle, was unbiased, straightforward reporting. It described the
bloodstained disarray of the hotel room and informed its reader-
ship that after more than a month her body had not been found.
A short auxiliary article below her picture flanked the lead story
about the tragic circumstances of her father Jack Winslow's
recent death.

Richard found the story in The Daily News on page 15.
Using their seamier, sensationalistic style of reportage, their
headlines had a slightly different focus.

Society Policeman Pirouettes
Around Family Client's Disappearance

Not only did the article question police efficiency, it alluded
to the previous investigation and inquest of her father's recent
untimely death on Cape Cod. The reporters stated the dirty

question, rather than leaving it for readers to surmise. 'Whether there might be a vendetta against this wealthy, but secretive family?' One they assumed the police may have missed or were covering up? Unlike the Times, the article listed the names of the police officers in charge of investigating Mrs. Winslow-Whitney's disappearance, labeling Richard Crane 'the Society Policeman' who was coincidently the son of one of the partners in the law firm Abernathy, Huntington, Crane, & Associates, who represented both the personal and professional interests of the Winslow family.

After reading both articles, Richard immediately returned his grandfather's call.

"You'll note that there's no mention of the mayor's having personally requested I be awakened at three in the morning on my day off to handle this case. There's no mention of how damned hard Stan and I worked to come up with zip. Nor how Banner in forensics has spent an exorbitant amount of taxpayer money to find a lead on this woman." Crane was hot, but the implications of the Daily News really made him steam.

"Now calm down, son. It's all right. After all, you know the average American can't take a steady dose of reality. These kinds of stories sell newspapers. In a day or two the media will be onto something else and forget all about it."

Richard knew his grandfather was right, but it was still degrading.

"Has my dad seen this?"

"I called him before I called you."

"And?"

"He says Abernathy, et. al., will bite the bullet. Frankly, he and your mother were quite amused. Your mother thinks this

new media handle, 'Society Policeman' is a bit more sophisti-
cated than your last, 'The Dick with the Trick.'"

Richard winced at the reminder of the indignities he had
suffered from that little news moniker. All because some petty
crook and his prison inmates had described Richard, who had put
them all behind bars, as a Dick who had lots of tricks to arrest so
many and make it stick. The press loved it and like kids playing
the telephone game, by the time it got back to Crane through
the department grapevine, he was bombarded with the presses'
shortened version. He knew his sister, whom he had enjoyed
calling Emily, the horse girl, when they were younger, was going
to give him a hell of a time tomorrow during Christmas dinner.
"I think I'll hang up and salvage as much of my Sunday as I can."

But Richard couldn't retrieve his day. The media had irrevo-
cably blemished it. Asia Winslow, whom he had put out of his
mind since the evening before, had this morning invaded his
most precious private time.

Sundays were for schmoosing with the Times crossword,
reading the comics, taking in museums, and walking in Central
Park. If a case was going to screw up your day, it ought to be
because of confusing leads rather than no leads at all.

Crane put down his paper and re-evaluated their original
leads. Stan had checked out Cynthia Ryder's alibi. It was iron-
clad. Forensics had gone over all the Winslow-Whitney cars
and they were clean. Of course, Ian Whitney could have used a
rental, but that didn't pan out either. On the previous Friday, he
and Stan had spoken with Doctor Hansen in Provincetown, who
had repaired Ian Whitney's arm.

"The man's arm was imbedded with small, fragments of
glass, riddled with them." He mused. "One of the more uncanny
accidents, I've seen. It was as if he had purposely smashed his

extremity into the mirror." Richard recalled the doctor's comment and how he shook his head as if bewildered at the thought.

On Saturday morning Stan had reluctantly left Jeanie to relax
at the Inn, while they finished their inquiries. Mr. Weatherspoon,
a long, lean, shaggy old duff, who was the Wellfleet property's
caretaker, showed them the hacked fireplace mantle, and the
frame with what was left of the mirror.

"Had no idea there was this secret compartment," he
explained as he showed the two detectives the damage. "A bit
curious, but these old houses often have their own little idiosyn-
crasies. Mr. Whitney claimed he'd found the damage done to
the mantle when he arrived and had tripped over the mirror."
Weatherspoon continued. "But, I woulda' sworn the last time
I checked the house, that mirror was hangin' just where it had
always been."

"And when was that?" Stan had asked.

"Saturday week, before Mr. Whitney's visit."

"I see," Stan paused. "Did the Whitney's use the place often?"

"Not much after she married, although often times we'd
hear him roarin' up the road in his fancy car. He'd come alone
for a few hours or over night. Never knew what he was doin'
here all by himself, but we're a small community and although
we're not nosin' into others affairs, we keep our eye out for
the unusual; what's goin' on. What the man did weren't none
of my business. But any comins' and goins' to this house was."
Richard smiled as he recalled the gruff tone of proprietorship in
the man's words.

"That's my job," he had continued, "to keep the place in good
repair and to keep an eye out. That's what Jack Winslow paid
me for and that's what I did." Mr. Weatherspoon rambled on as
he bent down to pick up an almost imperceptible piece of glass

that lay deep in the carpet nap. "How one trips on a glass mirror hangin' on the wall, …"

"Hmm," Crane remembered looking from Stan to Mr. Weatherspoon and saying, "It is puzzling." At the time he had sensed that the two other men had the same gut feeling; that Whitney was the culprit.

During that trip, all they came up with was that Whitney was looking for something important that he had not found, and the image of a spoiled individual prone to temper tantrums when things didn't go his way.

Richard mused at how he and Banner had played hardball back and forth with the facts for weeks. All they had was a messed up hotel room with no prints, a blood tainted elevator with lots of prints including Whitney's, and a lot of randomly spread fresh blood, albeit it was the same blood type as the missing woman's … 'When I find her, I'm going to give her hell!' Crane abruptly stopped sipping his cold coffee and subliminally watching the Brown Thrasher pluck seeds from the seed bell he had hung on his lone fir.

"When I find her, I'm …" It was as if a comic strip light bulb had flashed in his brain. Maybe there was no body because there was not supposed to be one. Crane began to reassess the lack of facts and the unusual configuration of blood. Someone had obviously faked the trail of blood to put them off track. That's probably why it was so easy to get her out. They walked her out. But who? If it were for money, someone would have received a ransom note by now. If so, would Whitney have told them? Maybe she had done this by herself, or she and Whitney were for some reason in cahoots. Maybe that was why, although they could not pin anything on Whitney, the few current facts pointed to him and he remained the only suspect.

This case was going nowhere fast. Yet Crane was damned if he would let it go entirely. It was like a jigsaw puzzle he couldn't finish, not because the pieces wouldn't fit but because some were missing. And he was sure that whatever had been secreted in the mantle cache was the key.

It also continued to nag at him that he had met this young woman sometime in his past. Like a pesky gnat on a summer's night, each time he'd swat at it there was only thin air. During dinner recently, his father had said their families belonged to some of the same clubs. Since returning to the City and joining the force, Crane had had little time for tennis and yachts. As a kid, when he wasn't working at the Stuyvestant Yacht Club, he spent his time at the family's clubs with his friends. Asia was five years younger. He had better things to do than hang out with some snotnosed brat.

Crane could not let it go, and the case continued to whirlwind 'round his brain. He was glad this Sunday was different, that he was expected at the Sorsky's for a pre-Christmas celebration during the late afternoon, and for once he really appreciated the prospect of his mother's Christmas Eve buffet.

"Thank heavens this afternoon and tomorrow are full of distractions." He said aloud, unaware that he had disrupted the silence of the room.

Even though he was soon to see Stan with Jeannie and the boys, Crane decided to wait until Tuesday morning to share his theory with Stan. Richard knew he and Stan would move on with their caseload, and the Winslow-Whitney case would be put somewhat aside for lack of leads. Yet for him, it would continue to be a constant enigma in the back of his mind. Eventually, he knew someone would slip up and when they did, he and Stan would be there to catch the banana peel when it flew, and toss it in the garbage where it belonged.

CHAPTER 27

Richard phoned his mother reminding her he'd be late for their annual Christmas Eve get-together, and then headed off to Stan and Jeannie's with his holiday offerings. This year he had gotten plane tickets to Florida for the family during the children's Winter break. Stan would pay for the rest, and it would become a really nice vacation that a family of four might not otherwise have on a policeman's salary.

"We're going ta' Florida," Tommy shouted exuberantly, jumping up and down on the couch. "We're going ta Flo…"

"Tommy!" Stan's voice resonated authority and the couch was once again saved. Richard eyed Tommy and gave him the usual wink. Signals met, Tommy winked back.

Besides whatever travel gift he brought for the family, Richard always brought each of boys an inexpensive gift. This year for Tommy, the rambunctious, athletic one, Crane bought a basketball, and for Ben, who was studious almost to a fault, a copy of Ben Franklin's autobiography.

Tommy, who was eight, made Crane a rather too long yellow and green gimp-lanyard-keychain, while Ben, twelve, wrote a series of poems which he had bound into a book. Both of these, Richard believed, would probably be this year's favorite gifts. Jeannie and Stan gave Crane beautifully soft doeskin driving gloves and a handsome leather steering wheel cover for his new car. Crane smiled to himself at their thoughtfulness. After sampling Santa's cookies, eggnog and hugs all around, and wishing the boys good luck with Santa, off he went to his own family's annual buffet.

Unlike other families' tight knit holiday get-togethers, the Christmas Eve buffet at the Cranes was rather a strange affair. As her children had gotten older, Mrs. Crane used this holiday eve as an opportunity to invite those whom she considered "less fortunate than we, who would otherwise spend the holidays alone." That was the way she described the affair. Richard's father called it her 'Christmas Eve soirée for the Indigent Rich.' Although there were many of the same lonely souls, every year, the guest list did vary. New faces were added. If some new acquaintance tugged on Mrs. Crane's heartstrings, they were added to the guest list.

As Richard walked in, he noticed his grandfather chatting with Ben Huntington, a partner in the family law firm, whose wife had died recently, and Barnaby Levin who arrived annually with his Irish wolfhound, Simon. Simon always hung out in the kitchen with Emily's three dogs, Bowser, Beauregard and Bear who all worked together feverishly doing the invaluable job of licking scraps off plates.

No one ever explained to Richard the relationship of the three men. Yet Barnaby was somehow an old friend of both his grandfather and Ben Huntington. Richard had never been allowed to be privy to the connection. Barnaby's educated graceful eloquence and demeanor belied his generally clean, yet tattered clothes and ravished appearance. Tonight however, for Barnaby, he was elegantly dressed in a worn dark corduroy sport jacket of excellent quality and grey woolen slacks, maybe half a size too large, clenched at the waist by an Italian leather belt. It wasn't that his elders were trying to keep a deep dark secret from Richard. It was just that while growing up, every time Richard had asked about Mr. Levin, he was always told, "to wait until later" or "when you're older." Richard had finally stopped asking and now that he was older, he guessed that everyone had forgotten that he didn't know. Yet, Mr. Levin remained one of Richard's favorites among his family's older friends.

Waving him over, Richard joined the three on his way to see his sister, Emily, whom he knew was in the kitchen.

"Mr. Levin, I just realized, I met a friend of Simon's the other day. An Alistair Sloane." Richard smiled as he recalled that the contact he had been given by Alistair Sloane was actually Barnaby's dog.

"A sad case, Sloane, but yes, he and Simon are great friends. One of Simon's closest."

"You should have brought him tonight," Richard continued.

"He isn't ready."

"I understand."

"Try your mother's shrimp…delicious."

Richard nodded and by way of the shrimp, he headed through the group toward the kitchen.

On his way, he greeted Mrs. Philips, who lived two doors down. She was another fixture. Touted to have been a young chanteuse in Paris during the twenties, it was reputed that while there, she married a titled German industrialist. Then in a fit of love or lust, one was never quite sure, she ran off with what she thought was a poor American doughboy only to find out his family owned half of Staten Island. Occasionally, she was referred to as the Countess. Whether it was true or not...

Richard spied his mother across the room dressed in her flowing holiday caftan of Pucci patterned reds and greens, surrounded by half a dozen rich and lonely friends, who looked forward to this yearly event. They waxed expansively over the likenesses and differences of the last year's menu and often called ahead to find out if mother would be serving their favorite dish. There were younger people too; young widows and singles, strays whom his mother had 'picked up' here and there, an old school chum's child who had just moved to the city and could not get home for the holidays. It was the usual array of this's and that's, all yearning for some holiday company.

Whenever Richard's father suggested that because the children were grown they might consider a Christmas vacation, his mother was adamant.

"Absolutely not! Those people would have no Christmas festivities at all, Edward and you know it." Of course, he knew she was right. Not that any of these people couldn't afford it, rather, it was that their lethargy mixed with holiday depression would not allow it. Besides, one of the highlights of their whole year was Christmas with Richard, Emily and her pets.

Richard finally maneuvered his way to the kitchen to see his sister and the dogs. There they were, a tails wagging foursome, each working feverishly to guarantee that no morsel was left, nor crumb accidentally dropped to be left uneaten.

"Hi there, Sport." Richard affectionately bussed his sister's cheek.

"Society policeman, hey?" Emily giggled.

Richard flicked her on her ear.

"Why you!" Richard heard Emily's voice in the background as he headed out to the punch bowl to fortify himself for the evening ahead.

Brandied eggnog was always a good starter for evenings like these, and as he turned…

"What are you doing, following me?" The angry words cascaded out, and Richard knew exactly their ownership.

'Is there no God?' he wondered as he turned around to see Ian Whitney's hard-edged sneer.

"Eggnog?" Richard inquired graciously, knowing this would rile the man even more. But what the hell, after all, it was his house….

"Is there no end to your police harassment? How the hell did you get in here anyway? I'll bet Mrs. Crane has no idea you're a flatfoot. When she does you'll be thrown out of here so fast…"

"Well actually," Richard began.

"Oh, Richard you're here!" Interrupted by his mother, he reached his arm around her waist and leaned to give her reddish brown hair a gentle peck.

"Oh! I see you two have met. How nice. It's not often we have anyone here on Christmas Eve near Richard's age."

"Are you aware, Mrs. Crane, that this man is a policeman?" Whitney almost spat out the words, obviously too angry to comprehend the situation.

Richard glanced over to see his father glance toward the ceiling.

"Well, of course, I'm aware of that! Although we do tend to refer to him as Detective." His mother responded a bit flustered. "After all, he is my son."

Ian Whitney stood wooden; his only show of anger was the almost imperceptible tightening of the muscles in his neck and a brief spasm of his clinching fist. "I see." Turning toward Richard, "Of course, you set this up. How clever." Begrudgingly.

"I'm afraid I'm a little confused, Mr. Whitney. Richard had no idea you were coming. I invited you because of your missing wife, and of course our families' long connections over the years." She paused eyeing one and then the other. "Anyway, I don't understand what difference it would make. Unless, of course… you have already met under unpleasant circumstances?"

"Oh, no mother, it's fine," Richard, aware of the worried tone in his mother's voice, smiled and extended his hand. "Nice to see you again, Mr. Whitney." Whitney lamely reciprocated, his former limp handshake replaced by an 'Aresian' grip.

Richard's mother seemed relieved and, smiling again, patted her son's arm and slipped quietly off to other guests.

"Eggnog?" Richard offered again. "A couple of these, and neither of us will care about anyone's occupation."

"Why not." Whitney responded, resigned to the situation. Both men knew Ian Whitney would leave as soon as it was politely possible.

CHAPTER 28

On Christmas day, Richard arrived on his parent's brownstone doorstep on seventy-third, just off Central Park, laden with packages. His sister Emily, who opened the door, was surrounded by a whirlwind of the three bounding dogs on their way out. The pets that converged on the Crane household with Emily, who always arrived the day before Christmas to help her mother with the final cooking and baking, and the Christmas Eve Buffet, were a replacement for the Winslow's yet to be produced future grandchildren. As neither Richard nor Emily had found what they considered suitable mates, their mother had made a quest of introducing each of them to every "potential partner' she could find. Which meant they both placated their parents by attending numerous cocktail parties and dinners, which had so far been not only a bust but also in their eyes, a big waste of time that could have been used in more interesting pursuits. That as it may, they both humored their parents and allowed their mother to continue what she believed was the mantra of her life, that of securing her children's true happiness.

The numerous packages under the tree were each family member's accumulation of a year's searches for that special something that exactly fit the recipient. No one ever took the near misses back, so the tree was surrounded by a marinade of colors, scents, bobbles and sparkles that delighted the eye and tickled the nose in anticipation of the onslaught ahead.

When Richard and Emily were small, they were only allowed to open one package from a family member on Christmas Eve, then it was the long anticipated wait for Santa, creating for the children one of the longest nights of the year. As adults, the Crane's holiday celebrations were planned around the children's schedule. One year, Emily's mare Tess gave birth to a new foal on Christmas Day. Most years the schedule revolved around Richard's duties with the NYPD.

"This is just perfect," Richard's mother gushed enthusiastically upon his arrival. "It's just like old times, isn't it Edward," as they greeted Richard, who had arrived weighed down with presents, most of which were commercially wrapped by the stores where they had been purchased. The ones that weren't had obviously been unceremoniously dropped in gift bags, taped and labeled.

"Looks like you've got some great stuff there." His grandfather observed as Richard casually dropped half the packages into his arms.

Together, they carried them into the living room and literally dumped them under the tree.

"Oh you men, so disorganized," Anna Crane laughed.

"Bowser! Beauregard! Bear! Come along!" Emily's tones made no impression on the three frolicking dogs as they returned bounding up the snowy steps back into the house, wrapping their leashes around Emily's legs and shaking the snow off their heavy coats.

"Emily and the girls are back." Edward called from the hall laughing and cajoling the dogs as he helped Emily untangle herself from the leather constraints. Once she had finally returned, everyone converged in the living room with muffins, hot chocolates, coffees and toddies in hand.

"Whatever were you thinking, getting me an orange riding crop?" Emily laughed as she flashed it around for all to see. "Is this the 'society policeman's' idea of a joke?"

"I saw it at that campy thrift shop on 57th." Richard smiled, "It said 'Buy me for Emily the Horse Girl' so I did."

"It is luscious, Richard." Emily and learned over kissing him gently on the cheek.

The Judge, Grandpa Abernathy received his requisite first edition, Edward, lots of ties, and mother more recipe books and her annual gift certificate to her favorite spa from her doting father.

"Anna, I have no idea why you think you need to go to a spa?" Gramps exclaimed. "You get more beautiful every year!"

"It's to get a rest from all of you." Mother laughed.

"Ump." Was the Judge's yearly response?

Bowser, Beauregard, and Bear, got wrapped in ribbons, bows and bells, then were relegated to the pantry where each received a soup bone, while everyone helped with the final dinner preparations.

As usual Christmas dinner at the Cranes was a jolly, sumptuous affair filled with laughter, love and lots of food; oysters on the half shell, roast turkey with brandied chestnut dressing, orange whipped sweet potatoes, wilted spinach salad, cranberry soufflé, and assorted vegetables.

"No one's eating." Anna complained, as she did every year, as if it was everyone else's fault that she had as usual cooked too much food. Of course not one family member refused to 'help her out' by taking home leftovers. Even Emily with her five foot six waif like body and pixie face, who could pack away food like a truck driver, was always willing to help out and take leftovers off her mother's hands.

As for desserts, every one had their favorites, so there were many but the menu never varied; traditional pumpkin pie laced with brandy or rum, was Edward's favorite, as for the Judge, it was old fashioned applesauce cake, Emily just loved the mixture of holiday cookies and candies, mother opted for fresh berries and Richard, during his Michigan days had acquired a taste for plum pudding and hot buttered rum sauce, which his mother imported yearly from Sanders in Detroit. As for the dogs, they would take anything anyone would sneak to them under the table.

After dinner, Emily and mother took the dogs out for an evening walk, while the three men headed upstairs to the library.

CHAPTER 29

Richard gazed out and watched as the chilling winds blew wisps of the new fallen snow across the park below. Its powdery pristine texture carpeted the dirty hard packed snow that had accumulated over the last few weeks, making this one of the city's harshest winters in years. Still, Manhattan's festive holiday lights turned the Park and the surrounding area into a vast surreal winter wonderland. Richard and his grandfather, Judge Abernathy, quietly shared the winter view below.

"Cognac is it?" Richard's father asked rhetorically as he poured the snifters each a third full and passed them around. The three men sunk into the rich wine velvet couches, as they watched the slow burning fire's dancing flames create rippling shades of light throughout the room.

"His father came to the firm back in the early thirties. 'Ole man' Winslow that's what everyone called him." The judge, staring directly into the fire, whirled his cognac gently around in its glass. "He once told me the original business had been bought from a New England chap, Revere. Paul as I recall."

Richard and his father smiled. "You're funnin' with me, Gramps."

But the elderly gentleman continued. "Seems this Revere, among his other accomplishments, engraved the first colonial banknotes for the Massachusetts Colony during the Revolutionary War. Got the paper from the old Crane Paper Company."

"Arthur is this true?" Richard's father questioned.

"The boy might be interested in the background of the Winslow family." He said nodding toward his grandson.

Richard smiled and nodded back.

"Like fine paper, banknotes are made from cotton that's been soaked in water, cut then beaten into tiny fibers. The fibers are dipped in a mold and the excess water removed. Then they are hung to allow the sheets to dry completely. Most of the books one buys today are made from wood pulp, which eventually decomposes and rots away to the great distress of librarians and historians. But bank note paper is still made in much the same process as they did in ancient China."

"That's amazing!" Richard exclaimed.

"Not only that," his grandfather continued, "Ole Winslow once told me there were counterfeiters as early as the mid 1800s and at his father's request, Crane Paper developed the technique of inserting silk threads into the banknotes to foil the thieves."

"So these people have been clients of the family firm since the thirties and I've never even heard of them." Richard tried to conceal his miffed tone.

"Keep in mind son, the Winslows have a very secretive business with many private as well as nefarious clients." Richard's father paused.

"Many of whom we are not at liberty nor would we care to discuss." His grandfather chimed in. "But we can give you more family background than you currently have."

"Why didn't you do this when I came to you in my official capacity?"

"Because we were asked not to, lawyer, client privilege."

"And now?" Richard was pissed, this from his own family.

"Things change; and I suppose concern for the fact that you have not found a body." The Judge explained.

Crane had already made some surmises about no body, and although these two men were family, they were at this moment in his eyes, almost hostile witnesses. Rather than get really angry, Richard decided to lean back, relax and enjoy the free ride.

"First, so you understand the relationship, your grandmother and Aunt Grace used to play bridge every Wednesday with Ole Winslow's wife and his sister."

'I would have liked to have eavesdropped on those afternoons,' Crane thought to himself.

"Pretty tight, those four old gals."

"When Jack Winslow grew up, he married one of Albert Amon's granddaughters, the Swiss banknote inks king. Amon had the distinction of being the richest man in the international banknote business. Whoever controls the inks, controls the industry. The Amon Company still has that monopoly on the inks. You won't ever find their name on any Forbes multimillionaire list. They are a private family company that is very secretive and totally quiet about their business and personal lives."

"There were the usual prenuptials. Nothing like the Hollywood kind." Richard's grandfather picked up the story where his father had left off. "These were solid. He could under no circumstances ever be involved in the Amon Company, nor get any financial gain from that company. Any inheritance Mrs. Winslow might receive would skip the husband and go directly to any offspring they might have. Although it was a great business match, it was a love match as well. Jack Winslow didn't care a hoot what he had to sign on that paper, this girl was the love of his life."

"But didn't Marcella die in child birth?" Richard's father interjected.

"No it was a riding accident, but the child was only five years old."

"That's right, and when the grandfather, Albert Amon died the child…"

"Asia Winslow?" Crane sat forward in his seat so as not to miss anything.

"Asia Winslow," continued his grandfather, "came into a vast fortune, not stock from the Amon Company because that stays with direct working heirs, but stocks and securities from international markets around the world. Assets probably more valuable than all of Jack's private holdings and World Wide Banknote combined."

"And I suppose that when her father died she got all of these assets as well?" The more he heard the more intrigued Crane became.

By now grandfather was refilling everyone's glass and his father took over the story.

"Not all of it. Ole Winslow's sister, who has a daughter, son-in-law and three grand children, owns Forty eight percent of WWB. Their only interest so far seems to be in receiving their dividends and keeping in touch during the holidays and summer vacations. Nice people, loving, but not even curious. Whereas Asia is like her father, smart, hard working, tough in the clinches, a real dealmaker if you will, yet honest and gracious to all comers. A really nice young woman."

"And what about her husband, Ian Whitney? How does he fit in to the picture?" Richard asked having seen few of the qualities described in him.

"He's a La Rue, the English banknote family. Not a direct heir but he came with a trust."

"I was on the bench by then, but Edward here informed Jack that the young man had had a small family skirmish of sticking his hands in the 'till.' But by then it was too late. His charm, and the fact that he was a La Rue had overwhelmed Jack. As for Asia, she was very young and quite innocent, and believed anything her father said must be true."

"Jack wanted to see the future through rose colored glasses, and he believed that if he gave the Whitney boy a high enough salary and a title there wouldn't be any problem."

"Was there?" Richard could not hide his eagerness for the answer.

"We really can't say."

"Can't or won't?" Richard was sounding more like an interrogator then a son.

"Richard," his father sighed. "We are only the attorneys, not the accountants. We aren't even privy to all their clients. World Wide Banknote keeps their own private accountants right at their Park Avenue premises. They play it very close to the chest."

Just then, Bowser, Beau, and Bear bounded into the room.

"We're back," Richard's mother and Emily trudged into the room, both ruddy cheeked as they collapsed on the couches, exhaustedly happy to join the men in front of the fire.

CHAPTER 30

Like so many others who make an extra buck working holidays, Captain Billy White and his wife, who owned White's Towboat Towing Company on City Island, were no different. They found that having their tug on call New Year's Eve was lucrative enough to pay for Christmas for their three kids, and cover the spring term school tuitions that were due every January 30th.

Generally it was the owners of yachts and sailboats docked down at the 79th Street Marina whose New Year's Eve revelers, having over indulged, decided they'd have a great time on a celebration cruise on the East River or up the Hudson. Between the coldness and the drink, these little excursions often ended in disaster, and Captain White and his crew had to come to the aid and rescue of many of these overenthusiastic holiday voyagers.

It was well into the early morning hours, after one of these annual debacles, that Captain Billy stood huddled in the lea of the companionway door and the Cabin bulkhead. Wrapped in warm winter clothes and oilskins, he hunched over his well-deserved thermos of fresh brewed coffee. Not counting the cash, it was a small reward for one hell of a New Year's Eve. The small yet sturdy tug, Lady Jo, named after his wife, slugged up against the tide through the choppy, icy cold East River. Soon they would go under the Throgs Neck Bridge, out into Long Island Sound and then north into Eastchester Bay, homeward bound.

White listened to the steady grind of the GM 671 engines as the Lady Jo knifed her way slowly through the heavy current coming out of the Sound. Just their luck. They had ended their job as the tide had turned against them. White knew it would be slow going and there was no help for it.

The glow of his cigarette was almost indistinguishable in the dawning light as the sun arched its way over the crisp icy horizon. Occasionally, a wall of water slammed into the Jo's hull head on, and the boat yawed slightly to port because of the direction of the waves.

Going under the bridge was particularly unpleasant. The bridge supports created a narrower passage through which the water could flow, slowing the boat to a sluggishly reduced speed. Lady Jo was almost dead in the water, as Kippy Kretzer began steering the boat tenuously past the bridge's first set of massive cement supports. As the boat's cabin house moved under the bridge, a colorful round object between the first set of bridge struts caught White's eye. The movement of the current and the force of the boat passing through the feeder forced it into a spinning motion. Curious, White reached out his boat hook hoping to snag it in mid whirl.

Hooked! At first White thought he had caught some kid's marbled rubber balloon lost in the desperate disappointed excitement of play. But the bulbous, swollen cherry like black eyes staring out of the bloated plasticine face would give him nightmares for years to come. As Captain White stared, the head slipped off the tip of his boat hook back between the cement supports.

"My God! Call the Coastguard!" He shouted. The eyes seemed to bore holes through his soul.

"What? Didn't quite catch that," Kipp replied, totally unaware of White's distress. "These engines are revvin' pretty high."

"God damn it! Call the Coastguard! Now! Mayday! Mayday!" White grabbed the ship to shore mouthpiece out of Kipp's hand. "This is the Lady Jo calling. Come in please. Over."

"This is Coast Guard Cutter, Thistle, how can we assist you, Lady Jo? Over." The calm matter a fact voice filled the air.

"I think we've found a dead body caught under the Throgs Neck Bridge." It was then that White realized there wasn't a body at all, only the head. For the first time in his life, Billy White leaned out the companionway, over the side of the boat and regurgitated into the bellowing waves.

CHAPTER 31

Maybe it was because the call came in during that momentarily bleak time between moon fall and sunrise when the iciest chill fills the air and even the most vigilant might doze off or idly break for a much-needed cup of coffee. Whatever the reason, fortunately for the police, when the Coast Guard received Captain White's early New Year's Day morning call, no one was monitoring the frequency. This gave rise to the current sick joke around the department: 'That lucky break had given the police a "head" start.'

"Female." Banner announced immediately. "We certainly have been getting some real doozzies lately," Banner mused as he surveyed the contents of the container.

Detective Ethan Ross from the 109th precinct, who had experienced Banner in action previously, delivered the head to the morgue. He reacted to Banner's statement with a nod and tried to engineer himself out of the lab as quickly as possible. Scraping bodies off sidewalks was one thing, but jawin' about the remains was more than his job description warranted.

"We're in luck on this one," Banner said. "The head's only been in the water a short time... few days to a week." Banner looked up at Ross and smiled with the pleasure of a man who enjoyed his work.

Ross grimaced.

From the corner of his eye, Banner surreptitiously noted the detective's discomfort. "The fact that the skin is still on the face, the eyeballs have not been eaten away, the protrusion of the lips and the fact that they are still there at all are all indications of the length of time the head has been submerged."

Banner, with obvious enthusiasm, ignored Detective Ross' eagerness to leave. Picking up a small pointer, he bent over the head and continued explaining, maintaining an oblivious professionalism to Ross' discomfort over what he considered Banner's enthusiastically morbid interest.

"See. The sea-life infestation here and here, they're minimal." He pointed to the orifices. "Here again, also because of the short amount of time in the water. However this is also in a large part due to the icy cold temperature. You know the old saw," Banner mused, "the colder the water, the longer it takes for a body to become a floater."

Ross, who had turned a putrid green, was barely able to control his urge to retch. Banner, seeing his little joke go flat this time, became serious. "But the real question is, if we're dealing with separated body parts, where are the rest?"

Detective Ross turned without a word and walked out. Ignoring Ross' abrupt departure, Banner continued his study and thought about the great criminological discussions he and his

friend Crane would have had if it had been he who had brought
the head in instead.

Because of the odd, lopsided slice of skin that hung almost
like a mantle where the neck should have been, Banner guessed
that the head had been severed from the body after it had entered
the water. The randomness of the slant of the decapitation also
indicated that the separation of the head from the rest of its body
was probably not the act of the killer, but rather was caused by
a sharp blade-like object such as a small boat propeller. Jarred,
the boat skipper probably momentarily slowed his boat curious
about the cause of the bump to his boat's prop, and then went on
his way unaware of his part in the whole event.

What really confused Banner was that in cold, crisp, winter
weather and the ice cold water, it would take at least a couple of
months for a body to float to the surface. However, there was
no indication that the head had been in the water that long and
a boat propeller could not have severed a head from a body that
was on the bottom. The river was too deep.

Although Banner, because of the condition of the head,
considered it a waste of time, the police dragged the East River
near the Throgs Neck Bridge for two days with no results. Then
Dixon and Hart, two divers from the department took over.
They found what they were looking for about fifteen feet offshore just north of the bridge.

The left foot of the crab-infested body was plastered into
a cement block in the water about twenty feet deep. The base
of the block was judiciously placed next to an old piling just
north of the Throgs Neck Bridge. A nylon line secured around
the upper torso was tied loosely to the pile. This suspended the
headless torso and free right leg in an upright position with just
enough slack to allow the body parts to sway back and forth in

the water like a handicapped marionette performing a gruesome danse macabre.

Dixon had done a lot of diving for the department, but this grotesque underwater grotto beat all. It was the first time he actually wavered. His partner, Sammy Hart, caught Dixon's arm and the two watched in morbid fascination as the grotesque, sea-life infested form moved rhythmically to the river's silent song.

The skin from the torso's right shoulder had been torn away with its head, and underwater crabs and small predacious fish were fast working their way through the exposed flesh to the collarbone beneath. Tattered bits of cloth where clothes used to be, hung randomly, pasted to the naked torso as it undulated in the flow of the waves and tide.

The nylon line was beginning to cut through the upper body below the breasts and here, too, small turtles, recently spawned during the early tides, were beginning to ravenously invade the rotting open flesh. It was as if the small sea-life had equally divided the spoils of an unexpected feast. Dixon and Hart both knew that if the nylon cord had sawed the upper torso and arms loose, they would have sunk to the bottom. Then a couple of months later, when the gaseous vapors had bloated them and the sea-life had fed on them beyond recognition, what was left would have either settled in a briny grave or surfaced at some unknown location to become a more gruesome missing part of an already hideous puzzle.

It was obvious that this was not the work of a novice diver. Some analytical, fiendishly sick mind was at work here. A meticulous planner, who understood the river, and except for the quirk of fate of the accidental severing of the head from its host, whoever it was had devised a foolproof plan. Hart surveyed the body more closely, and then rose to the surface.

"Its like a grotto down there, an underwater sea-eaten Venus de Milo. Somebody's idea of a sick joke."

Having been overheard describing the situation to his chief, Dixon refused to give his name to the press.

The Post and Times' headlines could not help but smack of gruesome sensationalism. Even the wire services outside the country picked up the story, and TV news channels rocked the nation with hearsay and morbid descriptions of the body, sans head, found standing upright attached to an offshore piling near the East River's Throgs Neck Bridge.

Of course there were photos, the media was told. "There are always crime scene shots for forensic use only; you boys know that," the press was told. "Once we've done our job ... then we'll see."

Reporters had always been a pushy crowd. It was the nature of the business, but since the rise of television, the news media seemed to be losing all constraints. Indeed this was hot. So hot, that eventually the cordoned off area had to be enclosed from the prying press as the body was raised and taken away to the morgue to be reunited with its head.

After placing the head in properly refrigerated storage, Banner returned to his office and mulled over the questions that puzzled him most. Who was she and what could she have possibly done to deserve this?

CHAPTER 32

Crane read about the service in the obituary section of the Times. A memorial service for Asia Winslow at St. Thomas Church was to be held the Monday after the New Year at 10 a.m. His schedule had caused Crane to arrive after the service had begun and he slipped in quietly, standing silently in the back.

"We are gathered to honor Asia Winslow-Whitney, who over the years has honored us with her caring goodness …" As the rector eulogized high in the oak carved canopied pulpit, Richard leaned against one of the large stone pillars in the back of 5th Avenue's St. Thomas Church.

He had a mixed opinion about this woman. Yet, surveying the large crowd packed in the historic old church, he realized that she had certainly made an impact. During his youth, Crane had attended two of these kinds of services. They were not really funerals but rather opportunities to honor and remember. One had been for a family friend, whose dad had disappeared, gone without a trace. The other, for a ne'er-do-well uncle believed to have drowned at sea, a victim of a downed plane. After months of searching when neither individual had been found, each family had a service of remembrance to ease their pain and bring closure to the unfortunate situations over which they had no control. That's what he was attending again today, not a funeral, but a memorial to someone these people could not lay to rest.

Crane knew that some mourners came because of the family and some out of curiosity. Some were employees, and some came to be seen. However, at this time of year, to come out on this cold, early January morning, most must have attended because of Asia Winslow herself. Although he did not remember all their names, he recognized faces here and there. Many were members of New York's social register, as well as a large cross section of individuals from the financial district and government communities who had come to pay their respects. He spied Ben Huntington, now one of the senior partners from the family's law firm, seated across the sanctuary with his own grandfather whom Crane knew was here representing the family. Earlier in the week, his grandfather had asked him to join them; however, Richard had declined. He was attending in an official capacity and wanted to be unrelated to anyone, to remain insignificant among the mourners.

He watched, looking for that one person who did not seem to fit, the face in the crowd, whom he knew, and by its very unique presence might give Crane the missing lead he needed. After all, he and Asia Winslow were only five years apart. They had grown up among the same social set. They were near enough in age that, as Richard still believed, their personal paths had crossed. Crane was looking for that individual they both knew, maybe at different times who could give him some real insight into the young woman, or better yet, the missing link he so badly needed. After two months, his investigation had come to a halt and with no leads. It was dead on arrival. He, however, stood by his gut feeling that she was still alive, and unbeknownst to these mourners, this service was just a sham. How many others in this sanctuary felt this too? He didn't know, but he believed there was at least one. So Crane listened and watched.

"And may the Holy Spirit have mercy on her beloved soul, that by some unmitigated luck she could be returned to us, unscathed and safe. If not, may the Lord in heaven accept her soul and cherish her in heaven as we have on earth. For Asia Winslow-Whitney had the ..."

People here seemed genuinely saddened by this young woman's apparent demise, a young woman, who was an enigma to Crane. Flowers of remembrance lined the chancel steps between the podium and the high oak-carved, New England pulpit, from where the rector spoke. Numerous people, one after another, stepped up to the lectern and spoke of the pain of their loss.

Finally, Crane seated himself in the last row of the old wooden pews next to a frail elderly lady in a worn black coat, the stoic type, whose emotions were concealed only by their breeding. Yet, her lower lip trembled as each person spoke, and a tear ran down her cheek in an avalanche of quiet passion. She didn't wipe it away, but kept her hands tightly clasped in her lap, and caught the tear on her tongue and swallowed her sorrow, leaving only the light streak of damp discoloration to give away her pain.

Sobs drifted throughout the church. These people really cared and Crane sensed an emotional heaviness, the weight of an anvil throughout the crowd. It crawled inside him, curled up in a ball and nested itself in the pit of his stomach. Like an old fashioned wake, someone needed to stand up and scream to break the pressure, but these people were too polite.

"Although this is unusual for our parish, and even though we are not yet sure of God's wish for Asia Winslow-Whitney..." How totally Presbyterian, Crane thought, as the minister continued. "It was Asia's last wish that we sing, and as Asia, to the end, will always be Asia ..."

A shock wave ran through the sanctuary, as Asia demonstrating kindness, even in her absence, broke the tension as the grand organ resounded with the unexpected 'And When the Saints Come Marching In.' After the initial shock, a knowing sigh rippled through the church, and almost everyone stood, sang and clapped. This Asia Winslow must be quite something. It was at that moment that he saw Captain Sanderson, his old sailing master from the Styuvestsant Yacht Club on City Island.

Finally! Was Sanderson the common thread he was so desperately seeking? Had Crane found the ivy in the chink in the wall?

But what about the old girl sitting right next to Crane? Who was she and how did she fit in? He knew he'd be welcomed at the captain's anytime, so he stayed put. They sat together in silence a long time. As he waited, Crane watched for other faces in the crowd as people left through one or another of the big oak doors. As she sat, an occasional mourner paused and nodded to her then went on. Finally she moved and Crane silently offered his arm.

He barely felt a weight as she pulled herself up and he guided her out of the pew toward the opened doors.

"Tea?" He inquired. "I'll get a cab."

"No, walking is perfectly fine, young man," she said as she directed him toward a small neighborhood coffee shop down the block. He was surprised by her robust tone, and squirmed a bit, feeling rather like a small boy in short pants.

CHAPTER 33

"You're different than the rest of us." The old woman's eyes bore a hole through him as if to read his soul. Then she turned and momentarily gazed out the window as the waitress served the rich black Chinese tea. Waving the girl away, she poured him a cup in the stately manner of one who had performed the task all her life.

"You're Crane's brat. The odd duck aren't you?"

Although amused, Richard was not quite sure if this was a statement or a question.

"I often saw you playing as a small boy. You've grown up to be quite sturdy, I see. And well educated, I understand." She paused to sip the hot aromatic tea, and then began again.

"My God! Why couldn't someone like you have married her instead of that sorry sod of a man? Jack was besotted by Ian's mother, always was, after his wife died. Of course, she is

2 1 5

a La Croix, which was no small factor in the matter. Banknote families are a closed shop you know, a separate kind of royalty. They stick together, keeping their business private. When one is dealing with heads of state, some ever changing, with stiff competition from an inner circle of players, letting outsiders in could mean letting in spies. It's a tough business, and although the parties involved are friends, they are also shrewd. When they are after a banknote order or an order to print lots of notes, friendship is left at the business door. You understand?"

Crane nodded. It was certainly a different perspective on the banknote business than Cynthia Ryder had presented.

"Somewhat like a sports competition. So what better union than a Winslow and a La Croix-Whitney. The British and American banknote companies united. Two of the largest banknote companies in the world, and the Fair Trade Commission could not do a thing about it. Of course the two companies have never actually merged, but my nephew thought himself rather clever at the time. He just didn't realize what a viper that young man is."

"Then you're her aunt?"

"Consuelo Winslow Blake," she extended her hand across the small round coffee shop table. "Great Aunt on her father's side. Why haven't you married?" She asked bluntly, "you look old enough."

Crane smiled at her forthrightness. At least she had done her homework. Mrs. Blake was obviously one of those Grand Dames who made the rules.

"Just didn't meet the right girl in college." He confided. "All those Buffys and Muffys my mother has in the wings are a bit too boring."

"Well. You certainly didn't pick a career that would appeal to most young women."

"True.   They're more interested in corporate attorneys or bankers; the Vineyard every summer and Klosters or the Caribbean in the winter."

"Certainly not a husband who's out at all hours and misses family social events; birthdays and anniversaries."

She was right on the ticket there, he thought.

"Are you sure my mother didn't send you?" Crane teased. It was the first time he had seen Consuelo Blake smile.

"If ever Asia's father did her a disservice, it was that marriage to Ian Whitney."

"Did he kill her?"

"He could have.   However during the Settlement House Charity Ball he was more apt to be debauching some frivolous young girl. There are such good pickings at those affairs," she sipped more tea, "and he was the ultimate opportunist. Would he have murdered her? Probably, when he was ready. But not there. It would have cramped his style. You've met him?"

Crane nodded.

"Vain, pretty boy. Moreover, he's a single topic man … however; he can only concentrate on one at a time. Money, sex or himself."

"It's obvious you like him a lot."

She ignored his statement.

"Isn't it a little soon for a memorial?" Crane moved on. "She's only been missing two months."

"It was Ian's idea. He, with Cynthia's backing, pushed for it. I was so appalled by the breach of etiquette, I was not even going to show up."

"And that's why you were sitting in the back rather than with the family." Crane surmised aloud.

She nodded, than continued. "Both he and Cynthia believed it was better for the stability of the business. Their public rationale for the service to the rest of the family was that if the clients thought something was amiss, they might choose another banknote firm." She paused.

"But if banknote companies function as you described, wouldn't Ian have steered the business toward his own family's British firm?"

"No! Jack found out too late, Ian is the black sheep of that family; because he has been ostracized from La Croix, he probably believes if he's slick enough, he will end up with World Wide Banknote instead." She paused. "You know Mr. Crane, she may not be dead."

Crane wanted to jump up and down with elation. Finally, here was someone who was expressing his own secret opinion.

"Leave it to Asia," the old woman continued, "when she had a problem, she would often solve it in an obtuse way. She's a shrewd one, sometimes making up the rules as she goes along, much like her father. That's why they were both so successful in the business. It was their keen sense of timing. Like you finding the right woman."

Crane smiled; she was quite a shrewd old bird herself.

"I have also always wondered about Jack's death." She paused.

Now we're getting someplace Crane decided.

"We are a family of genetic longevity. He was too hardy to have just up and died."

"You think she did it?" Crane was good at his job because he understood that if you just let people talk, they generally would.

But he was tired of her controlling the conservation, and he was beginning to see signs that the conversation needed to be spiked with a bit of prodding. She may have had all day, but he had work to do.

"No! Of course not!" She answered indignantly, eyeing him with shocked amazement.

"But even though he'd had a little problem with his own family, Ian Whitney was Winslow's fair haired boy." He led Mrs. Blake on, even though his opinion of Asia's husband was much the same as hers. In his mind, Ian Whitney was a bastard. But he wanted to get an uncontrolled response from the old girl, so he stuck in the knife.

"Are you telling me, you hate Whitney enough to create a family scandal and a crime?"

"Young man, I hate no one. However, I know human nature, and if you are anything like your grandfather, so do you. My nephew did not die of natural causes, and I strongly suspect Asia found out. It's your job to find the truth, Mr. Crane." She looked at her watch, got up and walked toward the door. Crane barely had time to slam down a 'tenner' and catch up.

"I suggest you check the company ledgers." She offered as she entered the long silver gray limousine that had hovered at the curb. It figures, Richard thought. He knew he had crossed the line but so had she.

"We don't have enough evidence against anyone to get a warrant to open the books." He called to her through the car window.

"As a board member of the company, you may have my authorization. You may pick it up from your father's office later today."

"Thank you," Richard replied, as if he were still the small bright-eyed boy who had just been given a large bowl of ice cream. "By the way, how do I contact you?" Although he already knew.

"Ask your grandfather." She waved him off as the electric window closed and the car pulled away into the late morning traffic.

CHAPTER 34

Crane did not need directions to Exit 8b, through Pelham Bay Park and over the drawbridge to City Island. He had been coming here ever since he could remember. City Island Avenue was the Island's only through street, and he drove slowly past the row of rundown single story buildings on either side. He was saddened that the village had fallen on such hard times. Farther down, toward the Barton Park section near the end of the island, Richard turned right into a side street and drove to the end. The three identical dusty, ochre-colored stucco cottages stood in a line along the Bay in a park-like setting. Instead of a driveway to each property with individual parking, access was by footpath, which ran across the front of all three tree filled lots. Like Richard, the inhabitants had to use on street parking and walk along the small walkway to their homes. The captain's house was the last one in the row. Before stepping out into the chilly, damp cold January air; he paused to gaze across icy Eastchester Bay, called 'the water' by the locals.

"Come in, come in, my boy." Captain Sanderson was expecting him and was genuinely pleased he had called. The captain hung Crane's coat on a hook in the entry by the front door and put his arm around Richard's shoulder. The staunch ramrod straight old gentleman ushered him into the miniature living-dining room made cozy by the crackling fire and a large picture window that looked out upon the bay.

"Sit, and tell me how you are. A fine detective, your grandfather tells me."

Crane sank into the broad flowered chintz armchair and relaxed, accepting accolades as Sandy handed him a hot toddy laced with cinnamon and warmed his hands toward the fire. "I'm fine, but I don't have much time for sailing. Unfortun ..."

"You're a sight for sore eyes," Sandy interrupted. I remember when Hank brought you down for the first time. You in your short pants ... your eyes aglow at seeing your first 12 Meter. I would have thought you'd have sailed around the world at least once by now. Brain won over brawn, I guess." They both laughed.

"That was one of the goals. Other things have just gotten in the way." Crane too, recalled his first visit to Nevins Yacht Yard to see the Columbia, the United States America's Cup 12-Meter entry. That was also the first summer he had come to Stuyvesant Yacht Club for sailing lessons with his grandfather's old friend, Captain Sanderson. Richard was a natural sailor and had a room full of trophies from every sailboat class contest he had entered. He recalled when, during his late teens, he was hired as a summer sailing assistant at SYC and earned enough to buy a Nevins 20 Victory Class sailboat, a long, lean thirty-one foot cedar hull, that sailed like a knife through the water. One of his greatest pleasures had been to take out one or more of his family members for what he considered the indescribable experience of the forces of nature pitted against man and his Victory. Most often his mother and sister Emily begged off, more eager to go back across the bridge to the Pelham Park bridle paths where they could go riding gracefully through the park, rather than be tossed about on a soggy adventure.

As Richard gazed around the cozy room, he found that not much had changed since his last visit. There were a few new pieces of seafaring memorabilia and a fresh stack of mariner magazines on the floor by Sandy's chair, but it was much the same as it had always been.

"What can I do you for?" Sandy kidded. "A busy New York City police detective doesn't take part of his work day off and come calling out of the blue. So out with it lad."

When Richard had rung earlier, he had the niggling feeling that Captain Sanderson had expected his call. Now he was sure of it.

"It's about a girl? Actually a young woman," Richard paused, "Asia Winslow. You came into Manhattan yesterday to her memorial service. She must have been pretty special for you to have left the island."

"Asia Winslow…" Sandy repeated her name softly. "And why would you be wantin' to know about her?"

"I'm the detective assigned to her disappearance," Richard had the odd feeling that Sandy already knew this, "and we have no leads."

"None?"

"Zilch."

"Ah, Asia Winslow, best little sailor I ever had," he paused looking out of the corner of his eye at Crane. Nonplused,

Richard sat expressionless. "Scrappy little piece of mischief," Sandy continued. "Took sailing lessons at SYC. You should remember her. She was around when you worked summers out there. You even raced her once." At this, Sandy couldn't suppress the glint of a smile. "She was about fourteen at the time."

"THAT was her?" Know her? He sure as hell did! How could he forget? Now that his memory was jogged, he remembered her as if it were yesterday, sturdy body... pinched nose, and two long blond pony tails that distractingly bounced every time she moved, which was a lot because of her animated delivery. She slung her sentences through the air like torpedo launchers hitting their target with explosive patterns of speech and ideas. The same way his sister Emily talked about horses and riding, she extolled the glory of sailing. She laughed a lot, giggled really, and he knew instinctively that as she grew older, she would attract attention.

Richard remembered that he was cleaning out the boats that day when she kept tacking back and forth, and having nothing better to do, babbling non-sequiturs and baiting him about her sailing prowess. Finally, when she had annoyed him to a point of exasperation, he decided to put her in her place. With a mouth like hers, she had made herself fair game.

"Ok, how about a little race?" He suggested.

"I'm game." While he positioned himself and his boat, she laughed and shouted toward shore. "Hey, Sandy, we're going to have a little race."

"A race eh! To where?"

"Hart Island!" She shouted. "Give the signal."

Richard, red faced, remembered how she had outmaneuvered him on every tack.

"Oh, yes. I do remember Asia Winslow." He said aloud, as he relived the moment. "Miss all guts and all glory."

"Eat your heart out chump." She had shouted as she sailed past him toward the dock.

"Talk about hurting a guy's ego! I was damn mad. It wasn't so much my losing, as her lack of humility about winning." No wonder he had suppressed his memory of the little wench.

"You didn't come to work for a week. Probably the only race you ever lost. Wasn't it?"

"Don't rub it in, Sandy." Crane pleaded.

"Real pistol, at fourteen. She was one ugly duckling who grew into a swan."

"I wouldn't know. All I've done is clean up her blood and meet her friends and relatives."

"I can assure you, she is a lovely young woman."

"Is? Then she's still alive! Just as I thought." Crane would lay odds that Sandy knew more about this little shrew's activities then he was letting on. "Did you see her often?" He asked already knowing the answer.

"She used to come up and visit occasionally. You two were the best sailors I ever had … nearly evenly matched. But if you had let her have a rematch, you would have taken her any time. In that first and only race, you simply weren't prepared for a kid to be that good. You went at it too casually and she took you with the element of surprise, not skill."

Richard smiled. Nice thought; however that was then and not now. He needed some answers. "How recently?"

"I'd say a few days before her disappearance."

"Did she give you any indication she was in trouble?"

"She'd talked about that husband of hers, and she implied something was missing. However, I never knew what. I got the impression it had something to do with her father, Jack, and the company."

"But you're sure she never mentioned what it was?"

"No. She never did. Had something to do with that place they own up Wellfleet way. Didn't tell a soul."

Now Richard understood the destruction at the cottage. And why Ian had gone alone. He had obviously gone ballistic when he found that something he had hidden was gone. That he had been caught red handed.

"Why didn't you come forward immediately when you saw the newspaper articles about her missing?"

"And have Whitney on my case? Not me! I am an old man, Richard. I stay out of other people's troubles."

"Hogwash, Sandy!" An expression he hadn't used since the cowboy movies when he was a kid around SYC. "She's alive, isn't she?"

Captain Sanderson sat quietly. Suddenly, he became an old carcass of a once vigorous man.

"She's alive and you helped her."

"It was her belief that her husband, Ian, was somehow responsible for her father's death. After all, with only the two of them at that cottage."

"What did she do? Sail out of here? Is she holed up down in Cape May or up at a marina near the Cape Cod Canal?"

The old man said nothing.

"Sandy, I can find out. I can interview every ship's chandler and every marina hand on the island. Or maybe old Chief Harry Hummer. He's still alive. Should I start there? No matter how tight you all are on this island, someone will crack. Is that what you want me to do?"

Sandy sat quietly.

"I'm only here to help her, which might include saving her life. You know as well as I do, if I've figured it out, Ian Whitney can't be far behind, particularly if he has a score to settle."

Almost inaudibly a single word came out. "Bermuda."

"Bermuda? She flew to Bermuda? We checked every commercial and charter flight!"

"She sailed to Bermuda." The words spilled out. "It's where her Godfather lives."

"Well I'll be damned!"

"Richard, with her father, she was docile – did everything he asked. After all, he was all the family she had. She adored him. However, she is just like him and when he died, the bright, street smart, hellion you met, surfaced again. She's a pistol, but a good one; just trying to right a wrong in the most expedient way she knows how."

"If I'm going to help her, I've got to go and talk with her. What if Whitney figures this out and gets there first?" Richard waited patiently as the old sea captain sat contemplating the flames.

"She's at Sir Aubrey Tinkerton's in Hamilton," he said finally. "I'll call Aubrey and let him know you're coming." Pausing a moment, Sandy began again haltingly as if measuring his words, "Ian, her husband, he's a bad one," Sandy said. "The biggest mistake of Jack's life, and both he and Asia paid the price."

Richard nodded. A tacit silence had taken over the room, and he knew it was time to leave. The two men rose, each struggling with his own thoughts, and shook hands as the old mariner showed Richard out.

At least everyone was in agreement about one thing in this case, Richard thought as he let himself into his car and drove away in the bleak winter morning haze.

CHAPTER 35

"The press has already skewered me once during this case. Once is enough. I'm bowing out on this event." Stan couldn't blame Richard for wanting no part of the legal maneuvers between his father's law firm, the courts and World Wide Banknote. "I'm going to City Island, no more potential run-ins with the press for me." Crane had said earlier that morning.

Stan had agreed, and took Davis instead to serve World Wide Banknote with a warrant from the court subpoenaing the company's books. There was not much Ian Whitney or Cynthia Ryder could say to a court order.

"Where is Detective Crane? If he were here ..."

"Detective Crane would what?' Stan stopped her in mid sentence. "It's all legal, Miss Ryder, and as for Detective Crane and me, we have a vertical line of power, his presence would make no difference whatsoever."

"You'll hear from my solicitors." The idle threat in Whitney's highbrow English accent could be heard in the background as Stan and the officers carrying away the books stepped into the elevator.

"Fat chance," Stan replied under his breath as the doors closed behind them. Stan knew the attorneys for World Wide Banknote and Mrs. Blake were one and the same. It was through them that the affidavit of authorization signed by Mrs. Consuelo Winslow Blake, allowing the police to subpoena the books had been executed the previous afternoon. This had given the judge the legal power to issue the warrant.

Abernathy, Huntington, Crane, & Associates were going to have a swell afternoon. As for the old lady, the way Richard described her, Stan was sure she could hold her own.

"The accounting boys have got 'em. It was all nice and easy," Stan said waving to Crane as he walked in from his visit with Captain Sanderson. "Seems the one that's all legs and skirt, the Ryder dame, thought you could stop history, but I put her straight."

Richard laughed. "Asia Winslow's alive. Anyway, she was, as of this morning. For how long, I don't know. I think that might be up to us."

Stan clasped his hands behind his head and leaning back, propped his feet on his desk. "And this woman is where?"

"Bermuda."

Then Stan gave Crane one of his long penetrating stares. These were usually reserved for his kids when hard questions needed honest answers, which were often when dealing with two devilish boys. "And you remember her from where?"

"Oh, that's not important." Crane grimaced.

"That painful, is it." An almost imperceptible smile crossed Stan's face. "By the way," Stan said as he reached down and casually picked up a sheet of paper lying in one of the unruly stacks that had been accumulating on his perpetually messy desk, "Banner called. He has something he wants you to see. Don't wanta guess what that is," he said as he scanned the sheet. "Oh! Shit!" Stan tossed the paper over to Crane. "Twelfth one down."

Crane picked up the single sheet and scanned the page. "Let's get Banner off our list, then we'll deal with this," Crane suggested.

"Getting any visit to the morgue over with is ok with me," Stan said as he watched Crane slowly fold the sheet and place it in his pocket.

Stan loathed even the thought of the morgue. The queasiness took hold even when he had to visit Banner's office. This time he knew he couldn't get out of it. After all, he was a cop, for God's sake.

. . . .

"Don't you ever do any work?" Crane asked as they walked in to find Banner with his feet planted solidly on his desk, reading so intently he had not heard them enter.

"At least I put all this stuff to good use," Banner swung his arm around the room pointing to the volumes of books and other materials.

"On government time." Crane countered with a smile. "I'll have you know, I have found Asia Winslow."

"However, where he knows her from is still a deep dark secret," Stan interrupted. "Not his. Ours. Lad's not talkin'."

"Well, now… a mystery within a mystery. When this is all over Stan, We'll take him out and get him drunk … that's the only way he'll talk. So the facts man. Then I've got something rather unusual to show you."

Crane told Banner about his morning visit as they walked toward the morgue.

"And the 'Society Detective' wins out again. Has the same sort of ring as 'the Lone Ranger Rides Again,' doesn't it Stan?" Banner led the way down the hall through metal, oversized, double doors.

"Stuff it!" was Crane's only reply.

"I think I'll pass, if you don't mind?" Stan said, turning to walk away as Richard finished filling Banner in.

"No, not this time, Stan. You might actually find this interesting."

There was nothing for it but to stay. Lagging behind, Stan had small hopes of getting to their destination in time to miss the show.

"Have I got a cadaver for you." Ignoring Stan's reticence, Banner flipped the handle to the stainless steel, rectangular, metal door and pulled out the drawer.

Richard looked down at bulging eyes and a bulbous face surrounded by a mass of tangled black hair. Although it was obvious the head had been severed from the body, it had been carefully placed atop the partially gnawed shoulders to create the visual concept of a proper connection. It appeared to have been severed from the rest of the partial chunks of torso and the extremities. Crane's reaction was one of fascinated revulsion.

"How did this happen?" Grizzly was what came to mind as Crane surveyed the rest of the masticated cadaver. The body's severed chunks and partial pieces had been placed by the pathologist in much the same way a paleontologist might reassemble a dinosaur find from a dig, given the limited ability to make it whole again due to its missing parts. "The body from near Throgs Neck?"

Banner nodded.

"Word is, one foot was encased in cement."

"Yeah, we had to cut it off and grind as much of the cement off as we could. Then we placed the foot back with the rest of the body."

Crane turned away, afraid he'd be ill. He heard the rollers skate softly across the track as the drawer shut and the metal door slammed into place. Banner was ready to leave and Crane followed.

"You know who she is?" Crane asked.

"No idea."

"Bloome. Annie Bloome. Angelina Bettonelli, twelfth one down on the list of missing persons." Crane pulled the sheet from his back pocket. "The looker from the Settlement House Charity Benefit." Richard continued.

"You mean 'the climber'?" Banner asked as he walked past the operating table toward the doors.

"That's the one."

"She had a bad fall."

"Last rung off the edge of life," Crane replied as he walked into the hall. "Stan, I think we ought to go back to the office and make few calls then go out to Quee ..." But Stan wasn't there. Only the swinging of the morgue exit door attested that he had ever been present.

CHAPTER 36

Asia's days in Bermuda were a respite after the tension she had endured during her last days in the City. Here the cloudless days flowed, one after another, with a quiet resonance that she had not enjoyed for many months. Asia looked upon her stay at Tinkerton House as a time of sanctuary. At first, she was euphoric, amazed she had succeeded this far; then she became pensive about what the future would hold. She enjoyed mornings lolling around in bed. But after a week of rest, Asia had taken Aubrey up on his offer and was at the bank every morning at nine o'clock sharp.

"Asia, you are a wealthy young woman, even without World Wide Banknote. Let's put that money to work. With my business connections and employees at your disposal, and your fiscal ability, you could show the world what a bright woman can do.

As a serious voyeur, I think I shall watch the fun." A devilish grin crossed Aubrey's face.

"You truly enjoy making money, don't you?" Asia said.

"Best game in town."

A young man who looked more liked a rugby player than an expert in finance entered Aubrey's office as if on cue.

"This is Roger Pickney," nodding toward the boyish new-comer, who was brushing aside an unruly shock of sandy blond hair that had fallen into his eyes.

"With the aid of his staff, Roger will work out a financial plan and teach you the nuances of the reinsurance industry, while pulling together the paperwork necessary for you to become a player."

"Reinsurance?" Asia paused. Aubrey had used the term before.

"It's insurance that insurance companies buy to insulate their businesses from the payouts on policies they've written from major catastrophes. You know floods, hurricanes, tornadoes, that rare event that happens only once every few years. You as the re-insurer get to reinvest all those yearly premiums for your own benefit. It's like taking candy from a baby," Aubrey glowed.

Pickney remained stone faced during his boss's explanation, but that changed to a roguish grin as he squired Asia into a series of adjoining offices.

"You're as bad as he is," Asia grinned back.

"Caught us out, you did. After all, it's just a big game, that's all, only the stakes are much higher because they're real," Roger laughed, "and if I screw up here …" Before she could ask, "Why?" he continued. "It's sort of like your little ocean sail. The odds are fifty-fifty but the thrill is one hundred percent."

During their days working together, Asia found that Pickney, who hailed from the U.K., was typical of the expatriates living in lesser-developed countries, hired because of the weak pool of able locals. Roger was one of those financial whiz kids whose international orientation and outlook gave him a keen understanding of global markets. As Asia spent more time at the bank, she found that the young Americans had guts of steel for the trade and the risk, but were more short-term players. Adversely, English and Irish chaps were able to cross the time zones of cultural thinking and deal as financial futurists.

Aubrey had obviously observed that by adding Pickney's global expertise to Asia's American brashness, it would make her unbeatable. Pickney, who saw the plan, occasionally shuddered to think of the outcome to her future financial adversaries. He often thought, 'To look at her ... they would never know what hit them.'

The weeks in Bermuda moved on quickly. Mornings were spent with Roger and most afternoons working on Onika. The average December temperatures in the high sixties were too cold for swimming, but that did not prevent her taking long walks on Elbow Beach, where the soft pink sand was without the graininess of New England beaches.

"Hey Lady! Catch." A well-packed solid ball of pink sand came hurling toward her.

"Hey, yourself, and back at yea!" Asia called out to the snot-nosed boy who had tried to take her by surprise with the ball of sand. The boy threw it again and Asia was ready giving as good as she got. Although the boy didn't know it, this was no new game for her. As a kid, she and her Bermudan friends had made solid balls from the sand and played catch for hours. After that first time, Asia saw the boy often, and it was always the same. When he thought she least expected it, "Hey lady or heads up," and after the warning shout the game ensued. But he never caught her off guard, nor did he ever miss her returns.

"You're pretty good at this.' The boy conceded one day after one of their more furious games. "Most adults aren't. You play sports or something."

"No." Asia laughed. "Just played this as a kid, just like you, on this very beach."

"Well, if you're ever looking for a job, you might consider the majors." The boy grinned.

"When they make beach sand ball throwing an Olympic Sport, I just might try it. Otherwise, I prefer to maintain my amateur status." She smiled back.

After leaving the beach she would wonder who he was, but whenever the game began, they were both too busy to exchange names.

'Maybe it's better this way,' Asia decided, 'a joyful anonymous memory with no strings. Life offered so few.'

After a few weeks, Asia moved Onika to Mill Creek Marine boatyard in Pembroke parish for a little TLC. It was much more convenient having the boat nearer to Hamilton, just across the harbor from Tinkerton House. Rather than having to take the bus over to Georgetown, a water taxi cruised across harbor daily, and she was at the landing everyday.

"Asia, my dear, you might find the Metro Section interesting," Aubrey said as he handed the New York Times to her across the breakfast table on the Sunday before Christmas.

"Finally! Somebody's taking an interest," she sighed. "Why has it taken so long?"

"Suddenly, Aubrey let out a guffaw that filled the room. "It's Crane's boy who's on your trail." He laughed again as he handed Asia one of the New York tabloids. "Here, get a load of this 'scandal sheet.'"

"Society policeman?" She said as she perused the page. "Should I know him?" She asked quizzically.

"Only the son of your family and business solicitor, my dear. I'm sure that went over well this morning in their household."

"You mean, Mr. Crane of Abernathy Crane ..."

"One and the same. The Cranes have a son; highly intelligent, independent lad, I've been told. Fine education, as I recall. Became a New York policeman. He chose to play cops and robbers rather than read briefs. You've met your match with him. He's dogged, won't let up until he knows the truth, I'm told." Aubrey could see Asia tense up. "This is not necessarily a bad thing. Kind of fellow who will get to the bottom of Jack's death if there's any getting to be done."

"But finding me too soon might not be such a good idea."

"Young Crane's help can't hurt, Asia. You just might also find him a catalyst to help clean up that little mess you left at the Plaza."

Asia winced.

"Your example, I know, of a purely pragmatic act," Aubrey said as he finished his breakfast, gave her a light kiss on the forehead and went off, leaving her to contemplate what he had said.

After reading the news article, Asia's sense of urgency to leave Bermuda, to sail away, was stronger than ever. She was happy here but she had serious concerns about Sir Aubrey's safety as well as her own. During the last months before her surreptitious departure from New York, Asia had seen Ian's temper. Breaking out in a clammy perspiration at the thought of what might happen to her, she felt as if her skin were withering from the inside out. She knew it was only a matter of time before Ian figured out where she had gone.

Christmas Day was celebrated with a trustworthy clutch of old friends. Now that hurricane season was well over, Asia moved Onika across Hamilton Harbor to the dock in front of Tinkerton House, in the lee of White Island. There she began reprovisioning. Within days of bringing Onika to Tinkerton House dock and watching her waterline lower from the amount of gear and provisions she stashed aboard, the little boat was ready.

Every time Ian's name came up, Aubrey behaved as if he could fight anything. "That young devil comes around here and he'll be out on his tail before …"

"Oh! Aubrey! You're are all bluster and mush, Mon;" She would tease back.

The first week in January, Asia read the Times notice about the memorial service. "My God, Aubrey! I'm dead," she laughed, but an unsettling snaking sense of foreboding coiled inside and constricted her internally, leaving her outer shell with no revealing marks.

Asia spent the next day at the Botanical Gardens among the physical and emotional shade of the park's tropical fauna of Camfer trees, Bermuda Cedar, and Casuarinas. The restfulness of their hues relaxed the inner warnings that stirred inside.

"Captain Sandy called today," Aubrey informed her casually that evening at dinner.

Asia flinched. Her instincts told her, that people were getting close. Her defenses went up.

"Oh," she responded casually.

"Says the young Crane fellow, whom he has known since he was in short pants, is on his way. We think you should talk to him," he paused to get his point across. "For your own safety."

There was the mention of Richard Crane again. To hear Aubrey tell it, Crane was going to be her knight in shining armor. Aubrey kept sending her dual messages; she was bright enough to manipulate money, but not much else. Look at where listening to men had gotten her so far. Anger welled up in her at the thought of allowing men to control her decisions again. 'Knight in shining armor, my a...!' She thought, taking stock of her present situation.

"I see." Was all she said and, feigning exhaustion, Asia called it an early night.

CHAPTER 37

After leaving the morgue, Crane and Stan tracked down Detective Ross at the 109th precinct, the officer on duty New Year's morning when Annie Bloome's body had been pulled out of the bay.

"Most ghoulish darned thing I've ever seen. As for that 'patho' guy, Banner over in forensics, he fits right in."

Crane smiled. He could hardly wait to share that statement with Malcolm the next time he saw him.

"Finally found the rest of the body parts, what was left of them. Freak accident, the head being sliced off like that. That psycho pathologist said it must have been done by a boat prop, one with a hull shoal enough to get close to the piling." Ross continued, "Not many people out on the water this time a' year. We put out an all call but no one came forward. Probably didn't want to get involved or just didn't remember. Hell, maybe it was kids."

Stan laughed. With two boys he could relate to that.

"You boys know who she is? You got a case where she fits?"

"Actually, we think she's part of the heiress' disappearance that happened a while back. You know, the Plaza?" Stan commented.

"You guys gotta' be takin' the heat on that one." Ross eyed Crane then Stan, soulfully.

"It keeps us on our toes," replied Crane, stone-faced.

"Glad it didn't happen on my beat," Ross paused. "I'll ask my chief to release the file, glad to be rid of it."

Crane and Stan left the 109th knowing this was going to be an afternoon of dirty work. Dealing with a victim's family was the worst part of their job. They had promised Banner they would bring in Mrs. Benetonelli to identify her granddaughter's body. As they headed out to Queens, they both knew breaking the news would be hard.

"You've found Angelina?' Mrs. Benetonelli asked almost before both the detectives had walked through the front door.

During the ride downtown, Stan asked her about her granddaughter's personal life.

"She was very hard working. She go to work, she come home. Sometimes she'd work late and spent the night in the city. But she always called."

It was obvious the old woman knew very little about Annie's private life.

"There were no Mafia boys. I know that for sure," she continued. "Occasionally they'd come siffin' around, but my Angelina, she had no truck with that scum." About this, Mrs. Benetonelli was adamant. As for February 25th, the day Jack Winslow died, it was Mrs. Benetonelli's birthday.

"She always made it a special day. Such a good girl. Took me to Mazaluna's Restaurant, like she did every year." The tears streamed down her cheeks and she wiped them away with an old fashioned, hand sewn white lace trimmed handkerchief. She was sure the officers had made a mistake. "It can not be my Angelina," she kept saying all the way to the morgue. When they arrived downtown, Mrs. Benetonelli was asked to identify the body. With a gasp, her withered body collapsed. After her recovery, the two detectives drove the weakened, sobbing, old woman home and deposited her into the arms of a kind neighbor.

The next item on their day's agenda was perusing the missing person's report for any leads. Although they were now quite sure, from their reports back from accounting, that Annie had probably helped Ian Whitney cook the World Wide Banknote Company books, neither detective could understand why anyone would cause her to endure such a brutal death.

Missing Person Report:
December 23, 1983

Mrs. Benetonelli, grandmother reported one Angelina Benetonelli (a.k.a. Annie Bloome) missing at eight o'clock, P.M., December 23rd. She was to have been home by four o'clock. Mrs. Benetonelli was told to contact the police again if her granddaughter did not show up within twenty-four hours. Hysterical, Mrs. Benetonelli continued to call. Angelina Benetonelli had still not returned by eight o'clock, Christmas Eve.

An officer was dispatched to the residence.

Grandmother stated Angelina had gone into work as usual the morning of the 22nd and planned to attend the annual Christmas party after work. Because it would be late, she decided to stay in Manhattan with a friend that night. Then she could finish her last minute Christmas shopping in the City the next day. She never came home. Mrs. Benetonelli did not know the name of the friend.

World Wide Banknote, her place of work, had been contacted, but most of the employees were on vacation until the second of January. They interviewed one Edward Meeks from the accounting department, who explained that there had been an annual holiday bash at the apartment of the Officer in Charge of Operations on Fifth Avenue and East Eighty Third, one Cynthia Ryder. Annie was there. Mr. Meeks did not know her plans. He received his Christmas bonus check and left at about nine thirty. As far as he knew, Annie was still there.

Police officers returned and interviewed the full staff on January 2nd. The reports from everyone were much the same. The Christmas party was an annual affair. It had always been held at Mr. Winslow's Park Avenue apartment situated on the top two floors of the Banknote business office. The party was always held on the evening of December twenty-second. This year everyone assumed it would be held at the Whitney's townhouse belonging to his daughter and Ian Whitney, which they were all eager to see. The untimely disappearance of Mrs. WInslow-Whitney changed all that and it was held at Miss Ryder's apartment instead. It was here that the annual Christmas bonus from the company, a generous check, was given out. This was the last workday of the year for Banknote employees. Except for a small staff that rotated yearly, everyone had the week and a half off between Christmas and New Years.

No one, including the hostess, one Cynthia Ryder, had any idea when Annie Bloome had left. Nor did anyone know her plans. Two individuals noticed she spent quite a bit of time talking to Mr. Whitney. Three others noted she was a little high, had 'slightly slurred speech,' and was somewhat wobbly in her movements'. It was stated that this was extremely unusual and totally out of character for the young woman, as Ms. Bloome rarely drank.

Currently, no leads have surfaced regarding Miss Benetonelli's disappearance.

CHAPTER 38

"So what've we got?" Stan asked as he put the file down on his desk. "A group of people having a good time. They're happy, they got money in their pockets and they got the week off. She's ripped. Probably any number of the others were too, and nobody knows a thing. Sounds like a typical holiday party to me." Stan's analysis was probably right on target. "Although I do find it strange that Bloome, supposedly a non-drinker, got tipsy. We need to look into that."

"We also have evidence that Whitney was in the hotel room at the Plaza with Annie Bloome the night of the gala. We have Mrs. Benetonelli's statement that Annie was going to stay with a friend in Manhattan. There is no evidence that she was close to any of her co-workers. Who could that friend have been?" Crane asked aloud.

"The only friend she has in the company, Ian Whitney?" Stan paused. "What do ya think, shall we pull him in?" A big grin crossed his face.

"You'd like that." Crane responded.

"Wouldn't you?"

"It's not as much fun, but let's go over and confront the guy now. He will hang himself eventually anyway."

World Wide Banknote was closing just as they arrived.

"What is it this time?" Whitney sneered when he saw them walk in.

"A few questions for you, Mr. Whitney, to tie things up."

Crane could hardly hold back his smirk as Stan used an officious tone he had never heard before.

"I'm tired of you barging into my offices anytime you please," Whitney retorted as he got up and began putting on his coat. "Anyway, I have an appointment. Sorry gentlemen, this time you will have to leave."

"Mr. Whitney, it's about time you begin to understand what we're about. I would not hesitate to cuff you and take you downtown. Or … you can take off your coat, sit down and talk to us here. Your choice." Stan's words caused Whitney to stop in his tracks.

"Your job should be finding my wife, not harassing me with stupid questions," Ian responded with an acid vehemence, as he removed his coat and turned toward his desk.

"Annie Bloome is dead, Mr. Whitney." Whitney stopped statuesque.

"Her head, minus her body, was found New Year's Day. The rest of her was found tied to a piling near the Throgs Neck Bridge," Crane continued.

Whitney turned back toward Crane in shocked disbelief. "You mean 'The Head'?" He asked as he fell back into his chair.

"Yes, the head." Crane paused to give Ian Whitney more time for the image to sink in. "We are trying to determine her final movements. We know that you had sex with Miss Bloome in room 309 at the Plaza Hotel the night of the gala.

"That's a bold faced lie," he shouted.

"Mr. Whitney, we have a wine bottle, a room with both your fingerprints, and bed sheets full of semen."

Ian's jaw dropped like a guy who was literally caught with his pants down, Stan observed later.

"Now shall we start over?" Crane asked.

"What do you want to know?" Whitney asked with resignation.

"Were you the one Miss Bloome was going to spend the night with on the 22nd, the night of the annual Christmas party? The night she disappeared?" Crane asked.

"Yes," he responded slowly, "but she never did. I decided I did not want her in my home."

"Why was that?"

"I don't know. It was as if a wave swept over me. I didn't want her there, near my things. I wish I could give you a better answer but I can't."

"Did you take her to a hotel?"

"No. I guess for me, the relationship insignificant as it was, was over."

"Was the 'relationship', as you call it, over or didn't you need her anymore? You see Mr. Whitney, I'm beginning to think your relationships last only as long as they're useful to you."

Whitney shot daggers at Crane but he refused to be baited.

"Did she leave with you?" Crane continued, seemingly oblivious to Whitney's reaction to his last statement.

"No, I left at about eleven fifteen and Annie was still there."

"And you went directly home?"

"Yes."

"Can you prove that, Mr. Whitney?"

"Don't blame this on me because, I didn't do this!" he screamed, his voice welling deep with anger.

"This what, Mr. Whitney?"

"Nothing, none of it," Whitney said putting his head in his hands.

"Thank you, Mr. Whitney. We'll be in touch." Crane said as he and Stan walked out.

.

CHAPTER 39

As his flight neared the Bermuda coast, Crane looked out the window and watched the seas become a rainbow of color as the waters, sprinkled with pebble-like shoals, shown with hundreds of luminous hues. The translucent shades ranged from brownish-yellow, doughnut sandholes to dark rich, indigoes depending on the ocean's depth. The morning flight from La Guardia was a two-hour milk run with more locals and businessmen than tourists at this time of year.

Richard passed through Customs without a hitch. Unlike New York, which had just experienced a winter snowstorm, it was another balmy Bermuda day with temperatures in the mid-sixties and a 10-knot breeze. Richard was glad he had not worn a suit or encumbered himself with a heavy overcoat, but had dressed in a navy cashmere turtleneck, camel haired sport coat, and heavy twill khaki slacks.

As he passed through the Immigration Gate, an older, stocky, black local, who was leaning against the front fender of a Rover sedan eyeing the passengers as they came out, slowly walked over. "Mr. Crane?" he asked, as he made an overall survey of Richard, which ended in a nod of approval.

"Yes."

"I'm Harold Ingham, Sir Tinkerton's driver. Have ya been to our island before?" He spoke in the typical clipped Bermudian accent as he squired Richard toward the Rover parked by the airport curb. Before Richard had a chance to answer, "Ya got no bags, Mr. Crane?" He grinned.

"No, I'm only here for the day, Mr.?"

"Call me Harold, everybody does."

Richard smiled.

"Named after my Uncle Walter Ingham, famous for ferryin' passengers across da harbor in his row boat. He started in '02 and retired in 1952. Died long since he did, and inspiration to us all. It's my first name dat's Walter. Too confusin', dat's why I go by my middle name."

As soon as they were in the car, Crane heard "I feel good, so good," by Ray Charles, crooning from the car radio as Harold headed toward the airport exit.

"See dere," Harold pointed behind him as he drove toward the causeway, "Dat over there is da US Naval Station. Takes up most of David Island, but our airport's connected to it so it keeps all da noise and commotion in one place." Harold spoke over the radio which was now playing "Who was makin' love to your wife last night when you were out makin' love," and Richard was glad Asia Winslow had found such a whimsical place to run away to.

"We're on Harrington Sound Road now. Dose is da caves over dere and Tucker's Town is just over to your right. Lots of rich Americans and Brits have houses along Tucker's Town Bay way." Harold was a regular little travelogue.

"It's Smith's and Devonshire parishes we comin' to next." Harold rambled on.

As Harold drove south on the fishhook shaped islands, and the road paralleled the windward Atlantic shore, the vegetation became less lush. There were no large hotels, only a very few cottage colonies and private clubs. The landscape was dotted mostly with private homes built in the typical Bermudian style and painted in pastels. Their white washed slate roofs were lined with gutters to guide the rainwater that was collected and stored in cisterns below the houses, the only access to water on the islands.

"I'll have my driver take you directly to my home. Then the three of us can talk in privacy and comfort," Sir Tinkerton had said when they spoke on the telephone the previous evening. "But I must warn you, Asia is not happy about your coming. She feels that if you've found her, Ian can't be far behind."

"I understand, and I can't agree with her more," Richard sighed, "but please reassure her this is in her best interest."

Although Harold drove at a steady pace, he did not exceed the Islands' thirty-five miles per hour speed limit and, as he neared the Waterville Roundabout, he slowed to the required Town speed of fifteen miles per hour. Driving around most of the circle, rather than heading for downtown Hamilton, Harold took the Harbour Road on the opposite side of the harbor through Paget Parish just past Lower Ferry. The long, low, rambling, two story yellow house sat on the shore side of the road. Harold drove down the drive to the house and dropped Richard opposite the entry.

The front door opened almost immediately upon his arrival and Richard was ushered into a long, low, inviting library.

"Glad to meet you, young man," Sir Aubrey extended his hand. "Know your father. Heard interesting things about you."

"And you, Sir. What a wonderful room!" Richard exclaimed surveying the unusually odd sized used bricks of the library fireplace, and the well organized neatly lined shelves of books.

Aubrey beamed and waved his hand to sit. "Call me Aubrey, my boy.

Coffee?" he asked as he poured himself a cup.

Crane salivated, "Yes thank you. About Mrs. Whitney." He began.

"I might as we well tell you straight out, she's gone. Got up this morning and she and the boat were gone. There you have it."

"Gone where? Do you have any idea? Did she leave you anything, a note?" Richard's questions seem to tumble out.

Aubrey slid a small envelope across the coffee table between them. Crane opened it and found it full of all the appropriate words, 'I'm sorry... safety... love.'

"Her original plan was to leave at the end of December. Sign some papers then sail on to what she considered a safer *modus operandi*. It was my fault really. I convinced her to stay against her better judgment."

"But from December through April the Atlantic is riddled with gales and freak storms. What was she thinking?" Richard's voice was full of shocked concern.

"Thinking. I believe it was fear, Richard."

"Fear! What could be more fearful than being in a small boat during the Atlantic's January weather?" This woman and her antics were getting to him.

"Ian Whitney. You must understand that if you are here, she believes that Ian cannot be far behind. Since her father's death she has seen his anger and it paralyzed her. She was not only afraid for her own safety, but for mine as well. Hogwash, of course. We take care of people who behave badly on our islands. But she obviously didn't believe me."

"But the Atlantic. Now?" Richard paused exasperated by the whole situation. "We have already seen an example of Ian Whitney's temper."

"Then you know. Asia is sure Ian caused her father's death and prior to leaving, she found a tap on her phone."

The two men sat across from one another helpless. For one it was the concern for a loved one, for the other the professional and moral responsibility to keep her safe. But there was nothing either of them could do.

"Do you have any idea where she was going?" Richard asked.

"Her original plan was to go to the Virgins. She had no worries that World Wide Banknote was in good hands with her friend, Cynthia, at the helm."

Richard sighed. He had reservations about that call too, but this was not the time to go into it.

"So her idea was to cruise the American and British Virgin Islands during the season, while you chaps sorted out the whole mess. Where she's headed to now is anyone's guess."

"Surely you have a chart of the Atlantic," Richard said.

Aubrey nodded, left the room and returned with a NOAA chart of the Western Atlantic and the two men poured over her possible ports of call.

"For obvious reasons, I think we have to assume that she didn't sail back to New York." Richard considered.

"Her choices are slim to none," Aubrey sighed, surveying landfalls and their vast distances.

"It's approximately a thousand miles to both Florida and the Virgin Islands from Bermuda." Richard calculated using the dividers and parallel rules Aubrey had handed him.

"She could sail to the Bahamas, but knowing Ian's family has a house at Lyford Cay, I don't think she'd consider that as a viable choice," Aubrey said.

"So bottom line, it's either Florida or the Virgins. My bets are on St. Thomas. Less chance of being noticed, lots of little coves and anchorages to hide out in, and a whole down island chain in which to move about." However, Asia Winslow had Crane stymied. There was nothing he could do. He certainly couldn't call on the Bermudan government to send their Sea and Rescue to cruise out and arrest her for trashing the Plaza. Nor could he follow her. Actually he could. He could hire a fast boat and put it on a course due south for the Virgins because he was sure that's where she intended to go. Luckily, she had a weather window, but she was under sail, which meant that she was probably only about fifty knots offshore by now. But, what would he do if he did catch up with her? Kidnap her away from her craft? That thought was unrealistic as well as illegal. His other option was to join the cruise. Tempting, but not with her, she was one woman he had no desire to be stuck with in the middle of any ocean alive or dead, particularly for seven to ten days.

Over lunch the two men discussed her chances of a safe sail this time of year.

"Other than the fact that Bermuda is a good jumping off spot for the Caribbean and that you are here, you have failed to explain to me why she came here." Richard stated feeling that friendship was only part of the answer for her Bermuda landfall, not the key to the whole picture.

"Do you know what we do here, Richard? What our major businesses are on the Island?"

"Tourism and money. It's a tax haven."

"A very select, discreet, and impeccably run tax haven of offshore personal and company trusts. However, there is a lot of competition from the Caymans, the Bahamas, the BVI, and the granddaddy of them all, Switzerland, to name a few. We are also very rigidly unionized which has given us one of the highest standards of living in the world. This has also protected us from the problems of homelessness and crime that riddle so many other countries."

"Interesting, but it doesn't answer my question," Richard interrupted.

"Be patient with me Richard, I'm getting there." Aubrey continued. "Unfortunately, if our markets are depleted by competition or international financial down trends, our incomes are not flexible during a down turn. We are constantly on the lookout for new financial instruments. Our latest, most lucrative, is reinsurance. Do you know what the reinsurance business is?"

"Vaguely," Richard replied, now a bit agitated.

"Most people don't. It is one of the safest and most steady financial investments. It's when an underwriter reinsures itself against any added risk. They assume the liability on risks only for that amount of insurance that is over and above the stated sum. Reinsurance portfolios are no risk policies, which not only guarantee the insured a specific future payment from the premium paid, but also a steady income to the reinsurer from the investment of that premium. Asia Winslow found that Ian had been dipping into the business and family coffers over the years."

"To the tune of?" Richard asked folding his hands under his chin.

"Six million dollars."

"Now this is getting interesting."

"He put them in bearer bonds. Asia found them hidden at the Wellfleet cottage and mailed them here to me. Besides getting the money safely away from him, she had to put it to work. She mailed it to me, and I've held the bonds here in my safe in the house until she arrived to sign them properly into an account."

Crane gave a long low whistle, "and that's why she sailed here, to put Ian off the trail when he found out."

"Exactly!" Aubrey exclaimed. "We are dealing with an exceedingly bright young woman."

"Who can be a little too casual when it comes to taking risks," Crane interjected.

"Ah! But if you believe you are invincible, risks sometimes don't appear to be so dangerous. While she was here, she spent her time learning the reinsurance business."

"Not only has she got the problem of the Plaza to clean up ..."

"But that's a misdemeanor," Aubrey interrupted, "a slap on the hand. It would probably require a large chunk of cash, an apology and some very unpleasant publicity. A small price to pay when one's life's on the line."

"Now she has to add transferring well over five thousand dollars out of the country, which might come under federal Postal Fraud Laws."

"Not so fast, bearer bonds, just as their name implies, have no name on them and the FBI would have no way of even tracking them or that they even existed unless they caught her red handed. At this point, even with the evidence of my testimony, which you can't subpoena, you will not be able to prove they ever existed because in regard to Asia Winslow, they don't."

Richard knew Aubrey was correct. He looked at his watch. It was time to leave.

"They are only a problem to Asia if Ian takes her to court to get them back. But then, he'd have to explain where he got the funds to purchase them, and that's not going to happen. The only way he could have gotten them back was to kill her for them, and now it's too late." Aubrey said as he steered the car past the roundabout enroute to the airport.

"Smart lady, dangerous game," Richard said. "However, considering Ian's temper, she still may not be safe."

"Ian Whitney called Tinkerton House while we were having lunch. I am forewarned."

"When is he coming?" Richard asked.

"Tomorrow, on the same flight you took out of La Guardia this morning. As for Asia, I will call if I hear anything. I still believe at some point, she'll need your help," Aubrey said as he dropped Richard off at the Bermuda Airport.

During the plane ride back to New York, Richard Crane pondered Asia Winslow's predicament and the choices she had made. The little wench may have wasted the public's funds running circles around them all, but he had to grudgingly admit that without even meeting her, she was quite an impressive young woman. His opinion of her had gone from one of anger to agitated fascination.

CHAPTER 40

As the sun rose above the horizon, Asia was pleased with the increased speed she had gained by her slight tightening of the jib. She knew she was becoming a seasoned offshore sailor, but that didn't mean she could let down her guard. Although the sail to the Virgins was a simple matter of 'Dead Reckoning,' she still had to compensate for winds and currents. Then it was just a matter of determining the compass heading and pointing Onika on course, which was almost due south.

Asia was now used to the reverberating drumming sound of the waves against the fiberglass and the occasional yawing of Onika's hull caused by a particularly brash wave. Passing the odd bird resting on a twig or a porpoise's dancing dives as it cruised alongside Onika had alleviated some of the daily humdrum of the churning seas. Their white peaked waves moved endlessly ebbing and flowing across the ocean to a new harbor.

Once, she passed a freighter, homeport Iberia. Unlike most countries with their coast guards, equipment rules and obeyance to specific Rules of the Road, this ship's company had bought its registry from a country that had not signed on to these international shipping rules, but rather used the registry sale as a means of revenue with no concern for the integrity of the ship's hull, safety, or the crew and their conditions. Fortunately, the ship had cruised past at a reasonable distance, causing Onika only the briefest of hobby horsing as she crossed its wake, and the little boat carried on, steady against the gently pounding waves.

This was the first sign of human life Asia had seen in five days, so she hailed it on her ship to shore radio to check her position. Just as she had figured, Onika was right on course. Asia knew International Maritime Law required freighters and cruise ships to radar scan their course every fifteen minutes. But there were always a few rogue captains who didn't follow the rules. The laxness of these men and their crew caused an occasional small sailboat to disappear, plowed under the sea leaving no survivors. After already having weathered a heavy storm, to be run down by a ship because of an irresponsible captain and his crew, in Asia's eyes, would have been adding an 'insult to injury.'

Seeing this ship didn't mean that another large freighter would not appear, for she and Onika were crossing major shipping lanes, those first discovered by explorers when they began sailing the trades. Nor did it mean that another storm would not erupt. Out here storms happened often. They just came and went, creating a surge of seas and winds that registered on no man's radar, except those in the immediate vicinity. But this time Asia was ready, psychologically as well as physically. Yet as they sailed, she and her boat only experienced small squalls, thumbing Onika here and there as the sea rumbled on its path

north and west. The rattling sounds of china became common-
place, with the shifting motion of the seas against the hull. This
cacophony of discordant sounds above and below decks was
much like an orchestra tuning up for a grand finale.

Yet, most days, Onika just drifted on her windward sail, bob-
bing determinedly through the waves toward her destination.
Although there were no other beings aboard, Asia soon realized
she was not alone. The sky, seas, winds, and waves spoke to
her daily, as she learned to appreciate their connective presence.
Once Asia's body adjusted to their rhythm, they enveloped her
with their deep dreamy mysticism, as if telling tales of their past,
present, and future. It was then, she realized, she and Onika had
become accepted interlopers in the seas' endless determined
quest to lap the land on the opposite shore.

As Onika made headway against the ever-churning seas,
Asia worked on deck, baked, read, or watched the clouds as they
punctured the desert-like sky's marinade of blues. As Captain
Andy had predicted, she enjoyed her quiet days offshore. During
these lazy routine days at sea separated from the stress of her
other life, Asia felt safe in the ocean's womb-like presence. It
sang to her, grazed her face with teasing splashes and empow-
ered her to believe that maybe there really could be 'happily ever
afters.'

After eight and a half days, Asia made landfall in Gorda
Sound at the end of Virgin Gorda Island in the British Virgins.
The sound was a protected harbor on all sides with two small but
easy entries. One on each side of Mosquito Island with Virgin
Gorda and Prickly Pear Island each wrapping around, giving
shelter on the other three. In the pitch-blackness of night, Asia
cautiously eased Onika into the harbor. Silhouetted by a lone
shore light, Asia was able to make out the ghost like hulls and the

tall black masts of the few other boats already in the sound. After her long, arduous days at sea, Asia was thankful to be anchored in this safe, snug harbor and she settled into a deep uninterrupted sleep just before dawn.

"Afternoon." a voice carried across the sound as Asia poked her head into the cockpit, with a large mug of rich black coffee. Ignoring the voice, she settled down on the deck cushions and propped a smaller one behind her back.

"Welcome to paradise." The voice continued. Asia turned to spy a ruddy looking fellow grinning up at her from a rather scruffy, wooden dingy to Onika's port.

"Thanks," she responded aloud, wishing silently he would disappear.

"Where you hale from?"

"St Martin." Now, back in the real world, one couldn't be too careful.

"Alone?"

"What are you, from the newspaper?"

"Just being friendly, maam, that's all." Like a wounded puppy, the stranger slowly began rowing away.

"And I'm just being bitchy," Asia called out in a stage whisper. "My husband's below still sleeping. Check in with us later, after Chad wakes up, after I've had my coffee and a swim. I'm more pleasant after my daily ablutions." Where the heck did that come from Asia thought surveying the lone man as he dropped an oar on the dingy rim?

"Catch you later then." With an ear-to-ear grin, the puppy bounced back to normal and tried a cheery wave as he grabbed both oars and returned to his rowing.

But there wasn't a later, Asia made sure of that. It had already been after mid-day when she had arisen. She lay low during the rest of the afternoon and she made sure not to have her swim until early evening. Of course the slumbering Chad never surfaced, not even for dinner and soon it was bedtime.

The next morning Asia was up with the sun and sailed off before anyone noticed. She headed out of Gorda Sound past Anguilla Point sailing the long Virgin Gorda coast. As the sun rose, a brisk breeze filled her sails whisking her off past Beef Island, and into Roadtown, Tortola's main Harbor, the capital of the British Virgins, and the main-island among these pristine little jewels. Here, she checked in with customs and immigration.

"So you arrivin' ay?" The customs' officer barely paused. "And where you be comin' from?"

"Bermuda," Asia responded, softly as she handed over her ships papers. Customs demanded honesty and although she knew there were no spies here; she surely wasn't going to shout out her business.

"That's a far sail. Alone?" He questioned with a hint of respect in his voice.

"Yes. And you are certainly correct, it is a far sail." She responded as a brief smile curled about her mouth.

"And how long you think you be wantin' to stay?"

"I don't know. It's so beautiful, I'd like it to be a lifetime... but you know. Reality." Asia paused again. "I'm just going to gunk-hole a few days, then I have to move on." Asia grinned broadly. "But I do think I deserve some kind of a rest after that sail, don't you?"

Although anyone watching would have thought this young woman had not a care in the world, all she really wanted was to fill in the requisite forms and get the 'hell' out of there. Being back in civilization (if that's what one would call these magical little islands) was too new, and Asia because of past events, was again automatically wary of every new person and situation. 'As if Ian could have a spy in every port! Just damn paranoid foolishness,' she thought as she watched the customs agent stamp her papers and passport.

"A rest? I be sure of tad, ma'am." The slight black man in his khaki uniform agreed and with a broad grin, he passed back her papers and waved her on.

After filling-up on diesel and water at a nearby fuel dock, Asia sailed along the Tortola Coast. Unlike the shoal Bermuda waters, the Caribbean was deep. See the island. Sail to it. Line of site, and the prevailing eastern trades made cruising a dream. One could spend a lifetime. Although Asia's time was more limited, she knew exactly where she was headed. Sailing south past Sea Cow Bay and Nanny Cay, Asia continued on past Soper's Hole and between Great and Little Thatch Islands. Pleased to again see the little dollhouse castle high on its island perch, she rounded up between West End Point, Tortola and Great Thatch onto a northern heading. As she sailed, a seeping guilt told her that now that she had made landfall, she should give Aubrey a call. But that call would thrust her into the 'real world' again, a world she was not yet ready to face. Upon hearing from her, Aubrey, she knew, would immediately call that cop. Men were so predictable the way they took charge, hanging together. And no matter how cleverly they covered their tracks, Ian would be right behind them. A shiver ran the length of her whole body.

"Whether they know it or not, he's probably panting on their doorstep as we speak." Asia laughed, suddenly aware she was again talking to her boat. "After all there is always Cynthia." Asia continued her monologue. "Cynthia is the one person I can always count on. Thank heavens Banknote is safely in her hands."

Selfish or not, now that she had finally made it, Asia wanted her freedom in paradise to last just a wee bit longer before having to deal again with the rigor mortis of creeping reality. No, for once Aubrey would have to wait.

CHAPTER 41

It was just after noon when Asia spied Jost Van Dyke in the distance. Almost empty, White Bay's long, white sandy beach glistened in the afternoon sun. The ethereal, fairyland quality of the island had always made it her favorite Virgin. Robinson Crusoe-esque, that's what it was. One always felt like a lone beachcomber on Jost Van Dyke. Asia rued the day the developers stampeded the island and ruined one of the last visages of real paradise.

Anchoring Onika, Asia dove into the glassy clear water and swam ashore. Ignoring the few other souls on the beach, she walked to the end where the hillside met the sand. There were no houses on West End Hill at this end of the beach. Asia donned plastic sandals and laboriously climbed to the top. Feeling the hot sun on her skin soothed by the cool trade winds, she sat gazing across the few miles of Caribbean Sea that separated the

BVI from the US Virgins. Asia mused at how Mother Nature had smacked these charming, now extinct volcanic islands down not far from the equator creating a series of land barriers between the Atlantic and Caribbean Sea. Before the sun began to fade, Asia returned down the hillside to the beach and swam to the boat. Once there, she lowered her dinghy, tying its painter securely to a cleat at the stern. Removing her swimsuit, she dove into the water on the seaside of the boat, and indulged in a soapy warm sea bath. Refreshed, she scurried back aboard for a fresh water rinse and clean duds. Then she hauled up the anchor, and made the short sail over to Great Harbor where she reset her anchor for the night. It was Saturday night at 'Foxies.' Totally out of character, tonight, she was going to let it rip, maybe pretend to be someone else.

As she ate dinner in the cockpit, Asia watched as twinkling lights on St Thomas and St John, began to dot the islands' hill-sides. Well after nine, when the music from Foxies began to vibrate across the water, Asia finally rowed ashore. It was the 'season,' which meant that Foxies would be packed with the usual crowd of tourists, yachties, locals and the occasional 'Stone' or some other celebrity swinger. Asia's lithe, tanned body, skimpy multi-colored skirt and off the shoulder peasant blouse belied her age and the first of many bronze jocks began to make his pitch even before she got near the bar. Asia wanted to celebrate her successful sail and this had the beginnings of a great night.

The next day when she'd awakened, Asia had no idea what time she had come home. But her headache proved there was a reason why students left their college flings back on campus when they graduated.

'My God,' she thought, looking around the cabin, 'I didn't bring anyone back to the boat, did I?' She questioned. After all there had been some pretty close calls. As she relaxed over her much needed coffee, she recalled coming out of the Foxies ladies room, when a longhaired brute had grabbed her, pressed his body to hers and pinned her against the wall. Before she had time to react, his hand was under her skirt about to reach down into her silky bikini pants.

"We could do it right here, baby," the deep raspy whisper of his words culminated with his tongue in her ear. She could feel him getting hard. As he leaned back, the impact of his beer breath made Asia doubly sure, that after all she'd gone through to save her financial virginity from Ian, she surely wasn't going to let herself get fucked by this ape. Suddenly Asia pushed her elbows up in chicken-wing fashion forcing him just a little off balance. Then she kneed him in the crotch.

"OOH," he moaned doubling at the waist. "You bitch.... you mean little bit...OOH God Damn," unable to straighten up.

'The harder they are the louder they moan,' Asia mused as she wriggled away. She could almost feel his gaze drilling holes in her back as she hurried away from the back of the bar.

'Definitely time to leave,' she decided and she began maneuvering her way through the crowd. Just as she was almost home free, Asia felt a rough but gentle hand on her bare shoulder. Asia's heart sunk.

"You know, Charley Atkins over there isn't going to let you off so easily. Not after that little foreplay." The voice was vaguely familiar. Before she could disengage the hand tightened and the stranger turned Asia facing him then reached over to the bar and handed her a rum and coke. "Wasn't this what you were drinking?"

"Actually, I was on my way out."

"Without Chad, or is he still on the boat?"

'Damn,' Asia thought as she bit her lower lip. "Yes. Well…
who made you our cruise director?" Inflamed, she had responded
in kind.

Casually looking beyond her, suddenly he quickly grabbed
her hand, "Look there's finally a free table over there, baby." He
pointed, and before she had a chance to protest, he put his rough
hand firmly on her arm and stirred her to the vacated table.

"Take your hands off of me." She began to protest.

"I think we'd be more comfortable over here, honey." He
said as he plopped her down on the bench next to him. "At least
pretend you like me," he whispered.

"What the…"

"Well speak of the devil, here is Charley Atkins right now."
He said before she could get a word in, and a large hairy figure loomed over the table. "You wouldn't be making a pass at
my lady now would you, Charley? Because if you are or have
been…"The man paused, "I'll beat the living shit out of ya. You
got that Charley."

"Your lady, I had no idea."

"Well now you do. Be careful where you put your hands
next time when it comes to my woman or maybe you won't
have any."

"Come on, honey let's dance." A slow tune had just begun
and he pulled her up real close to dance.

"Are you trying to pick up where he left off?"

"No. I'm just trying to save your ass for Chad."

"Thanks, thanks very much, as a matter of fact I'm sure
Chad would thank you too," she replied with a genuine warmth
in her voice.

When they returned to their table, Charley was gone.

'Wow talk about close calls.' She mused as the coffee began to take effect. Clearing one's head was one thing, but remembering all the happenings of an all too eventful evening was another.

"Ahoy." A familiar voice spoke to her over the rail and there, in his old wooden dinghy, stood the same ruddy fellow from Gorda Sound and the previous night. In the daylight, he looked much older than he had appeared the night before. "Nice boat. Did you really sail it single handed from Bermuda?"

"Would you like to check the ship's log?" She answered before she thought. 'Gees, how much did I blab last night?' she wondered.'

"May I come aboard?"

Giving an affirmative nod, she figured she'd know soon enough.

"Coffee?"

"Best offer I've had all day. What did you say you did? Advertising? You must have taken a leave, or something."

"Or something," Asia barely got a word in edgewise.

"When do you have to go back? You got to admit sailing is much more fun than a New York office." He finally paused to give her a chance to reply.

"You're certainly full of a lot of energy this morning."

"Afternoon…" he corrected her.

Asia looked at her watch, surprised at the time, "Damn straight." She conceded.

He smiled.

"As to going back to the city, a girl's got to eat." More of the evening was coming back to her now, "Steve Hughes, travel writer." She laughed and pointed at him in a silly flirty way. "Last night did I, we, say or do anything we shouldn't have?"

"Only that there is no Chad, and that you were secretly proud of sailing single handed from Bermuda."

Asia just smiled. Thankfully, she had not been too forthcoming.

"I'd be proud too, if I were you. In fact, I'd like to write an article about you and your sail. I've been writing about cruising all over the world and there aren't many female single-handed sailors around."

"Well, I'd have to chew that one around for awhile. After all, I'm generally a pretty private person." All she needed was some jerk ruining everything. "But it's a lovely idea," she responded. She knew she still couldn't be too careful. She still had a mighty mess to clean up and besides, he was a writer. The scent of a good story, and they couldn't be trusted. "No. Not now."

"What about the next time I'm in the city, maybe we could get together? We could talk about it then."

"That's a lovely idea. Give me your address and after I get resettled, I'll write you a line. I'll certainly give you first dibs over anyone else. That's the least I can do after last night." But that was all she was willing to give. Although she knew she had no intention of ever selling her story to anyone.

"Fair enough. Maybe I could do a little more convincing over dinner."

"Now that I'll have to pass on. I really need to get to St John and clear customs today. I'm seriously running out of time. Be gone with you," she laughed, "or I won't have a job to go back to."

"I get the interview, for sure?" She nodded shook his hands and as he climbed into his dinghy, "Ok Annie Wise, but if I don't hear from you, the next time I'm in the city I'll track you down."

'Annie Wise, now Asia was doubly sure she was safe. Annie Wise, indeed!'

. . . .

'Yes, it was certainly nice to be in civilization again' she thought as she sailed through the Northwest Passage and into US waters to enter Customs in St. John. Asia anchored in Cruz Bay and rowed ashore just in time to make US Customs before they closed.

"Welcome home." The US Customs officer commented as he checked her ports of call. "Single handed eh? Must be pretty proud."

"Well, I don't feel too shabby about it." Asia laughed. Actually she was so thrilled she could hardly conceal her pride.

The next morning Asia headed through Pillsbury Sound between Great James Island past the Lagoon entrance and Frenchman's Bay to Charlotte Amalie and into St. Thomas Yacht Haven Marina. After docking, Asia called Aubrey as she had promised.

"Don't forget to call Captain Andy" were her last words as she hung up the phone. "Hey! I've just sailed more than seven hundred miles off shore out of sight of land. I'm a Blue Water Sailor." Asia laughed to herself. It was only then that Asia decided the next best thing to going to sea was enjoying a long hot water shower upon reaching your port of call.

CHAPTER 42

It was well past 9 p.m., when Crane walked into the precinct. "Nice threads." Davis shouted across the room. "Hot date, or is your only set of work clothes in the wash?"

"Yeah, yeah." Crane smiled, realizing he had forgotten to go home and change. "Got stood up," he said. "Came here to sulk." That got a laugh. Nevertheless, when he thought about it, the statement was truer than he would have liked to admit. She had gone sailing instead. That woman really ought to have boats taken away from her, he mused, as he sat down at his desk and picked up the file, Stan, who was long since gone, had left for him.

Crane, whose desk was perpendicular to the wall, swiveled his chair so he faced out toward the room, propped his feet up on his desk and began to read. As usual, the precinct was teeming with its twenty-four hour buzz, playing four-part harmony with Crane's brain, but his was the only part he heard.

He had already read the statements from the grand jury several times. The new information he'd acquired from Aubrey Tinkerton had given him a fresh viewpoint, which he believed might be helpful in seeing something in the report he had otherwise missed. After his visit to Bermuda, he was beginning to agree with Asia Winslow; Ian Whitney was not as innocent as he would have liked everyone to believe. Six million dollars, in whatever form, certainly increased the possibility of a motive. A possibility that might give rise to new questions, particularly after finding Annie Bloome's body dancing at the bottom of the bay. What began as a case of missing persons was beginning to look more like a double murder. By the time Stan had dropped Crane off at LaGuardia that morning, they had narrowed down their suspects to one, Ian Whitney. Yet Richard had questions about the others in the cast of characters in what he was beginning to see as a rectangle of personalities. 'Where was Cynthia Ryder the night of Jack Winslow's death? Did she know about the bearer bonds? And what about Annie Bloome? Was she aware of what Ian Whitney had done with the money she probably helped siphon from the Company?' Under the circumstances, the last question was much harder to answer.

Jack Winslow's autopsy stated there was a blow to the head. A blow to the head had to be within millimeters of the temple to cause death. However, the angle of the blow had not been determined. Might the definition of that angle make a difference in proving what caused Jack Winslow to fall, whether he was pushed or passed out? If Malcolm Banner said 'Yes', then a request for exhumation might be in order. The facts would have to be precise, and also be accompanied by a request written and

signed by the family. Crane doubted that Mrs. Winslow-Blake
would refuse to make the request if asked.

It was well after midnight when Crane climbed into bed.
Still, he tossed and turned, fitfully rehashing the events of his day.
Finally, he drifted into a troubled sleep, dreaming of Technicolor
file folders balanced on a thirty-three and a third RPM turntable
that whirled in his brain. He woke with a start. It was morning,
after 8 a.m. Wandering into the precinct about an hour later, he
headed straight for the coffee.

"Well, if it isn't Sleeping Beauty," Stan commented. "Where's
the dame?"

"Out sailing, God knows where. The woman's diabolical."
Crane sloughed off the question.

"You mean, I send you off to an island to pick up a broad
and you return with no dame, no tan, and I'll lay odds, no
Outerbridges Sherry Pepper Sauce."

"Oh, damn! I'm sorry," Crane said, and he genuinely was.

After his third cup, the coffee began doing its job, and
Crane's head began to regain the feeling of its normal orb-like
shape. A message from Banner reinforced his musings of the
previous evening.

"Six million smack-a-roos, that's a lot of bread."

"Is Damon Runyon your hero?"

"Here, have some coffee."

Crane gave Stan a weak smile and held out his mug. Then he
continued to fill Stan in on his 'Bermuda pleasure trip.'

"That could be one hell of a motive." Stan paused, "By the
way, seems your girlfriend, the Ryder dame, has an Advanced
Scuba Certification. A regular little Cousteau. Likes to spend
her vacations diving in Belize."

"Impound her car," Crane said matter of factly.

"I already did. Totally clean."

"What is it with these people, they all have clean cars. Aren't there any dumb criminals anymore?" Then Crane laughed and let it go. "How about rentals?"

"Already on it, every car rental company's central computer in the tri-state area for the month of December and the first week in January is on the job."

"What a team," Crane smiled. He was still tired, but he was pleased. At least they were no longer dealing with a dead end; in fact, things were beginning to take on a roller coaster kind of rhythm.

Crane had called ahead for an afternoon visit with Asia's great aunt, Mrs. Blake, and they arrived at her apartment right on time.

"Well, Mr. Crane," she said as she directed the two detectives to sit down in the worn, but pleasant room, with its mix of comfortable couches and Louis XIV antique chairs, armoires and tables. "It is obvious you have not married because your reputation for lacking a soft touch precedes you. It seems young women leave town before they have even met you."

Stan had never seen Richard squirm before.

"Then you've spoken to Sir Aubrey Tinkerton?" The answer was obvious, but Crane asked to be polite.

Mrs. Blake smiled and nodded.

"I have lost the girl, madam," Richard said rather theatrically, "but her choice of escape was not the most sensible. Not to scare you, but she picked what can be a very dangerous time of year to embark on a long cruise."

Stan was amused by the way Richard pandered to the old gal.

"I think I told you, Asia is not a young woman who always takes the easy way out."

"I'm learning that, Mrs. Blake," Richard admitted. Then he explained their request.

"Gentlemen, I am almost ninety years old. When I was a young girl and someone died, they were put in a box, buried, and you hoped with your prayers, sent off to their maker." She hesitated, "The first autopsy on Jack was a defilement of the body - and now you ask me to sign for a second. You want me to disturb Jack where he lies at rest. I don't know."

"We understand it's a very difficult decision. Would you like to take some time to discuss it with someone you trust?" Crane didn't like having to ask this of the old woman, but there was no one else. "Maybe you'd like to take some time and think about it," he said, although he didn't want her to take too long. "I know this is a serious and emotional decision."

"This should NOT be an emotional decision, Mr. Crane." She said emphatically.

Crane and Stan sat patiently. This was Mrs. Blake's call and they were not going to cajole her into anything. After all, what if Crane's theory and Banner's analysis of the expected outcome were wrong. This was not a cop movie on television; they were not required to fill a scene with dialogue. They were dealing with real people, real lives. The grandmother and the aunt in this case were victims too.

"In the past, I would have discussed this kind of situation with Jack. Ironic isn't it. He was not perfect, of course, but he had one quality I always admired, the quest for truth. Before he made a decision, he would seek the truth in every individual and situation. The one time he allowed his emotions to get in the way was in his evaluation of Ian Whitney. That one time, his quest may well have also been his downfall."

She paused as if groping for the right words. "You gentlemen are asking me to give you the power to determine just that, the truth. How can I refuse? I will call your father in the morning Mr. Crane, and be done with it. Now if you'll excuse me." The spryness in her step and the spirit she had exuded were gone. They had been replaced by a frail, suddenly very saddened old woman.

The two detectives let themselves out, hoping that in the next few days lab reports would give them the facts necessary to back up their theories.

Their days were spent tracking rental cars, solving new crises, and paperwork, while they waited for the lab report about Jack Winslow's remains,

"Hey, Stan, you looking for a rental car?" Davis shouted across from his desk, as the two detectives stopped in to check their messages before calling it a night. "I think I got one."

"One is all we need," Stan called back.

"Maverick, up in White Plains. A three-day rental, hired the 22nd of December. I sent a tow. Forensics got it about four this afternoon. I figure a Dewers at the Whitehorse would do it."

"You're on," Stan replied. "I think we're on to something great," Stan sang under his breath as he dialed Jeanie to tell her he was on his way.

"I'm going home to get some sleep." Crane yawned and waved as he made his way out.

CHAPTER 43

"I think you'll find this interesting." Banner's scribbled memo was attached to the rental car's lab report. Stan snatched it off Crane's desk, as a right of first arrival.

"How is it that I, who live in Brooklyn, can get here before you and you live around the corner?" Stan asked, not expecting an answer.

"Going to be one of those days, Stan?" Richard replied as he sat down at his desk with a brimming mug of coffee. "That's the ticket," he said as he inhaled the rich aroma and took a sip. Then he turned toward Stan. "Finding it worthwhile reading?"

"Bloodstains, Bloome's blood type, Bloome's hair follicles, plus particles of Sakrete, a bonding cement, found in the trunk." Stan looked up and grinned. "Hey! Get a load of this. Torn corner of a bank check with the last two numbers, 87, found wedged between the driver's seat and the shifting console. What was the number of the Christmas bonus check Bloome received?"

Crane leafed through his notes. "7187," Crane said matter of factly.

"Like frosting on a cake," Stan said gleefully.

"You really don't like Miss Ryder, do you Stan?"

"Lookit, everyday poor slobs pass through here, the dregs of society, 'sickos' too. Many of them just feeding a habit the only way they can. But this dame, she had it all, good looks, education, money, a cushy life-one hundred percent of the pie. The whole bunch of them are parasites. Why did she need more, anyway?"

"The sophomoric philosophical question. More seems to be a disease of many 'haves,'" Richard mused. "Greed, the human condition. You'd like to eat the rich this morning, wouldn't you Stan?" Crane laughed, "and there are some who should be, but it sounded to me like Jack Winslow was a fine person and good employer."

"Yeah, Well?" Stan groped his way off his soapbox. "And the 'Crane' isn't so bad either, for an absentee landlord."

"It's true, I do keep the tenants in my Upper East Side seventy-third street slum off my back." Crane laughed.

"Let's go arrest her." Stan got up eagerly. "Banknote?"

"Good place to start," Crane commented as he finished his coffee and let Stan get his aggressions out by leading the charge.

It was mid-morning when they arrived at the world Wide Banknote offices.

"I'm sorry gentlemen, Miss Ryder is not in," the receptionist said. "She left early yesterday afternoon and hasn't called in since."

"She has not communicated with any of the staff?" Stan asked.

Ian Whitney, who had been looming in the shadow of his office doorway, walked over to Stan and confirmed the secretary's statement.

"None of us has seen or heard from her," he said. "I had Miss Weston call her apartment this morning, but there was no answer. Once in a while she takes a break. It has been a bit stressful around here lately." He paused to sneer at the officers.

"Any idea where she might have gone?" Stan asked.

"None whatsoever. She'll probably call in later."

"And you'll let us know." Stan countered.

"Certainly." Whitney replied as he turned and walked away.

"I think she's onto us." Stan said as the elevator doors closed.

"No doubt. He may be too."

"Or maybe he just doesn't get it."

"Let's check out her apartment." Crane suggested, resigned to the fact that to catch up with Cynthia Ryder might be a long and difficult business. It was no surprise that there was no answer at her apartment. The super let them in, but the apartment was empty. The doorman had not seen her since the previous afternoon and her car was not in the garage.

Back at the precinct, a description of her car and the license plate number were sent out on the wires and Crane and Stan began the laborious task of contacting police units at the terminal parking lots of local bus and train stations. Commercial Airline departure manifests were also being checked along with charter flights.

The next few days they waited, receiving negative responses from their inquiries while making dents in the inevitable pile of paper in their inboxes. Crane had to go downtown to testify in court on a burglary charge; another one of the human fodder had been caught up in the never-ending downward spiral of drugs and detention. Crane and Stan both had a problem with the government's stand on addicts. They needed help, not prison. Nevertheless, it was Crane's job to uphold the law and he did. There must be a better way, he thought, as he walked out of the courthouse, his hands resolutely shoved in his pockets.

Grabbing a cab uptown, he contemplated the whole damned situation. Not Amsterdam, he thought, but maybe Copenhagen and Christiania, that seemed to work. However, US drug laws were not his problem; finding Cynthia Ryder was. The day had been one of tedious boredom; it was exhausting in a way that left Crane physically and mentally wasted. He left the cab at 58th and Columbus Circle. A little exercise might clear my head, he mused, and strolled across the park among the throngs, most of whom like him, were heading home.

"Evening, Richard." Barnaby Levin's voice resonated through his reveries and as Crane looked up, he felt the warm nuzzle of Barnaby's Irish wolfhound against his hand. Unlike Christmas Eve, the long, lanky, mustached man wore his standard camouflage fatigues, dark knot cap and fingerless gloves.

"Hi, Simon. How's your friend Al Sloane?" Simon wagged his tail as Crane patted the dog affectionately on the head.

"Minor advances, but still not quite ready for one of your mother's holiday parties." Barnaby laughed. "Any closer to finding your missing girl?"

"Actually, although I can't get to her, we know she's alive and hopefully safe. Tell Sloane we figured out what he saw, and to give me a call."

Barnaby Levin nodded as he and Simon continued on their stroll in the opposite direction along the path. That was the longest conversation Richard had ever had with this odd, mysterious man, who continued to surface occasionally on the periphery of Richard's life. Other than his name and that of his dog, Richard still knew little about him, and he decided to take the time to find out more about this man and his relationship with his grandfather. After all, mysteries were his business and Barnaby Levin, who had resurfaced in and out of his life since Richard's childhood, was one he was now determined to solve. In the past, Barnaby Levin had always been a transition rather than a distraction, but in the last few weeks that had changed.

Richard's focus returned to the problem at hand. Damn these women, he thought as he wandered home in the evening chill. One, sailing God knows where. At least he knew she was in the Atlantic, unless she had drowned, unable to weather a winter ocean storm. It had been fourteen days since his visit to Bermuda. Not having heard from Aubrey Tinkerton, he was becoming anxious. Meanwhile, Cynthia Ryder's whereabouts had him totally baffled. 'To hell with it. I'll find her tomorrow,' he thought, as he stuck the key in his lock.

That night he slept fitfully, waking at odd times, then dozing off dreaming of running in a continuous marathon in which he could never quite reach the finish line. Suddenly, he awoke with a start. He knew where Cynthia had gone, upstate to Union Center to World Wide Banknote's factory. Why, he wasn't sure, however he knew he was right. Maybe it was her megalomania; that in her sick, convoluted mind, she had a proprietary right to the company, and the need to be near the inner workings of something that was possibly hers alone.

Wide-awake, Crane picked up the clock. It was 6 a.m.

The phone rang.

"Sir Aubrey here."

"Yes."

"Sorry to wake you, however, I have just heard from my god-daughter. She's safe in St, Thomas. I told her you were coming."

"Absolutely," Crane paused. Everything was happening at once. "We have a little situation here I need to clear up; then I'll fly out. Thank You."

"Thank you and keep her safe."

"I'll do my best." Crane replied with a sigh as he hung the phone back on its cradle.

CHAPTER 44

Crane was out within an hour; the brisk morning air energizing him as he walked the few blocks to the precinct. His first call was to the Binghamton County police.

"That's right," he replied, "a 1983 black Mercedes, license plate N33 AB6 ... Yes, an unmarked car. You don't want to give her any warning that we're onto her ... I'll be waiting. Thanks."

When Stan walked in, he was shocked to find Crane there before eight. Within fifteen minutes of Crane filling him in, they got the call.

"Let's go for a ride," Crane said and they were off. Two hours later, they drove up to the factory and parked next to Cynthia Ryder's sleek, black, Mercedes convertible. Local backup was standing by to enter the lower section of the large brick building where the steady cadence of the presses could be heard even outside of the old, turn-of-the-century, red brick factory building. Accompanied by two local officers with a search warrant in hand, Stan and Crane walked up the slight incline toward the office level entry.

Crane tried the door. It was open. Quietly he walked in, followed by Stan and the officers. Slowly Crane opened the office door. Cynthia Ryder was seated at her desk.

I'll be with you as soon as I finish this memo," she said, as if she were expecting them.

Crane waved to the officers to remain in the hall.

She put down her pen and folded her hands. She stared at the two detectives for a moment as if she were having trouble focusing. Then, without warning she jumped up.

"Right on time," she said as she slowly gazed down at her watch. It was as if she were functioning in suspended staccato animation.

"Miss Ryder, we have come to arr …" Stan began.

"Yes, we wanted to be on time," Crane interrupted him.

"I appreciate that Detective Crane" Cynthia smiled. "As I recall, you are here for the tour of the presses."

Crane and Stan looked at each other, and then gave her a brief nod.

"That's right, Miss Ryder, we are here to see the presses," Crane reassured her as Stan edged slowly over toward the balcony door.

"But first, we'd like to talk to you about Miss Bloome."

"Bloome? I don't know anyone by that name," she responded in a perplexed tone.

"Annie Bloome. She works for you in accounting," Crane continued speaking softly. "Tall, dark hair. Think, Miss Ryder."

"I don't want to talk about her; she has nothing to do with the presses."

"She's dead, Miss Ryder."

"You're here to see the presses," she said as she walked toward the door as if she had not heard. Her hand went for the handle.

"You're not going out there, little lady," Stan said as her grabbed her arm, but she was too fast. Without a moment's hesitation, she locked her leg around his ankle forcing him off balance. Cupping her hand, in one sideways motion, she chopped him in the chest and was out the balcony door. Stan laid spread eagle on the floor before he realized what had happened. Crane gave him a hand up.

From his previous visit, Crane knew that between the noise of the presses and the thick glass between the room and the balcony that she could not hear anything they said in the office.

"I think we need an ambulance," Crane said, and the backup needs to move discreetly inside on the ground floor."

"And I'll send an officer in here," Stan said.

"But not until he sees that I've at least gotten out on the balcony. We don't want to spook her anymore than she already is."

"Right."

"When Crane saw the office door move slightly ajar, he knew things were ready. During the few minutes she waited, Cynthia had been leaning over the rail watching the presses. Crane reached for the balcony door handle and found it was locked. He knocked on the glass but knew she couldn't hear. Finally, he jimmied the lock and was in. Stealthily he reached out for her. Without warning, as if she were functioning with an inner antenna, she turned and kicked him in the chest. Crane fell back, catching the railing just in time to stop his fall.

"I'm a black belt," she screamed over the roar of the machines. Suddenly, with quickening movements, she spun around again.

Grabbing the support pole, she jumped up and balanced herself on the rail. Crane looked down on the monstrous press below. The massive rollers converged, one toward the other, pulling the rolls of paper in at one end and spewing out federal government food stamps at the other.

"You want to talk about Annie?" She shouted. "I'll tell you about Annie Bloome. She was a gold digging little bitch from the wrong side of the tracks, trying to play in the big kids' yard." Cynthia's pupils began to dilate and became glazed.

"Let me help you down," he shouted over the roar, as he extended his hand.

"Well it didn't work," she yelled, kicking out at his hand. "She had a cold, poor darling. So I was kind. I gave her cough medicine with codeine, probably more than she needed. Then I told her to drink a little wine. Annie was much more pliable when I got her down to the car. After all, I couldn't leave her to find her own way home. That would have been mean, particularly after Ian had already rejected her that evening. When it was time for her to stick her foot in the bucket, she was so out of it she thought we were playing a game. 'Put your foot in this squishy stuff,' I prodded." Cynthia paused catching her breath. "It was like taking a lamb to slaughter." Suddenly, with her mouth wide open, Cynthia threw back her head, her glassy eyes shone, her whole body shook and she exuded a raspish sound that Crane realized, as it got louder, was maniacal laughter. "Then I suited up. Do you know how cold it is diving in the dead of winter? Excruciating. I'm a kind person. I hit her in the back of the head so she wouldn't feel a thing. Not until the icy water made her come to and she was gulping water. Then it was turn about. I watched the dumb bitch writhe as she sucked it in. She found out who would get Ian and the money, didn't she."

Cynthia's eyes were glassier than ever. She had swallowed something. Crane was sure. A combination of Demerol and Valium?

"What money?" Since she was in a confessional mood, he felt this was too good an opportunity to miss and Crane went for it.

"You know, the six mil'," she shouted back, her voice filled with pride. "You think he figured out that little ruse himself. Ian's cute, but he's not a Rhodes scholar. But Jack got in the way. Moral bastard. But that didn't stop Ian! You should have seen Jack go down. That big powerful man. It was sweet." Cynthia's mad grin said it all. "You know, Crane, we could have had something beautiful, you and I."

Suddenly, she swooned. As she regained her equilibrium, Crane watched as she tightened her grip on the post. One of her flats slipped from her foot, and they both watched as it fell down and bounced off the edge of one of the machine's rollers onto the floor.

"Yes, we could have had a great thing going together, but we can't have anything if you're not down here with me," Crane pleaded. "Please, Cynthia, come down," he pleaded.

"Prison?" She yelled. "You won't take me to prison?" She paused, again catching her balance. "I wouldn't do well in the same clothes every day."

Crane could tell she was becoming dizzy. Her foot slipped again and her words were beginning to slur. She grabbed the pole with both hands.

"I don't want to come down," she said. "I want to fly." Suddenly her hands seemed to lose their grip and she extended her arms. Crane watched her go down. With her arms spread wide, it was as if she floated on her back. The angel of death had taken over and Crane watched helplessly as Cynthia fell away. As she landed on the press, her body bounced then lay still as her right arm became mangled between the two massive rolling drums and the machine stopped. Her broken body lay atop the press, like an offering on an ancient funeral pyre, and the press was silent.

CHAPTER 45

The early morning flight to St. Thomas was a 'nonstop bus ride on good roads' that landed at Harry S. Truman Airport right on schedule. Brad Henley, the local FBI agent, and Detective Creque of the St. Thomas police force were waiting when Crane disembarked.

"The boat's docked at Yacht Haven Marina in Long Bay across from the West India Company docks," Henley said as they walked toward the car. Richard was beginning to enjoy being picked up and chauffeured around, something he could personally well afford, but would rarely do.

"Detective Creque is your contact and is on call to supply you with backup if the need should arise," Henley continued.

"Whateva ya need Mon, ya just call," said Creque, a large black plainclothes policeman with a mouth full of teeth and a broad smile. He and Richard shook hands and exchanged cards.

The traffic on Veteran's Drive from the airport through Charlotte Amalie along the waterfront moved at a snail's pace. Unlike Nassau in the Bahamas, where speeding drivers had hit tourists, St. Thomians stopped for jaywalking tourists and vehicles turning left and right in and out of the waterfront road. Virgin Islanders had a leisurely outlook toward life on their Island paradise. As they passed the Virgin Islands Legislature, Long Bay came into view with boats anchored out, away from the Yacht Haven docks.

"This is Yacht Haven Hotel, on your right." Henley commented.

Richard turned toward a group of run down pink pastel buildings that were well past their prime.

"During the sixties and seventies it was one of the major hotel operations on the island, but lately it's become a financial albatross. Various subsequent owners have tried to return it to its glory days, but they've all failed," Henley said as they turned into the Marina entrance.

"She's gun shy," Crane explained as he filled them in during the ride. "Case of a greedy husband with lots of lovers and a rich wife."

"We ave dat plenty here too, mon. It cause a roogadoo when they be chasin' each other wit a machete all about. A mess I ca tell ya, mon!" Creque explained as a big broad expanse of laughter emanated from his elephantine frame at the domestic scene he described.

"I can imagine," Crane said as he and Henley joined in, laughing heartily. "I brought both of you a copy of this guy's picture and his vitae." Crane passed each of them a manila envelope. As I explained on the phone it's got to be a one-man operation.

However if Whitney shows up, your backup may be necessary, invaluable."

"If he arrives on the island, as we expect he might, he will have crossed territorial lines which makes it federal business," Henley interjected. "That's why I'm involved." He had turned toward Detective Creque as he spoke. "But it's your island, your police force."

Grabbing his small duffel, Crane stepped out of the car at the marina entrance. He paused and wrote down his own name on the back of Detective Creque's card to make sure that if someone needed to contact Creque for him, they'd have the facts.

Detective Creque understood and nodded in agreement.

"Thanks a lot," Crane said. Then he turned away, walked toward the parking lot, passed the Bosun's Locker Marine Store and headed down onto the docks. Near the end of the last tee, tied up alongside an inside finger pier, he found Onika, a sweet little fiberglass thirty footer. She wasn't one of the newer racing designs, rather more in the style of a classic John Alden. The occupant, with her back to him, was standing in the cockpit straight legged, yet totally bent over with her entire upper body parallel to her legs. Her hands coiled around her ankles. Amusing Crane thought, I've found a circus performer.

"Ahoy! Onika!" Crane waited for a response. "Quite a move," he observed as the body straightened into an upright position. A bronzed, amazingly attractive natural blond stood looking at him, wearing topsiders, short white shorts and a ratty navy cotton tee that didn't quite reach her navel. Provocative. Her hair was pulled back into a single ponytail topped by a white cotton sun visor.

"Exercise," she responded, "is a form of sublimation caused by lack of sex in a marriage."

"Asia Winslow?"" He asked trying not to laugh.

Shading her face from the bright Caribbean sun with her hand along the edge of the visor, she squinted at him momentarily.

"You're the dick," There was an edge of anger in her voice although she had tried to respond matter of factly.

"You could say that, but in public, I'm known as Richard Crane," he called back.

"Aubrey said you'd be along soon."

"Didn't make a liar out of him, did I?"

"Seems to me, I owe you a 'victory class' rematch."

"You could say that too." He was sure someone must have jarred her memory. But Richard was nearing his threshold on banal conversation. He had a job to do and time was running out. "May I come aboard?" He asked.

"Suit yourself," she said, turning toward the companion-way to the cabin, she went below. Richard rolled his eyes and jumped aboard. She had grown to be stunningly beautiful, but she still had the same little fourteen-year-old brashness to her personality.

Peering out from below, she gazed from him to the duffel. "Planning to spend the night?"

"I hope not." He had had about enough of her smart-ass repartee. Maybe I should just let Ian Whitney have at her, he thought.

"Coffee?" She asked as she handed him out a mug.

Things were looking up.

"I live on it, do you?" She asked as she returned above decks with a second mug.

"You don't seem very worried about your situation, Miss Winslow?"

Crane said as he put the first serious bent on the conversation. "A lot has been happening since you began your little sojourn."

"That's what I've been told." With the bluster gone from her voice, Crane noticed it had a soft, melodic, almost lyrical pattern, which under the right circumstances might be quite mesmerizing.

During the next hour, with Asia's added information, Crane was able to put the final pieces together to make a case against Asia's husband for her father's death. "You see," he explained, "the blow to the side of the head was at such an angle that only a push could have done it. Whereas, the bruising on the side and the back, originally thought to have been caused by the fall, could very well have been the result of a physical assault. Your father probably confronted them about the bonds, there was a tussle and your father was struck.

"Them?" She asked.

"Cynthia Ryder and Ian, didn't you realize they were both there?"

She stared down at the deck and shook her head. "And?" She whispered so softly, Crane wasn't quite sure she really wanted him to go on, but he had no choice. The truth would have to come out sometime. Better to get all the facts out in the open. Then she could begin with her final grieving, now, all at one time.

"She was there, alright. After it was over, she left Ian to deal with the authorities. She convinced him it would look more accidental, that the fewer people there the less questions would be asked," Crane paused to let it all sink in.

"My guess is Ian's looking at an indictment for second-degree murder, or at the very least, manslaughter. After all, Cynthia claimed they were at the cottage at your father's request. They had time to plan. Which one gave the actual push we may never know, but we do know that Cynthia was responsible for Annie Bloome."

"I am so sorry about Annie. Dad had decided to pay her tuition to NYU. No matter who actually killed her, hers was just another life wasted, manipulated by Ian's charms." Asia lamented.

"And what about your friend, Cynthia?" Crane asked curiously.

"Cynthia? Nothing. Anger. Annie fought for everything. Cynthia wanted for nothing. My father took her in, as a second daughter because I loved her. She was my friend, and he learned to love her too. I see now that I was not a friend. I was a stepping-stone. Sympathy. How can I have sympathy for someone like that?" She sighed as the tears welled. Then she smiled. "Excuse me," she said softly and went below.

Once she was back above decks, Crane figured he might have softened her up enough to approach the inevitable. "I need to get you out of here," he said.

"Why? You have all the information you need."

"Yes, I do. However, without you in the witness stand it's just hearsay."

"You want a sworn statement? No problem. I'll give you one, right now down at the police station in the Fort."

"Miss Winslow, I am also concerned about your safety." She was beginning to try his patience.

"Translated, you're here. I should fall into your arms? My safety is it. How is it I've gotten this far without your caring for my safety?" Her voice filled with anger as she confronted him and no one in particular.

"And you've done damn well! But time is running out. You said so yourself, in Bermuda to your godfather, when Crane arrives, Ian can't be far behind. Well I'm here!" At least he had her attention. He paused to let his words sink in. "We've got a plan." He began again before she had a chance to reconsider or respond with another wise-assed remark. He had little doubt she was scared. It was there in her eyes. Her sarcasm was just a cover.

"We. Who's we?" she questioned suspiciously.

"Me, with some help from the local authorities. I've arranged for two tickets on the evening flight back to New York. Once you're there we put you up in a safe house."

"I still see no reason to go, Mr. Crane," she replied stubbornly.

"Is your brain addled, young woman? What about your banknote business, for God sake!" Family disloyalty was something Crane could not abide. "Who's in charge, the office staff, a bunch of accountants? There is no one running the show except your elderly aunt, Mrs. Blake. Is that what you want, an old lady trying to keep your father's family legacy from going down the tubes?"

"You mean you bought a plane ticket in my name? That certainly isn't a 'red flag,' now is it?" Her voice was shaking with anger.

"We've got the ticket, but your name is not listed on the manifest."

"And I'm staying where?"

"At my sister's empty apartment, East Seventy Third, half a block from the Park. Round-the-clock surveillance until Whitney's in custody, which shouldn't take long." He didn't tell her it was his address too, and that he was the round the clock protection. He figured he had already spent his wad. Now he waited silently while she decided if she would let him buy the farm.

"I'll have to change and pack a bag. If you would secure the boat?" She asked almost docilely once she agreed to leave. "We'll stop at the dock master's on our way out."

"And I'll call for a car."

"A car?" She questioned.

"An unmarked car."

"No police cars. All the unmarked cars are like Hester's big red 'A,' on this island. A cab."

"Ok, a cab." He acquiesced. He'd gotten this far with her, why quibble. Skittish though she was, he just hoped his luck would hold.

Veteran's Drive was teeming with traffic as Richard raised his arm to hail a cab.

"No, not yet." Asia said.

"What?" She had to be kidding.

"I'd like to get a Dairy Queen to eat on the way. It's there just across the street." He followed her gaze to a windowed white building on a cement mound with a smattering of plastic white tables and chairs placed randomly in front.

"Are you crazy, woman?" Richard had lost his cool.

"No. I'm hungry."

"They'll get us something at the airport."

"What can it hurt? It will only take a few minutes; we have the light." She had already headed across the street before he could stop her.

He had gotten her this far. 'Why the hell not? Dairy Queen. Cab. Airport. Home. What could go wrong?' He thought as he raced across the street to catch up.

CHAPTER 46

"I haven't eaten this stuff since I was a kid," Crane mused as Asia and he walked out of the building toward the slight incline that led to the sidewalk below.

"Good isn't it? Maybe you ought to try kid stuff more often. That's one of the things I've learned on my forced adventure." Asia was beginning to feel safe with this man.

"Enough of this," he said, suddenly snatching away her cone.

"Hey! What are you doing?" Asia began in shocked surprise.

Throwing both cones into the trash receptacle, he clasped her hand in his and led her quickly down toward the Sky tram ticket booth next door.

"Let's see the parrot show," Richard's voice was full off spontaneity as he pointed to the sign.

"You don't have to get carried away with the idea immediately," Asia retorted annoyed and a bit confused.

"Asia, do as I ask you, please," Richard's voice was definite. "I want to see the parrot show at the top of the skyway."

Her eyes followed his gaze across the street. Ian was walking fast out the marina entrance, his eyes scanning the area.

"I love parrots." She responded coyly.

"Walk casually toward the ticket window. If our backs are to him he may not see us," Richard said. "Is he familiar with what you're wearing?"

"He may be, I don't know?" He could sense her voice tense.

"Relax, it's going to be all right. We'll ride up the tramway and get a cab at the top." He reassured her. "Just don't look back."

At the ticket window, there was one couple ahead of them. The guy's money was out, but the wife was full of numerous questions.

"I don't know if this is really what I wanta do, Artie," she whined. He hesitated with the cash.

"Oh, come on, Mavis," Artie begged, "It'll be fun."

Crane guessed Artie begged a lot. "Look, I go on this every time I come here, lady. It's like Disney World only better," Richard said, trying to move things along.

"How often do you come?" Mavis asked turning toward him. Her large fuchsia framed rhinestone studded sunglasses said it all.

"Every six months for the last eight years," Richard lied. "We get off the boat and come over here first thing. Isn't that right, honey?" Richard turned toward Asia for affirmation.

"Damn straight!" Asia chortled.

Richard looked at her. What was that all about he wondered? He could see the 'sky lift' cars coming down into view. He saw how they glided continuously without stopping. He wanted to get on. He wanted to move, now, before the three cars were shunted up toward the top again, and Asia and he had to wait for the next trio of cars to come down.

"Would you mind if we bought our tickets, while you're deciding?"

"Not at all." Artie moved out of the way still arguing with his wife.

"Thanks a lot, buddy," Richard said as he laid down his cash and scooped up the two tickets. Seizing Asia's arm he steered her up the steps to the second level just as the first sky car was about to make the U-turn on its trip back up to the top.

"I think he's seen us," Asia paused looking around to make sure. "He's coming this way," she said as they reached the lower loading platform.

"He's got to buy a ticket. Maybe Artie and Mavis will stall him with their bickering."

A young St. Thomian in neat khaki shorts and flowered shirt held out his hand for their tickets. "Good afternoon," he said with a broad grin. "Glad ta ave ya wit us today." The attendant caught the car door so the cab slowed down long enough for them to leap in. Richard saw Ian running up the stairs to the cars, shoving Artie and Mavis out of his way as he came.

"Call Detective Creque and tell him I need backup. My name's on the back. Crane. He'll understand. It's an emergency! Police business." Richard said in a tone no one would disobey.

"Sure, mon, right away." Wide eyed, the young man let the door fall closed and peered down at the card. Just as he turned, Ian clambered onto the platform and began reaching for the handle of the next sky cab door.

"You need a ticket, mon!" The young man shouted as he moved toward the gondola car.

"I don't need jack-shit!" Ian shouted as he pushed the attendant out of his way. The attendant grabbed at him. Ian let go of the door handle and punched him in the face. Before the fellow regained his balance, Ian hit him again in the chest, sending the poor young man slamming into the wall behind. Asia and Richard watched in horror as he slid down onto the platform floor unconscious. Crane watched furtively as Detective Creque's card slid out of the attendant's hand in cinematic slow motion to lie on the cement floor beside him. Ian ran, gripped at the door handle of the second car again and this time jumped inside just as it began its seven hundred-foot accent up the mountain.

"Artie, you can't let him do that to us!" Mavis screamed in high-pitched nasal as Artie raced up the stairs. The attendant was lying in a pool of blood and the last car was already past the passenger-loading platform following the others on its circular upward route.

"Mavis, get the ticket seller." Artie ordered, as he reached the top step. Mavis eyed the blood soaked attendant and froze. "Now!" He shouted. Instead, she stood paralyzed, pointing upward and screamed.

The man in the ticket booth and passersby came running up the stairs. Artie slapped her hard across the face. Mavis, reeling from the slap, stopped screaming, and slumped down onto the step quivering, her face in her hands, and began to cry. "I can't look." She moaned, her whole body shaking hysterically.

"Oh my God! What is he doing?" Someone in the crowd shouted. Everyone stood at rapt attention as they watched the door of the second gondola swing open and Ian peer out.

"We gotta call the police." Artie picked up the platform phone hoping 911 would work. As he did his foot kicked Crane's card and he picked it up. As he read the card, Artie looked up toward the couple in the upper most cab, and dialed the number. "And we have an injured man on the lower level," he said. "He may be dead." Helpless, Artie hung up the phone and watched, mesmerized, with the rest of the crowd.

The three skyway cars were suspended in stationary positions on a giant cable equal distances apart, each hanging on massive, solid steel, elbow shaped arms. The cable, propelled by an engine on the lower level was strong enough to move all six cars, three in each set, from the bottom to the top of the mountain and back. Via a series of three sets of pillars placed on each side, situated an equal distance apart midway up the mountain, an enormous doughnut shaped wheel, on the top of each pylon, kept the cable taut while together they guided cable to the wheel at the very top, and around on its downward route.

The crowd stood frozen as Ian opened the cab door and slung his body atop the car. Resting momentarily to get his breath, he grabbed the cable between the first and second cars and began moving slowly, hand over hand, toward the first gondola.

"Rock the cab!" Richard instructed. "As hard as you can!" The car began swaying back and forth. Slowly, Ian was getting nearer and nearer. Instead of the cab swinging to and fro toward Ian, it rocked perpendicularly. He did not have to avoid the cab's movement but rather judge the parallel swing to heave himself aboard.

The cable was grinding closer and closer to the first support strut. Any nearer and Ian's fingers would be crushed between the giant cable and the massive wheel. Just before the cable began winding itself over the mid-point of the pulley wheel, Richard and Asia heard the thud of his body as Ian swung himself on the roof of their cab. Sirens could be heard in the distance.

"Keep rocking, maybe he'll lose his balance!"

But Ian held fast. Suddenly, the cab tipped to one side. Holding onto one of the lipped edges that ran along each side of the top, Ian swung his body down and by using the whole weight of his body and his heavy steel tipped boots, smashed through one of the large rectangular viewing windows. His feet fell flat onto the inside floor of the cab with a thump, his extra weight causing the cab to tremble and spin in the air. Asia screamed. Then, in one swift movement, he reached inside his boot and pulled out a large knife, and bent his body backward outside through the broken window to waist level to gain leverage. He lifted his arm high over his head and lunged. The crowd below was spellbound.

"Move, Asia!" Crane shouted as he pushed her to one side of the cab. Before he had time to get out of the way, Crane felt the knife plunge into his shoulder with a painful blow. Thinking he had immobilized Crane, Ian pulled the knife out and with a swift movement turned toward Asia.

"You unmitigated bitch!" he yelled. His face contorted into a mass of inhuman, convoluted evil, gnarled and coarse. He stood staring at her with beady electrifying eyes. "How do you like being cornered, you scared little bitch?" he snarled. As he raised the knife over Asia's head, Crane raised himself and grabbed Ian's arm from behind. Throwing him off balance, Crane slammed Ian's arm down hard, banging it against the edge of the broken window imbued with chards of broken glass. Sweat poured down both men's faces. "You son of a bitch!" Ian screamed as his bare arm struck the sharp pieces. Crane slammed his arm again and Ian's hand fell opened. They both watched as the knife fell to the ground. Suddenly with a burst of strength, Ian broke Crane's grasp. He smashed Crane in the face and clenched his hands around Crane's throat. Richard knew he was losing blood and he could feel the air going out of his body. Ian had him halfway out the window, but he hadn't considered Crane's loose arms that as a last gasp effort squeezed Ian's torso in a hammerlock with what appeared to be a rebirth of super-human strength.

'If I'm going to die, it's not going to be at the hands of this guy,' Crane thought, as Asia slammed Ian in the back of his knees using the whole force of her body, falling on the cab floor as she did. By forcing Ian to lose his balance, his hands loosened on Crane's throat. His body flipped over so that he was suddenly on the bottom being pressed, by the full weight of Crane's body. The impact had smashed Ian through the opposite window suspending him as if levitated on his back by a magician.

There he hung half-in and half-out. Crane's body weight was the only thing keeping Ian's hanging body inside the cab. Ian could feel the excruciating pain of the sharp shards of glass impaled in his back. His arms flailed in the air with the gyrating motion of the wings of a wounded bird. Finally, Richard fell back and Ian's body gave way, losing whatever leverage it had. Slowly, his feet somersaulted over the rest of his body as if in suspended animation. As Ian fell to the ground below, a crumbled mass of death and destruction, the sky cab lumbered on up toward the upper level tramway stop.

Richard looked up at Asia, who sat with his head in her lap, as blood streamed down her right cheek. She smiled and brushed his hair from his eyes.

When the jammed gondola door was finally unlatched, Detective Creque found Crane and Asia laying in a mass of broken glass and splattered blood.

"Are we in time for the parrots?" Crane asked and passed out.

CHAPTER 47

Richard Crane awoke swathed in white. 'I'm dead,' he thought, 'floating in a cloud.' As his sight began to connect with his brain, he realized his whole body ached. 'No one could be in this much pain and be dead.' He could feel an acute throbbing emanating from his right shoulder, also encased in white, which impeded the movement of his right arm. He reached his hand to his face and found a bulbous swelling on his lower lip, which smarted at the touch. Running his hand along his lip he could feel tightness around the corner of his mouth, puckered together by the pulling pressure of a scab forming on a cut.

Painfully turning his head, he gazed through a window. Unaware of the media circus outside, his outside was a bare, brown, treeless field in need of rain. Finally, he realized he was in a hospital. Asia Winslow sat in a chair over to one side reading.

She looked tired and worn, but serenely beautiful as ever. She would not be sitting there if Ian Whitney were still alive.

As he watched her, he knew he had finally met the right woman. He also knew there could always be a lot of garbage between them. He had no doubt that he would see her again when they were both back in the City. She was the right person, but in the wrong circumstances… 'What a hell of a way to end one's day,' he thought as he closed his eyes and fell back to sleep.

As his eyes closed, she looked up as if subliminally aware of his thoughts and smiled a knowing smile.

AFTERWORD

Still anchored in Great Harbor, Jost Van Dyke, Steve Hughes sat in the cockpit of his boat reading a day old Virgin Islands Daily News. The story jumped out at him like a man-eating tiger.

'HEIRESS, HUSBAND, POLICE IN FATAL
DEATH DEFYING FIGHT.'

This was the kind of headline the media clamored for. Reporters swarmed onto the island, along side an entourage of paparazzi.

Hughes smiled as he realized little Annie Wise wasn't as innocent as she pretended. 'Go to St Thomas and join that media circus. Not a chance,' he thought. 'I'll bide my time. When it all dies down, I'll get the real scoop.' This was one promise he was definitely going to collect.

INDEX

Bloom, Murray Teigh. ***Brotherhood of Money****, The secret World of Bank Note Printers;*
BRN Press. Port Clinton, Ohio, 1983.

Feinberg, Steven L. (ED), ***Crane's Blue Book of Stationery;***Double Day. New York, 1989.

For more information about single-handed sailors mentioned in this book, Sanders Candy Company and/or the author, please go to my website.

www.bklauren.com

15607179R00173

Made in the USA
Charleston, SC
11 November 2012